JOHN FANTE

THE
BIG HUNGER
STORIES 1932–1959

Edited by Stephen Cooper

ecco

An Imprint of HarperCollins*Publishers*

THE BIG HUNGER: STORIES 1932–1959. Copyright © 2000 by Joyce Fante. PREFACE, EDITING & NOTES. Copyright © 2000 by Stephen Cooper. All rights reserved. Printed in the United States of America. No part of this book may be used or reproduced in any manner whatsoever without written permission except in the case of brief quotations embodied in critical articles and reviews. For information, address HarperCollins Publishers, 195 Broadway, New York, NY 10007.

HarperCollins books may be purchased for educational, business, or sales promotional use. For information, please e-mail the Special Markets Department at SPsales@harpercollins.com.

First Ecco edition published 2002.

Library of Congress has catalogued a previous edition as:

Fante, John, 1909-1983
    The big hunger : stories, 1932–1959 / John Fante ; edited by Stephen Cooper.
        p. cm.
    ISBN 1-57423-120-0 (paperback)-
    ISBN 1-57423-121-9 (cloth trade)
    ISBN 1-57423-122-7 (deluxe signed)
    1. United States—Social life and customs—20th century—Fiction.
I. Cooper, Stephen, 1949 –   II. Title.
PS3511.A594   B54   2000   99-88227
813'.52—dc21   CIP

HB 06.08.2023

Contents

Preface

ON A SUMMER DAY in 1994 Joyce Fante ushered me into her sprawling ranch home on Malibu's Point Dume. Since our first meeting earlier that summer she had thrown open the door to me three or four times, always welcoming me with a brave smile. We would sit on the patio or at the dining room table drinking coffee and talking about her life with John Fante, the early days of their marriage in Los Angeles and Manhattan Beach and Roseville and San Francisco, and then the years here on Cliffside Drive, where the couple had raised their four children and where Joyce had remained after John's death in 1983. Since then her time had been filled with reading, composing her diary, and nurturing the world's recognition of John Fante as one of the great writers of the twentieth century; and on the days when I came she would tell stories which I knew the world would also want to hear, stories for the biography which I wanted to write.

But this day seemed different. After greeting me at the front door Joyce led me through the dining room and the kitchen, where her big gray tomcat was sitting sentry, and into a small, dim, dusty-smelling service porch. She wanted to show me something.

My eyes were still adjusting when she flicked on the bare ceiling bulb, and I saw the only things there were to be seen in that room. Four tall black metal file cabinets stood crowded against the wall, each fitted with four cavernous legal-sized drawers. Joyce nodded. At the touch of my hand the top drawer of the nearest cabinet groaned open. The drawer was stuffed with envelopes, letters, folders, notebooks, and ream after ream of typewritten and handwritten manuscripts. The second drawer was crammed with more of the same, and the third, and the fourth, and so on. Thumbing through the contents of one drawer after another I glimpsed photographs, baptismals, studio contracts, tax returns, canceled checks, carbon copies, old issues of *The American Mercury,* medical records, address books, scrapbooks, prayer books, even a sealed envelope labeled "John Fante's Hair"—as much evidence in one place as anyone could hope for of a person's life, all there, within my reach, in that room.

The moment felt so much like a dream.

And yet it was not just a dream. For when I looked back at Joyce her eyes told me that after our several

8

sessions of talk I was now free to begin my explorations. It came over me then, and I recalled the preface which Charles Bukowski had contributed to Black Sparrow's 1980 reissue of *Ask the Dust,* the part about his discovery of Fante's great novel in the Los Angeles Public Library. At that moment, Bukowski wrote, he had felt like a man finding gold in the city dump. And now here I was, in the goldmine ...

As I write these words it is the summer of 1999. In order to write my biography of John Fante I spent years sifting through the files in that room, tracing chronologies, piecing together fragmented manuscripts, filling in gaps large and small in the life story of a writer who often obscured the facts of his life. I learned things about Fante, not always pleasant, which I never could have learned without access to those files. Not least of all I found the stories in this book.

Contrary to the misconception that Fante saved nothing he could not use, I found that in addition to scores of screenplays, teleplays, and film and television treatments, most of them never produced, he saved dozens of unpublished short stories, as well as several others which had appeared in various magazines but which after his death had never been collected. Even Joyce Fante did not know of all of these writings in their entirety. Thanks, however, to her support and the enthusiasm of Black Sparrow's publisher John Martin, *The Big Hunger* now brings together seventeen "new" stories by John Fante, plus the untruncated prologue to *Ask the Dust.*

Readers wishing to learn more about the stories may find the notes at the back of the book helpful. But each piece is a revelation in itself. Taken together, the contents of this volume will strengthen the hold which John Fante continues to exert on imaginations around the world. Five years ago it was my privilege to step inside a dark and dusty room. Now the privilege is mine again, this time to help bring to light John Fante's last book—in some ways his youngest, and hungriest.

S.C.
July 15, 1999

The Big Hunger

Stories 1932–1959

Horselaugh on Dibber Lannon

DIBBER LANNON HAS a big brother. His name is Pat Lannon. Dibber told me his brother Pat was going to be a pope some day. Well, Dibber sure got fooled. Dibber said Pat would be the greatest pope in the world, even greater than Pope Pius. Horselaugh on Dibber Lannon!

This is why:

Pat Lannon was an eighth grader when me and Dibber were third graders. I remember him. Some big brother! Fooey! He was a snitch-baby, that's what he was. He was the champ snitcher of this school, and he still holds the record. Dibber doesn't know this. How could he? He was Pat's little brother, and how could a little brother know his big brother was a snitch? Who will tell him about it? Nobody. Well, horselaugh on Dibber Lannon.

I heard some of the old guys from this school talking about Pat Lannon. They knew plenty. They told about the time they went to Manual Training but didn't go to Manual Training, but played hooky instead. Everybody but Pat Lannon. He was too good to play hooky. What did he do? He got Mr. Simmons and brought him to the trestle bridge. The guys were under it smoking. Mr. Simmons flunked everybody but Pat Lannon. And that's the kind of brother Dibber Lannon's got. And he's the same brother Dibber said would be pope.

When Pat Lannon went to our school I was only a third grader. He was an eighth grader. But I remember him. He was a very screwy guy. He looked nuts. He wore glasses. His eyes wiggled. He looked at something, and his eyes went all over. He wore sandals. Some big brother! The old guys said that when Pat was in the first grade he even wore bangs! And he was going to be pope! Ho ho.

Every year our school gives a play. I remember when Pat Lannon was in the plays. The plays are never any good. I mean, they are very lousy. The sisters write them. They aren't even plays. They are pageants. They are very goofy things. They don't have any action, nobody gets killed, and nobody ever says anything funny. The girls are not allowed to act in them. The boys dress in robes made out of sheets. It is all very crazy. Everybody has a bum part. Like one guy will be Sin. The next guy will be Purity. The next will be Faith.

14

The next will be Mercy. This goes on for a long time. The whole thing is done in holy-talk, like Jesus.

Sin comes out. He says something in holy-talk. Then Faith comes out. He says, "Hail ye! For I am Faith! I cometh with a message!" Then out comes Hope. He tells the people who he is and what he does. And the next guy is Charity, or Humility, or something just as goofy. They all come out to the middle of the stage and wait. And for what? For Love! And who was Love? Pat Lannon! Every time! He came out and hollered, "Hail ye! For I am Love! I bringeth peace on earth, good will to men!" The people out front thought that was just too wonderful for words. They clapped and clapped. Some pope!

Pat Lannon had a big suck with the sisters. He had a bicycle. He ran errands for them. He stayed until night, doing things. He cleaned erasers and washed blackboards. He even corrected papers. The old guys told him they would punch him in the nose if he flunked them. But he had to flunk a few to make it look right. And what did he do? He flunked the girls. And why? Because they were the only kids in this school he could lick! And Dibber said *he* was going to be pope! Horselaugh!

Russell Meskimen was one of the old guys. He used to let the air out of Pat's tires. Once Russell had to stay after school for writing dirty words on the sidewalk. Sister Cletus was his teacher. She promised to let him go home if he would run an errand. Russell thought he was getting off easy, so he said sure.

But there was a hitch to it.

Sister Cletus said, "Go down to Gales' and buy twenty rolls of toilet paper, and have them charged to the Sisters of Charity.

Oh oh. That was a tough one.

But Russell couldn't say no. So he said yes. He didn't want to do it. Gales' is right in the middle of town. What would all those people think? One or two rolls didn't matter—but twenty! And for the sisters too! You know how people are. Gosh—they laugh right in your face for hardly anything. Russell went to get his bicycle.

At the bike rack he saw Pat Lannon.

"Hey Pat," Russell said. "How would you like me to promise not to let the air out of your tires anymore?"

"That sure would be wonderful," Pat said.

"If you'll go downtown for me, I'll promise," Russell said.

So Pat Lannon went down to Gales'. He didn't think anything of it. He went right in and ordered twenty rolls. And he's the guy who Dibber said would be pope! What a pope! Twenty rolls, too! When he got back Russell took the rolls and brought them to Sister Cletus. On his way out, Russell saw Pat's bike in the rack. He started to figure. He figured, if a guy is as dumb as all that, he doesn't need air in his tires. So he let the air out anyhow. Which proves something.

Bob Armstrong is another old guy. He and Pat were partners on the altar boys. They served Mass

16

together. Bob used to steal wine. One day he stole too much, and Father Walker got wise. He asked Bob if he did it.

Bob said, "No, Father. Honest."

Then Father Walker asked Pat.

Pat said, "Bob did it, Father. I saw him."

Well, well. A snitch-baby too!

After Mass, Bob laid for Pat. He jumped on him from behind the lilac bushes. What a fighter Pat Lannon turned out to be! A dirty fighter, because he kicked with his feet. And he even scratched! Bob got madder and madder. He knocked the hell out of him.

I used to go over to the Lannons'. Me and Dibber fooled around, doing things. We built a tree house and dug a cave. After playing around, Dibber took me to his house for something to eat. The Lannons have a swell house, one of the best in town. No wonder—Mr. Lannon owns a furniture store. They have carpets everywhere, even in the basement. They have a hard green carpet in the kitchen, and green chairs, and a green stove, and even green handles on the pans. It's certainly a swell kitchen. It's a lot better than our front room, even.

Pat Lannon had a den in the basement. I watched him play with his chemistry set. I stayed at the door. He didn't talk. He didn't like me to play with Dibber. He looked at me with his wiggly eyes. He scared me. After a while he pointed to a tube of green stuff.

"See that?" he said.

I said I did.

Then he pointed to a tube of yellow stuff.

"See that?"

I said I did.

He said, "Pour the green stuff into the yellow."

I did.

It went—*zoo!*

It burned my hair and fingers. It hurt. He laughed until his glasses came off. Then I laughed too. But I was only pretending. It wasn't funny. It was sad. I was sore. My finger hurt. I was mad. I hated that goddamn fool. Jesus, I hated him. Some pope!

Once I went with Dibber to the haunted house by the creek. We had slingshots to kill ghosts. We climbed all over, looking for them. There were cobwebs and bats, but no ghosts. We heard a noise upstairs and got our slingshots ready. It sounded like a ghost. But it wasn't. It was only Pat Lannon. He was fooling around. He took some chalk from his pocket and wrote on the floor:

Caution! These boards are weak. Caution!

"What does that mean?" Dibber asked.

He wouldn't tell. He said it was a secret. But he gave me a nickel and Dibber a nickel. He told us to go to the Scoutmaster and tell him what he had written. He said he would get a medal for it. Dibber went. I didn't. I thought it was another joke like the stuff in the tubes. I fooled him. I got another nickel and went to the show.

Pan Lannon had secret wires strung over his back-yard. Everything you touched gave you a shock and knocked you down. He said it was to keep out chicken robbers. But I know what happened to the chickens. Pat killed them. He was mean to kittens too. He put wires around their legs and gave them shocks. He would chase a chicken and chase a chicken and chase a chicken until it fell down, all pooped out. Then he shocked it. He mixed stuff in his chemistry set and killed kittens. There was an ant-pile in his back yard. He tied a kitten to a post over the ants.

After the sister school, Pat went to Prep. The Lannons had a Packard. Pat brought Prep school girls to Mass in it. They sat in the Lannon pew. They weren't Catholics. If you're a Catholic, you're not supposed to go with them. It's not a sin, but don't do it anyhow. They had swell legs though. Better than Catholic legs. They didn't hear Mass. They just sat. One was a red-head who chewed gum. I sat in the next pew the time she came. She kept asking, Why did he do that?—meaning the priest.

Dibber said the reason Pat brought Protestant girls to Mass was to try to convert them. Applesauce! Pat Lannon didn't try to convert anybody. I guess I saw him one time. I know. He came back from communion one time, and he was smiling. He rubbed his belly and licked his lips. The redhead watched him. "Marvelous!" he said. "Marvelous!" It is a sacrilege to talk like that. Holy Communion isn't marvelous at all. You can't even taste it. Some pope! Horselaugh on Dibber!

Pat Lannon's main girl was Dagmar Heine. He brought her to church too. I like Dagmar. She's keen.

Swell legs. Before she grew up and went to high school she used to go sleigh-riding on our hill with her Flexible Flyer. She had the hill record every year. Also golden hair. She lived near us, right by the hill. Her mother was dead. Her old man worked for the railroad.

A pope doesn't swear, but I heard Pat Lannon swear in front of Dagmar. It was on the Lannon tennis courts. Pat was playing Dagmar. She was beating him. She laughed at him. He fell into the net and she had to stop playing she laughed so much. Pat got mad and wouldn't play with her. He said he was tired. But I know why he quit. He felt cheap. He was in Senior Prep too. Some pope!

I asked to borrow his tennis racket.

He said, "Ask the bitch over there."

"Why Pat!" Dagmar said.

"Fuck you!" he said.

Some pope!

All summer he was with Dagmar. She came to his house. I saw them kissing and hugging. Pat took off his glasses to do it. There was a ditch across his face. Dagmar saw it, but she kept kissing. I couldn't see how she did it. I used to wish I was older so I could kiss her. But not after that guy.

If me and Dibber were in our cave, Pat and Dagmar used our tree house. If we were in our tree house, they used our cave. We tried to kick them out. They wouldn't go. Dagmar offered us money if we would let them use it. They gave us a dollar. Me and Dibber went halvers on it. I knew what they were doing in that tree house. I hated it. It rustled like an earthquake. Some pope!

Dibber always did tell me Pat was going to study to be a doctor. Once we asked Dagmar what she would do, and she said she would study to be a nurse for Pat's patients. Then all at once the whole town was talking about Pat Lannon going away to be a priest. I thought it was very strange. Father Walker didn't announce it the way he did when Rooney went. I didn't believe it. I asked my mother. She said she thought it was true. But I still didn't believe it. I asked Dibber. He said it was a fact. He said Pat was at a monastery in Kentucky.

Then Dibber started to brag. He told me about the letters they got from Pat. Brag, brag, brag. Once Pat wrote that he was working in the grape fields in the monastery. Then he was studying Chinese. Then he was peeling potatoes. Then he was in retreat for six weeks, and no more letters while the retreat was going on. A retreat is where you do nothing but pray. You can't write letters. I was glad of that.

Dagmar came to our house. She talked to my mother. She couldn't believe Pat had gone to be a priest. She told my mother she would never believe it. She cried and was very sad. Priests can't marry. That's why she was sad. She was stuck on the guy. Sometimes Dagmar brought my sister magazines. She would hang around and talk before going away. I asked her if she was still going to be a nurse. She said she didn't know.

I heard my mother talking to her. It was all crazy, what my mother was saying. She told Dagmar she should be very proud now that Pat was going to be a priest. She said Pat would light up Dagmar's life with sanctifying grace. She said Dagmar was the luckiest person in the world to have the prayers of a priest. Fooey! It sounded nuts to me. A priest is a good thing—like Father Walker—he's a good fellow. But not Pat Lannon. I knew him. He didn't fool me. I knew that guy. How he killed the chickens and kittens. I knew. Maybe he *was* going to be a priest, but he couldn't be such a hot one. I saw that dead kitten. You can't do that and be holy. Not in a million years.

Then it was wintertime again. The hill was covered with snow. Soon it was hard and bright and we cut down our sleds. After supper we were on the hill. Me and Dibber and my brother and all the guys. The tracks went past Dagmar's house. We saw her at the window. She watched us. We hollered for her to come out like she used to when she had the record with her Flexible Flyer, but she wouldn't come. The lights went out and the house was black. We pulled our sleds up the hill past her house and wondered what the heck.

We coasted until late. One by one the guys all went home. Then Dibber went home, and there was only my brother and me on the hill. We decided to go down one more time. It was my brother's turn, so he pulled the sled. The lights in Dagmar's house were still out. When we got to the top of the hill the lights turned on again. Dagmar came out on the porch in a fur coat. Old Man Heine was with her. They walked down the steps and through the deepest snow to

Reeves's Pasture. It was very screwy. There wasn't any path through the pasture. They waded in, bucking the deepest snow. After they reached the elm trees we couldn't see them anymore. I knew they didn't see us. That was why I didn't holler hello. I couldn't understand it. Me and my brother went to bed. I couldn't sleep thinking about Dagmar and her old man wading through the snow toward the elm trees.

Next day I told Dibber Lannon.

"That's funny," he said.

"Sure is," I said.

"Let's go see her," he said.

We went that night before coasting. The Heine garage was open. We saw Dagmar's sled with rusty runners hanging from the rafters. It was a sad thing. What a sled it used to be! The fastest sled ever seen on this hill! And there it was, rusty and old-looking.

Then Dibber whistled, and Dagmar came out on the front porch. She asked Dibber a lot of questions, mostly about Pat and what he wrote in his letters. Dibber started bragging right away. He said they were training Pat at the monastery to be the next pope, which was a lie because you don't go in training to become pope, they just elect you. Oh that Dibber! The horselaugh is sure on him. Dagmar stood there listening to him. She sure looked swell, with a fur coat pulled around her.

Then Mr. Heine stuck his head out the door.

"Dagmar!" he said. "Come in here!"

We pulled our sleds up the hill and started coasting.

23

We coasted until eleven. It was very cold. The guys began to go home. Me and Dibber waited on the hill. Nobody could see us from below. In a while Dagmar came out with her father. They started across the pasture, wading in the deepest snow. They didn't go anywhere—just a big circle around the elm trees and back to the house again. After that they did it every night. Me and Dibber were up on the hill watching them. We laid on our bellies and they couldn't see us. They didn't do anything but walk around. They never walked in a path. It was always through fresh snow up to their hips.

Then Dagmar went away. It was before Christmas. I heard my mother talking. She was very sore. She kept calling Dagmar a murderess. After New Year a letter came to our house for my sister. It was from Dagmar. My mother tore it into little pieces.

"That murderess!" my mother said. "That murderess!"

"Who did Dagmar kill?" I said.

"You mind your own business," she said.

If Dagmar killed somebody he deserved it. It's all right with me. Besides, it's all right for Dagmar to kill somebody because she's a Protestant and Protestants don't have mortal sins in their church. Besides, I like Dagmar. Besides, Dagmar has swell legs. Besides, she wouldn't kill a kitten the way Pat Lannon did. I know that.

That Pat Lannon! And Dibber bragged. Pat Lannon was a fake. I will tell you why he was a fake. After the snow, it came spring and baseball season. One night after practice me and Dibber were going home. Dibber was bragging. He had the guts to tell me Pat was going to become pope by summer. We crossed the street. A car went past us, lickety-cutting down the street. It was the Lannon Packard. Pat Lannon was in it. Dibber hollered. He didn't stop. He went right on down the street raising dust. Then Dibber said it couldn't be Pat. Because Pat was at the monastery studying to be a priest. But it was Pat all right.

When we got to the drugstore on Pine, there he was, in the Packard. The redhead who chewed gum was with him. He didn't look like a priest to me. His collar wasn't upside-down, and he wasn't wearing a black suit. He looked the same as ever. Dibber ran up.

He said, "Hey, do I have to call you Father now?"

Pat laughed.

"No," he said. "Call me Pat like always."

"Are you a priest now?" Dibber said.

The redhead laughed.

"Cut it!" Pat said to her. "You bitch!"

Dibber was sure surprised. It was the first priest *he* ever heard say that! Real priests are very respectful. They know plenty of dirty words, but they don't use them in plain talk.

"I shall never be a priest," Pat said. "It seems I was mistaken in my vocation."

Dibber was disgusted.

"Aw hell sakes!" he said. "And here I been telling all the guys you'd be the next pope!"

Pat laughed. He got out some money and handed

it to Dibber. "Forget it," he said. "Take Arturo with you, and get yourselves a milkshake."

We went up the street. Dibber was feeling pretty low. I didn't say anything for a long time. But when we got to the bank I had to say something.

"Some pope!" I said. "Horselaugh on you, Dibber!"

"Shut your damn face!" he said.

But I didn't. All the way home I gave him the horselaugh. I kept calling him Pope. All over school now they call him that. They used to call him Dibber, but now all you have to do is say Pope, and Dibber looks up. He doesn't mind though. He thinks it's better than Dibber.

Jakie's Mother

NOW IF I HAD a mother like Jakie Shaler's I would do something. I would do something very strange. I would go right out and find another mother.

Jakie is a swell guy to bum around with, but he does not talk very much. And his father is also a swell guy too, only we do not bum around with a guy's father. Mr. Shaler is not mean like Mrs. Shaler. He buys Jakie footballs and baseballs and basketballs and bats and boxing gloves and sleds and tennis rackets and bows and arrows and tools. Mr. Shaler bought Jakie a gun, too. So Jakie has all the things he wants, but he does not get to bum around with us on account of his mother is the worst one going. His father is very different. His father is a swell guy.

It is his mother who does all the lickings in that

house. She will not let Jakie do hardly anything. She will not let him go out of the yard on Saturdays, and on school days he has to come straight home from school. Before his little brother Petey died, Jakie had to stay home and play with him all the time. It made Jakie sore, because Petey was too little to play with. He tried to sneak away. But the minute he sneaked through the fence Petey would start hollering for all he was worth, and Mrs. Shaler would run out of the kitchen and chase after Jakie. She would get him and take him down the basement and pound the living hell out of him. You could hear him hollering all over town. She gave it to him with a special broomstick. She hit him with all her muscle. We saw blue marks on his ass and legs. He showed them to us.

Jakie felt bad about having such a wicked mother. She was worse than wicked: she was dirty, but Jakie did not say so. And when he was in school he hated to sit down after he got licked by her. He would sit down slow and easy. He sat down on his hands to not make it hurt so much. That shows the kind of a mother he has. That shows how much she hurt him. He could not run after he got a licking. After he got a licking he would umpire ball games, because the umpire always has it pretty easy. He would umpire games for a whole week straight.

Mrs. Shaler made Jakie eat soap two times, and she burned his tongue with a poker one time. Jakie had to eat soap because he swore, and if you think soap is so hot, taste it. The reason he got his tongue burned with the poker was because he got caught smoking. We were all smoking in the barn, a block away from the Shaler house. Mrs. Shaler did not catch us smoking for real, but she saw the smoke, so she knew. And it is lucky for Jakie that Mrs. Shaler did not find out the stuff we were smoking. Boy! I say it is, because it was horse manure.

This is how Jakie's little brother Petey died. One day he was playing in the yard, and an auto came by. Petey ran into the street. He ran square into the bumper. He was knocked down and run over and killed dead right now.

They had the funeral on Friday. Everybody in our room went to see little Petey at the Shaler house on Thursday. Everybody had to bring a nickel for flowers, because Petey was Jakie's brother, and Jakie was in the same room with us in school. Some of the guys did not bring their nickel. Robert Teale did not bring one.

Little Petey was in a white coffin. He had on a new suit. He smelled too sweet, and he did not look natural. He was so white in the face he looked like he was wearing a wig. They had the shades down, and candles were lit in the room, which made it scary.

We knelt down and said the rosary. Some of the girls were crying already. It was hard to keep from crying. After a while, the only one who was not crying was Robert Teale. Oh, that Robert Teale is a tough guy. He is the kind of a guy who will not cry at anything.

Mrs. Shaler came into the room. She had a black dress on, and her eyes were very red. She hollered and made a run for the coffin and put her arms around it and put her head on Petey's chest and mussed up his hair and cried and screamed to our Lord not to take Petey from her.

"Take me, God! Don't take this baby of mine. Oh oh oh oh oh oh oh oh oh." She went like that.

And it was sad. It was the saddest thing you ever saw. We felt so sorry for Mrs. Shaler. You know how she felt, being Petey's mother. I was wishing God did take her instead of Petey.

Some of the girls cried so hard that they started to beat it. Everybody cried but Robert Teale. You have to go some to make that guy cry. He is tough. But the girls should have stayed in the room, because they missed something. They missed the best part.

That was when Mrs. Shaler started to talk to Petey like he was not dead, but sleeping. She knelt on the floor and pulled Jakie down with her. She put her arms around Jakie's neck and pretty near choked him to death. You could see Jakie's face get red and then purple.

She cried, "Oh, my little Petey! Your mother hasn't been a good mother to you. Oh, come back, little son!"

Everybody but Robert Teale was crying. I was crying, even. The girls kept going out with their handkerchiefs in front of their noses. Petey's hair was all mussed up like he just woke up in bed in the morning. He did not wake up for real, though. He was dead in the coffin. He just looked like he woke up.

Mrs. Shaler started to scream. Every time she did, it made me sick in my stomach. I was more scared now. I was more scared now than sad.

"Oh God, bring him back!"

Jakie could hardly talk on account of crying so much.

He said, "Don't talk like that, Mother." I guess he felt cheap in front of us.

Mrs. Shaler screamed, "Regrets! Regrets! Regrets!"

She grabbed Jakie. She almost knocked him off his knees.

She said, "Oh Jakie, I promise you here before Petey, here before all your wonderful little friends, that I will be a good mother from now on. I promise you, Jakie. I promise."

Jakie said, "You already are a good mother, Mother. You are a swell mother, Mother. Honest you are."

Mr. Shaler came in. He picked up Mrs. Shaler and took her to the bedroom. Jakie went in when his father called him. After a little while Mr. Shaler came out and combed Petey's hair. He did not say anything. Then he went out again. Us guys and girls were all alone with the coffin. It was scary. We were kneeling down. We could barely see Petey's face and hands. Some of the girls wanted to go home, but they did not get up. It got hard on the knees, kneeling on the floor so long. One of the guys wanted to know what to do next.

Robert Teale got up. He started to go out. He sure has nerve. He went over to the coffin and bent down real close to Petey's face, and looked right at it.

Then he said, "Well, the rest of you can do what you want. I ain't going to stay here. I'm going home. Here I go." And he went out. Then everybody got real scared. We ran out of the house. It felt good to get outside. Everybody went home.

I kept on thinking about Mrs. Shaler. I was glad she promised to be good to Jakie from now on. That meant that Jakie could bum around with us if he wanted to, and we could use his footballs and baseballs and basketballs and bats and boxing gloves and sleds and tennis rackets and bows and arrows and tools. We could use his gun, too.

They had the funeral the next day. We thought we would get out of school to go to it, but heck no. This is a rotten school. The only one who got to go was Jakie. And the only reason he got to go is on account of Petey was his brother. This is a rotten school. My mother went to the funeral. She said the church was full of people.

She said, "I never saw so many pretty flowers. The Elks Club sent a great basket." I am glad the Elks did, because my father is an Elk.

My mother said, "Oh, I felt so sorry for that little boy Jakie. He knocked the candlestick over on the coffin when he passed by. He was so frightened. He felt so bad about it."

Jakie was at school on Monday. Nobody asked him about knocking over the candlestick. Everybody already knew it. The mothers of most of the guys went to the funeral, and they told them. We treated Jakie real nice, on account of the funeral was just a couple of days ago.

We chose up sides for the game later, and the other side chose Jakie. But Jakie would not play.

He said, "I can't play, but I'll umpire for you."

Robert Teale said, "Holy Christ! What kind of a mother you got, anyhow? Didn't she promise she wouldn't give you any more lickings? I call that a heck of a dirty trick."

Jakie did not talk very loud. We could barely hear him.

He said, "You guys don't know what I did. You weren't at the funeral, so you don't know."

Robert Teals said, "Oh yes I do. I know what you did. That ain't nothing awful. You never did it on purpose. You know, you got a hell of a mother."

Jakie started to cry. He did not cry out loud. He did not cry because he had a heck of a mother. He was crying because his little brother Petey was dead. You could tell.

The Still Small Voices

YOUR BROTHER shook you by the hair until you were awake. It was about two o'clock in the morning.

He whispered, "Wake up. Mama and Papa's started in again."

In the next room you heard the voices of the two. The door was open, but there was no light. The whole house was dark. The bitterness in the voices was the same as on the other nights. The fire in the voice of your father made you and your brother reach for the skins of one another as you lay listening to the inscrutable words of the two, sometimes inaudible English words, but mostly Italian you had never heard.

Your brother Pete, who lay beside you, who was ten, said, "This is a hell of a house."

In the next room your father said, "I'm through, that's all. I'm through."

Your mother said, "And what about the kids?"

Your father said, "Take them and get the hell out."

Your sister in the room beyond theirs began to cry. She called out to you in the darkness of the old house, and you answered, "What?" And your mother and father became quiet so that they could hear what your sister was wanting, and she called out again, her voice weaving through the doors to where you lay, "Go see why Mama and Papa are fighting, Jimmie. Please go see. I'm scared."

And your youngest brother Tommy, who slept in the bed with your sister, shouted to you who were twelve and the oldest, "I ain't scared, Jimmie. She's eight too, and I'm only six."

Your father roared, his voice vibrating the whole house, "If you kids don't shut up, I'll give you something to be scared about."

The brother who slept beside you said, "Tommy is sure a nervy little guy."

Your mother said to your father, "Now you woke up everybody."

Your father said, "Let 'em wake up. See if I give a damn."

Your room was between that of your mother and father and that of your grandmother, and now you heard your grandmother rising from her bed. She would come to your room as she always did when your mother and father quarreled in the night. With every

36

step she took, she moaned a strange "oh oh oh."

The brother beside you said, "Now here comes Grandma to butt in."

The door creaked, and your little grandmother was standing beside the bed, her very dry hand pawing the pillow in search of your head.

She whispered, and she was always crying on nights like this, "Go see, Jimmie, go see. You must make them stop. Your father will kill her."

Braggadocio, you said loud enough for your father to hear, "Aw, Papa's all right."

The house was quiet except for the "oh oh oh" from your grandmother's old bosom.

You said, "See? There ain't no more fighting."

Your father heard. There was the known sound of whining bedsprings, and your father sat up in bed and sputtered rapid angry words at your grandmother. It was that Italian of which you knew nothing. You did not catch a single ascertained word. Your grandmother went slowly on tiptoe back to her room, and her door closed, and the springs in her bed creaked.

Your mother said to your father, "That was a fine thing to say to your own mother."

From the room beyond, your sister said, "Mama, Mama, please don't start again."

Your little brother Tommy said to your sister, "Scaredy cat."

The brother beside you said in a whisper, "What did Papa say to Grandma?"

You said, "I don't know. Go to sleep."

The walls around the room were of lath and cracked plaster, and you could hear your grandmother in her bed. The strange "oh oh ohs" were round sobs that shook the bed now.

The brother beside you said, "Grandma's crying."

You said, "I'm not deaf. I hear her."

Your brother who was six said to his sister, who slept beside him: "Hey Jo, Grandma's crying."

Your sister said, "Well, you'd cry too, I bet, if you was her."

Your brother said, "Aw, how can I be her?"

The brother beside you said, "Listen to Tommy."

Your father asked in the darkness, "Who's crying?"

"Grandma's crying."

Your mother said, "His own mother."

Your brother Tommy said, "Papa, why's Grandma crying?"

Your father said, "You go to sleep, Tommy. It's awful late."

The brother beside you said, "Tommy sure asks questions."

Your mother got out of bed and put on her kimono. You heard her scrape through the room in her raggedy red slippers with the holey toes.

Your father said, "Where you going now?"

Your mother said, "Don't talk to me."

The moon was shining through the dining room windows, and you saw your mother pass them by. You heard the creak of the good rocking chair, and you knew your mother had seated herself by the stove. The embers in the stove were going out now, but she would not pour in coal because it made a kind of desecrating noise. The chair purred sweetly as your mother rocked to and fro, and pretty soon all was very quiet, and your mother was asleep in the dining room.

In the yard next door you heard the tumble of boxes, behind the grocery store. It was the neighborhood cats looking for meat scraps.

Your grandmother was asleep now. There were no sounds from her room.

Your father sighed. The springs in his bed whined angrily. Your father was fighting for sleep.

The brother at your side snored in the fresh sleep of boys.

Your little brother Tommy and your sister Josephine were soundless.

And after a little while, you heard your father whisper to your sister.

He called softly, "Jo, Jo ... Josephine."

She did not answer, and your father got up from his bed and went to the room where she slept.

Your father shook your sister until she woke up.

He whispered to her, "Josephine, will you be Papa's nice little girl and go sleep with Grandma?"

She said, "Oh, I like to sleep with Grandma."

"All right, you go. Just tell Grandma you wanna sleep with her."

Your little brother Tommy was awake now, and he said, "I wanna sleep with somebody. I'm scared to sleep alone."

Your sister said, "Scaredy cat."

Your father said, "You come and sleep with Papa, Tommy. Just you and Papa all alone."

And before they went to their different beds, you too were asleep.

Charge It

THE GROCERY BILL—I can never forget it. Like a tireless ghost it haunts me, though boyhood is gone and those days are no more. We lived in a small town in northern Colorado. Our red brick house was my mother's wedding gift from my father. Brick for brick he had built it himself, working evenings and on Sundays.

It took a year to build that house, and on the first anniversary of their marriage my mother and father took possession. I was the first son and the only child not born in the red brick house. In the first year in the new house my brother was born. The following year another brother was born. And then another. And another. And another. My mother gave birth to sons with such rapidity that my bricklaying father was sent spinning into a daze from which he never entirely recovered. There were nine of us.

Next door to the red brick house was Mr. Craik's grocery store. Shortly after moving into the new house my father opened a credit account with Mr. Craik. In the first years he managed to keep the bills paid. But the children grew older and hungrier, more children arrived, and still more, and the grocery bill whizzed into crazy figures. Worse, every time we had a birth in our house, it seemed to bring my father bad luck. His worries and his brood moved up a notch, and his income moved down. He was sure that God had a powerful grudge against him for earlier excesses. Money! When I was twelve my father had so many bills that even I knew he had no intention or opportunity to pay them.

But the grocery bill harassed him. Owing Mr. Craik a hundred dollars, he paid fifty. Owing two hundred, he paid seventy-five. Owing three hundred, he somehow managed to pay a hundred. And so it was with all his debts. There was no mystery about them. There were no hidden motives in their non-payment. No budget could solve them. No planned economy could alter them. It was very simple—his family ate more than he earned. He knew his only escape lay in a streak of good luck. His tireless presumption that such good luck was coming had stalled his desertion and kept him from blowing out his brains. He constantly threatened both, but did neither.

Mr. Craik complained unceasingly. He never really trusted my father. If our family had not lived next door to his store, where he could keep an eye on us, and if he had not felt that ultimately he would receive at least part of the money owed him, he would not have allowed further credit. He sympathized with my mother, and pitied her with that quasi-sympathy and cold pity that businessmen show the poor as a class, and with that frigid apathy toward individual members of it. Now that the bill was so high, he abused my mother and even insulted her. He knew that she herself was honest to the point of childish innocence, but that did not seem relevant when she came to his store to make additional increases on the account. He was a man who dealt in merchandise and not feelings. Money was owed him and he was allowing her additional credit. His demands for money were in vain. Under the circumstances, his attitude was the best he could possibly muster.

It took courage for my mother to go in and face him day after day. She had to coax herself to a pitch of inspired audacity. My father didn't pay much attention to her mortifications at the hands of Mr. Craik. Beyond expressing her dismay at again confronting the grocer she did not tell my father of Mr. Craik's cruelty in detail. It was too humiliating. And so my father was not fully aware of it. He suspected it, but that was the sort of suspicion one hated verifying. He naturally expected some trouble in obtaining additional credit. As his wife, that was her obligation. To his way of thinking, it wasn't *his* fault that there were so many children. He looked upon that part of it as a deliberate conspiracy between her and God. He was merely a man who worked for a living. He loved his children of course—but after all! And so she had to do her part, which he thought was awfully easy, since it had nothing to do with the sweat and toil of his trade.

All afternoon and until an hour before dinner, my mother would wait for the valiant and desperate inspiration so necessary for a trip to the store. She sat with hands in her apron pockets—waiting. But her courage slept from overuse and would not rise.

This winter afternoon was typical. I remember: it was late. From the window she could see me across the street with a gang of neighborhood kids. We were having a snowball fight. She opened the door.

"Arturo!"

I saw her standing at the edge of the porch. She called me because I was the oldest. It was almost darkness. Deep shadows crept fast across the milky snow. The streetlamps burned coldly, a cold glow in a colder haze. An automobile passed, its tire chains clanging dismally.

"Arturo!"

I knew what she wanted. In disgust I snapped my fingers. I just *knew* she wanted me to go to the store. Her voice had that peculiar, desperate tremor that came with grocery-store time. I tried to get out of it by pretending I hadn't heard, but she kept calling until I was ready to scream and the rest of the kids stopped throwing snowballs.

44

I tossed one more snowball, watched it splatter, and then trudged through the snow and across the icy pavement. Now I could see her plainly. Her jaws quivered from the twilight cold. She stood with folded arms, tapping her toes to keep them warm.

"Whaddya want?" I said

"It's cold," she said. "Come inside and I'll tell you."

"What *is* it, Ma? I'm in a hurry."

"I want you to go to the store."

"The store? No. I'm not going. I know why you want me to go—because you're afraid on account of the bill. Well, I ain't going."

"Please go," she said. "You're big enough to understand. You know how Mr. Craik is."

I did know. I hated him. He was always asking me if my father was drunk or sober, and what the hell did my father do with his money, and how do you wops live without a cent, and how does it happen your old man never stays home at night? I knew Mr. Craik, and hated him.

"Why can't August go?" I said. "Heck sakes, I do all the work around here."

"But August is too young. He wouldn't know what to buy."

"Well," I said, "I'm not going."

I turned and tramped back to the boys. The snowball fight resumed. She called. I didn't answer. She called again. I shouted that her voice might be drowned out. Now it was darkness, and Mr. Craik's windows bloomed in the night. My mother stood looking at the store door.

The grocer was whacking a bone with a cleaver on the chopping-block when she entered. As the door squealed he looked up and saw her—a small, insignificant figure in an old black coat with a high fur collar, most of the fur having been shed so that white hide-spots appeared in the dark mass. One of her stockings, always the left, hung loose and wrinkled at the ankle. You knew a safety pin supported a garter of worn elastic. The faded gloss from her rayon hose made them a yellowish tan, accentuating the small bones and white skin under them and making her old shoes seem even more damp and ancient. She walked like a woman in a cathedral, fearfully on tiptoe, to that familiar place from which she invariably made her purchases, where the counter met the wall. She smiled, as though at herself for being what she was: a mother, a prolific mother, and not a society lady.

In earlier years she used to greet him with a "howdydo." But now she felt that perhaps he wouldn't like such familiarity, and she stood quietly in her corner, waiting until he was ready to wait on her.

Seeing who it was, he paid no attention, and she tried to be an interested and smiling spectator while he swung his cleaver. He was of middle-height, partly bald, wearing celluloid glasses—a man of forty-five. A thick pencil rested behind one ear and a cigarette behind the other. His white apron hung to his shoe tops, a blue string wound many times around his waist. He was hacking a bone inside a red and juicy rump.

"My!" she said. "It looks good, doesn't it?"

He flipped the steak up and over, swished a square of paper from the roll, spread it over the scales, and tossed the steak upon it. His quick, soft fingers wrapped it expertly. She estimated that it was close to ninety cents, and she wondered who had purchased it.

Mr. Craik heaved the rest of the rump upon his shoulder and disappeared inside the icebox, closing the door behind him. She wondered why butchers always closed icebox doors behind them; and she guessed that, assuming you locked yourself in and couldn't get out, you wouldn't starve to death at least—you could always eat the wieners. It seemed he stayed a long time in the icebox. Then he emerged, clearing his throat, clicked the icebox door shut, padlocked it for the night, and disappeared into the back room.

She supposed he was going to the washroom to wash his hands and that made her wonder if she was out of Gold Dust Cleanser; and then, all at once, she realized she was out of *everything*.

He appeared with a broom and began to sweep the sawdust around the chopping-block. She lifted her eyes to the clock. Ten minutes to six. Poor Mr. Craik! He looked so tired. He was like all men, probably starved for a hot meal, and she thought how nice to be the wife of a grocer; but even if she *were* a grocer's wife she wouldn't allow anything but homemade bread on her table. That made her think again of how much money you could make if you had a little store downtown and sold good homemade bread, the big loaves like the ones she herself baked. She was sure she could handle such a business, and she couldn't help thinking how mad her husband would be if she went out and earned her living like so many of these women were doing nowadays. She could see herself in that little bakery store, with cakes and cookies and loaves of bread in the window, herself behind the counter in a white apron, society ladies from University Hill coming in and saying, "Oh, Mrs. Bandini! You bake such wonderful things!" And of course she would have a delivery route, too, and Frederick and August and Arturo would be the delivery boys, and later their brothers would follow; she wondered how much she would pay them as a start; and since Arturo was the oldest and needed most coaxing she would pay him six dollars a week, and August three, and little Frederick one. They would put their money in a savings bank and after that first store was a success she would ...

Mr. Craik finished his sweeping and paused to light a cigarette.

She said, "Cold weather we're having, isn't it?"

But he coughed, and she supposed he hadn't heard, for he disappeared into the back room and returned with a dustpan and a paper box. Bending down, he swept the sawdust into the pan and threw it into the box.

"I don't like cold weather at all," she said.

He coughed again, and before she knew it he was carrying the box back to the rear. She heard the splash of running water. He returned, drying his hands on his apron, that nice white apron. She smiled sympathetically, but he wasn't looking in her direction. At the cash register, very loudly he rang up NO SALE. She changed her position, moving her weight from one foot to the other. The big clock ticked away. Now it was exactly six o'clock.

Mr. Craik scooped the coins from the cashbox and laid them on the counter. He tore a slip of paper from the roll and reached for his pencil. Then he leaned over and counted the day's receipts. She coughed. Was it possible he didn't know she was in the store? He wet the pencil on the end of his pink tongue and began to add figures. Patting her hair, she raised her eyebrows and strolled to the front window to look at the fruits and vegetables.

"'Strawberries!" she said. "And in the winter too! Are they California strawberries, Mr. Craik?"

He swept the coins into a bank sack and went to the safe, where he squatted and fingered the combination lock. The big clock ticked like the beat of a small hammer. It was ten minutes after six when he closed the safe.

She was no longer facing him. Her feet had tired, and with hands clasped in her lap she sat on a box and stared at the frosted front windows. Mr. Craik took off his apron and threw it over the chopping-block. He threw his cigarette on the floor, stepped on it, and went after his coat in the back room. As he straightened his collar, he spoke to her for the first time.

"Come on, Mrs. Bandini. Make up your mind. I can't hang around here all night long."

At the sound of his voice she lost her balance and nearly fell off the box. She smiled to conceal her embarrassment, but her face was very red and her eyes lowered. Her hands fluttered at her throat like disturbed leaves.

"Oh!" she said. "And here I was, waiting for you! I'm awfully sorry. I never thought ..."

"What'll it be, Mrs. Bandini—shoulder steak?"

She stood at the counter, her lips pursed.

"How much *is* shoulder steak today?"

"Same price. Same price."

"That's nice. I'll take fifty cents' worth."

He tossed his head grimly.

"Why didn't you tell me before?" he said. "Here I went and put all that meat in the icebox."

"Oh. I'm awfully sorry. Let it go then."

"No," he said. "I'll get it this time. But after this, come early. I got to get home some time tonight."

He brought out a cut of shoulder and stood sharpening his knife.

"Say," he said. "What's Svevo doing these days?"

In twelve years the two men had rarely spoken to one another, but the grocer always referred to her husband by his first name. She always felt that Mr. Craik was afraid of him. It was a belief that secretly made her very proud. Now they talked of Svevo, and she told

50

again the monotonous tale of a bricklayer's misfortunes in the wintertime. She was anxious to get away; it was so painful to give Mr. Craik the same report day after day, year after year.

"Oh, yes!" she said, gathering her packages. "I almost forgot! I want some fruit, too—a dozen apples."

It was a bombshell. Mr. Craik swore under his breath as he whipped a sack open and dropped apples into it.

"Good God!" he said. "This charging business has got to stop, Mrs. Bandini. I tell you it can't go on like this."

"I'll tell him," she said hurriedly. "I'll tell him, Mr. Craik."

"Ach. A lot of good that does. I'm not running a charity."

She gathered her packages and fled for the door.

"I'll tell him, Mr. Craik. I'll tell him. Good night, Mr. Craik. Good night, sir!"

Such a relief to step into the street! How tired she was! Every cell in her body ached. But once more, and for another day, the problem of food was solved. She smiled as she breathed the cold night air, and she hugged her packages lovingly, as though they were life itself.

The Criminal

THAT SUMMER we lived on Madden Street, down near the high school. It was the best house we ever had, with a bathtub and jets for a kitchen range. A gas range was one of the big dreams of Mama's life. The jets brought it nearer realization. Now, all she had to do was get a range.

The rent for the Madden house was twenty-five a month, five more than we ever had paid before. It was a three-bedroom house of red brick with a real lawn in front. At last we had room to spare. Mama and Papa slept in the main bedroom, Grandma had the one off the kitchen, and my two brothers and I slept in the middle bedroom. Everybody had a bedroom, which was quite a development in our family.

Not many Italians down on Madden Street.

Besides our family, there was only Fred Bestoli, who was more bootlegger than Italian. Once Fred had been a friend of the family, but now that he was a lawbreaker my mother didn't want him around. Grandma too had been fond of Fred Bestoli before he sold booze. Like herself, he was from the province of Abruzzi and they had people and places in common. But now she hated him because he persisted in getting arrested and not caring for the reputation of other Italians.

When Papa brought Fred to the house she would greet him in Italian. She'd say, "Good evening, Dog Dung." Or, "Look at what came out of some woman's stomach."

Fred Bestoli was a melancholy, taciturn Italian, but my grandmother always brought out considerable fight in him. He would answer, "Kiss my buttocks, old woman," and Papa would encourage him.

"That's right, Federico. Tell the old slut to mind her own business."

Raging, Grandma would turn on Papa and say it would have been better if her womb had produced a pig rather than himself. Papa would answer that, since she was his mother, he was surprised that he had *not* been born a pig. This violent obscene language never meant anything one way or another. They just talked like that.

Every fall my father made wine and stored it in the cellar. He never had much luck with the wine. It was either too sweet or too sour. He had no patience, and if the vintage had possibilities he downed it before it had a chance to age. Thus he was always going down the street to Fred Bestoli's house, where the bootlegger lived alone in chaotic squalor. On these trips Papa carried his bricklayer's toolkit, a heavy canvas satchel. But he fooled nobody. The neighbors watering their lawns along the street looked at him brazenly, assuring him they knew what was in the bag.

We kids were fascinated by movie criminals, but Fred Bestoli was hardly the fascinating type. He neither killed nor robbed. He carried no firearms, nor was he hunted by the police. He was in and out of the Boulder County jail so much that we too despised him.

He always came to our house by way of the alley. Standing behind the coal shed, he whistled for Papa. If we were having supper, Papa would go outside and tell Fred to wait. This created bad feeling at the table, Grandma grumbling and slamming things, cursing America, saying she should have drowned Papa the day he was born. Mama would stop eating, her body freezing in resentment, her eyes fixed on Papa, who started slamming things too, saying he wished he had never married, had never come to America, had never been born to a jackal like his mother or wedded to a fool like his wife. If any of us kids so much as breathed heavily during this spell of fury, Papa would snatch a knife and threaten to slit our throats, and though this frightful warning was shouted three or four times a week throughout our boyhood, the nearest he came to carrying it out was the night he flung a meatball at my brother Dino.

Dinner finished, the kitchen would be cleared and Mama would order us into the dining room and lock the door, and Grandma would go to her room. But Grandma was always full of fight. She made it a point to encounter Fred Bestoli, if only to spit at his feet or insult him in some way. He returned spit for spit, insult for insult, until my father shouted for peace. Then she would retreat, whimpering, to her room, beseeching God to burn down the house and everyone in it.

One evening while we were having supper there was a knock on the front door. Papa answered. Who should be there, his arms loaded with packages, but Fred Bestoli?

"Hallo," he said, frightened as he glanced at Mama and Grandma. There was something new and shining about him, and it wasn't the new suit and green necktie. It was in his face, an eagerness to please, a friendliness. He even nodded to us kids. Grandma spoke up.

"What do you want, jackass?"

He tried to smile.

"Throw him back in the gutter," Grandma said.

He turned piteous brave eyes on Papa, who moved closer to listen to some whispering. Papa kept nodding and smiling. Finally Papa slapped him on the back.

"Good," he said. "Good boy, Fred."

As he would a bashful child, Papa led Fred into the dining room. He stood before us at the table, his teeth clenched, his arms around the packages.

"For you," he said, pushing a long gift box toward Grandma.

She withdrew as if he held a snake.

"Take it!" Papa commanded.

Grandma scowled and snatched the box.

Fred searched his packages and found one for Mama. She hesitated, but Papa tore the box from Fred's hands and shoved it into Mama's arms. There were three other packages. They were identical and Fred handed one to each of us boys. The thin boxes looked suspiciously like neckties. Carlo tore his fingernails into the paper, but Papa told him to wait. With clean, shining black eyes Fred Bestoli looked to my father, who cleared his throat as if he was about to make a speech.

"Fred Bestoli has been my friend for thirty-five years," Papa said. "He was born ten miles from my hometown. He came to America when I did. He worked hard in this country. Hod carrier. Coal miner. Dug ditches. Hard work. No money. He's got no trade. So what does he do? He sells a little whiskey. A few bottles of wine. Is that bad? I say, no! But the law says yes. So he goes to jail, three, four times."

Fred coughed. A fat, silvery tear rolled from his eye, slid down his cheek and went crashing toward the floor. His emotion touched Grandma. She made a bouquet out of the corner of her apron and put her nose in it. Papa was pleased with his effectiveness. He raised his voice, lifted his hands and eyes to the ceiling.

"Up there," he said, meaning heaven, "is where they judge what's right and what's wrong—and up there Fred Bestoli's got friends—even if he's got none down here."

Mama, Fred and Grandma were all crying now, and Papa was so moved that he sobbed. My brother Victor snickered in embarrassment. This brought such a twisted silent snarl to Papa's lips that Victor lowered his face and stared at the floor.

"But Fred Bestoli's a different man tonight," Papa shouted. "He's reformed. He's all through with boot-legging. He wants to be friends, like before."

Grandma jumped up and tossed her fat little arms around Fred. "Thank God!" she said. "Ah, thank our heavenly Father."

Laughing through his tears, Fred smacked a loud kiss into Grandma's grey hair.

"My Federico," Grandma said. "My son. Better, so much better, indeed, than my own flesh and blood."

"Can we open the packages now?" Victor asked.

Papa nodded, and we pulled the paper away. Neckties they were. It was extremely difficult to feel gratitude, but Mama forced us to thank the man. Grandma's package contained a black shawl. She was overwhelmed as she put it around her shoulders.

"Thank you, *figlio mio*," she said, the tears bursting from her eyes. "A thousand thanks." Then she glanced at Papa. "Ah, that God had made you my son instead of him. Forty-five years, and he has never given me so much as a chamber pot."

Fred's gift to Mama was a grey coat-sweater. We watched her put it on. She buttoned it up, pleased, and rubbed her hands over it.

"How about some dinner for our friend?" Papa said.

The question brought a flurry of activity as Grandma and Mama made a place at the table for Fred. Mama got a plate from the good china, and Grandma went to her room and returned with a linen napkin. Papa disappeared into the cellar for a pitcher of new wine.

Through the front door Carlo saw something in the street.

"Look!" he gasped.

Parked in front of our house was a brand new Packard sedan. It was a big black job, so new it loomed like a shining animal. It was Fred Bestoli's car. He had bought it that day, only a few hours ago. We rushed outside and examined it closely, opening doors, pushing buttons, honking the horn. None of us had ever ridden in such a new car.

"Let's ask him," Victor said.

In the house Fred was seated before a stuffed pepper and a glass of wine. Mama and Grandma hovered over him and Papa sat across the table. We asked for a ride in the new car.

"No," Papa said.

"We didn't ask you," Carlo said.

"I'm *telling* you."

But Fred was expansive. "Sure. I give you a little ride."

"They'll ruin your car," Papa said.

Fred shrugged. "How?"

"I don't know. They'll find a way."

But he gave in finally, and said we could go. There was a condition, however. We had to "get ready." This meant we had to change clothes, put on our Sunday stuff, with a necktie.

"What for?" Victor demanded.

"You don't ride in a new car looking like that," Papa said.

We looked at one another. We were in corduroys, our school clothes. It was silly. But there was no arguing with him. Either we got ready, or we got no ride.

The long hateful preparations began. We had to bathe, the three of us in the tub, Grandma supervising. She used a washcloth the way a carpenter used sandpaper, tearing away the flesh back of our ears. She could get a corkscrew effect by twisting the corner of the cloth, stuffing it into an eardrum, and twisting it. She removed scalp dirt by ripping it out with her fingernails. When the ordeal was over we went into the bedroom where Mama had arranged our clothes—fresh underwear, clean shirts, clean socks. That night, as a tribute to Fred Bestoli, we were trussed up in the new neckties. Starched and strangling, we were ready in half an hour. We trooped out of the bedroom and into the dining room. There sat Papa and Fred. Twice in that time they had emptied the wine pitcher. Their faces and voices showed it.

"Go wait in the car," Papa said.

We waited an hour. We were glutted with waiting,

our bodies aching. The night had come. The street was in darkness. Through the front door we looked hatefully at Fred and Papa as they leaned heavily on the dining room table. The new wine had mowed them down, and they had succumbed uproariously. Though only four feet apart, they shouted at one another and banged the table with their hands. They were beasts, ugly beasts.

"Look at them," I said. "They make me sick."

"What a father," Carlo said. "Nuts to him."

"I'm leaving here some day," Victor said. "I've had about all I can stand. Wait'll I'm twelve—you'll see. I'll be gone. Then they'll be sorry."

Finally Mama intervened. We couldn't hear what she said, but her gestures indicated an appeal for us.

"Let 'em wait," Papa yelled.

It brought a shriek from Carlo, a long wild eerie howl of pent-up exasperation that turned his face blue as the cords of his neck tightened and the frightening wail penetrated the night. It was so terrifying that Fred and Papa stopped shouting and gaped at one another, sobered a moment. Papa arose on rubbery legs and Fred lurched out of his chair. They came through the house and down the porch stairs like men dying of thirst, groping at shadows for support. They almost fell on their faces as they reached the sidewalk, but as they approached the car a touch of dignity stiffened them and they pretended to be sober.

Papa pushed his head through the rear door and smiled disgustingly at us, his eyeballs floating.

"All set?" he drooled.

We didn't answer. Fred Bestoli had staggered around the car to the driver's side, but an odd impulse had made him keep going. Across the street he wandered aimlessly, talking to himself. After a fashion, Papa went to his rescue. We could hear them yelling under the apple tree in front of the Whitley yard. Fred had forgotten that he owned a car. As they shouted, the lights on the Whitley front porch went on. It chastened Papa, bringing out a last remaining spark of human decency as he quieted down and laboriously helped Fred back to the car. We could hear the two men gasping and reeling, their feet tangling as they stumbled toward us.

We weren't interested in a ride anymore. Fearing for our lives, we tried to get out of the car. But Papa wouldn't let us. A ride we wanted, a ride we would get.

"But he's too drunk to drive," I said.

"*I'll* drive," Papa said.

We groaned. My father had never driven a car in his life. Papa got Fred into the car just as Mama and Grandma came down the porch stairs. Fred was asleep, with Papa trying to get the car keys out of his pocket. We opened the rear door and jumped out. Mama appealed to Papa not to drive. He ignored her, searching for the keys, pushing Fred about like a sack of onions. We were clear of the car by the time he found the keys and as he groped the dashboard for the ignition Grandma stepped forward with a broom. She pushed it through the door and beat the keys out of

Papa's hand. They fell to the floor. As he searched for them Grandma banged him on the head with the broom. The incessant whacking infuriated him. He seized the broom, twisted it from Grandma, staggered out of the car, and charged her. But she held her ground, her arms folded defiantly, her lips spitting epithets. Toe to toe they stood, battering one another with insults. Mama reached in the car and put the keys in her sweater pocket.

By now nearly every porch light in the block was turned on. Neighbors stood in doorways and watched. Papa and Grandma suddenly stopped insulting one another. With Mama's help, they pulled Fred out of the front seat and led him into the house. Mama pulled down the blinds and turned off the lights in the front part of the house. One by one the porch lights along the street went out, and doors were closed and bolted. The night was quiet once more.

They stretched Fred Bestoli out on the sofa. He snored with his mouth open. Papa went into the bedroom. His shoes thumped the floor as he kicked them off. Soon he was asleep too, his snores as loud as Fred's.

Disconsolate we sat in the kitchen, Carlo and Victor and I. Grandma came in. She smiled as she opened her coin purse. She handed each of us a dime.

"Go to the movie pitch," she said.

The movies! We swarmed over her, kissing and hugging her. She pushed us away and we pulled off our neckties and hurried from the house. It was the best house we ever had.

A Bad Woman

WE WERE HAVING DINNER when Uncle Clito arrived through the snowstorm. He pulled off his overshoes, breathed into his cold hands, and came into the dining room.

Papa asked him to have some *pasta e fagioli*, but he didn't want any. Straddling a chair, his chin on the back-rest, his alert brown eyes studied the table. He noticed the wine, the amount Papa had drunk, the amount of butter spread on our bread, everything. Mama preened herself, pressed her hair into place. For you had to be very careful around Uncle Clito. He had a talent for discovering trouble. We kids hid our hands, lest he observe our unkempt fingernails.

Uncle Clito was a barber. He was Mama's oldest brother, the only brother born in Italy. He spoke a broken English. His shop was the best in Denver's Little Italy. Though he was a rich man, Uncle Clito's excuse for not marrying was that he could not afford a wife.

Everybody was afraid of him. He could diagnose trouble out of the most trifling symptoms. When we went to his shop for haircuts Mama made us dress in Sunday clothes. That was because Uncle Clito once saw my worn shoes and deduced Papa was gambling again. He was correct. Mama's brothers and sisters descended upon our house, demanding to know if Papa was neglecting us. Passing Uncle Clito's shop on Osage Street, we made sure he saw us wave as he worked the first chair by the window. There was reason for this too. Once my Aunt Teresa passed without waving. She crossed the street and passed the shop with her head turned away. Immediately Uncle Clito phoned Uncle Julio, Teresa's husband. Julio closed his butcher market and met Clito in front of the barber shop. Together they walked down Osage, peering into every bar and café. Sure enough, at Zucca's they found Teresa in a booth with Tony Mongone, the bookmaker. Aunt Teresa was playing the horses again. Julio dragged his wife into the street, slapped her face, and sent her home in a taxi. Later Uncle Clito smiled with cunning and explained why he had suspected Teresa of gambling again. The way she had walked, he said, her nervousness, the fact that she had not waved at him.

So here was Uncle Clito at our house once more, coming through a snowstorm to tell us something.

"How's business?" Papa asked.

Uncle Clito shrugged. Then he nodded at us kids, indicating that he wanted us to leave the room. We went away contemptuously. What did we care? All we ever got from that old skinflint on Christmas was long underwear, socks, and other useless junk. We trailed into the kitchen, Papa closing the door after us. Immediately we piled against it, our ears pressed against the door crack. Uncle Clito spoke.

"Anybody see Mingo, lasta few day?"

"He hasn't been around," Papa answered.

Mingo was our favorite uncle, Mama's youngest brother, and the most famous person in the family, for he played piano in the Denver Symphony Orchestra. His Christmas presents to us included air rifles, electric trains, baseball bats, and sleds.

"Pretty soon Mingo get marry, for to have wife," Clito said.

"Mingo?" Papa doubted it.

"You wait. You see."

Through the keyhole I watched Uncle Clito's mysterious smile. His face twinged with pleasure.

"Who's he to marry?" Mama asked.

"Some *puttana*, no doubt," he said in Italian, "Some harlot or other."

"How do you know this?"

"I know lotsa thing." He smiled. "Lotsa, lotsa thing."

Mama and Papa were silent, afraid of his wisdom. I could hear wine clucking in Papa's throat as he drank.

"I'm glad Mingo's getting married," Mama said.

"He's so lonely, living by himself in that terrible Roma Hotel."

"Lonely?" Uncle Mingo grinned. "Live all by his self?" He shook his head. "Mingo not so all alone like you tink. The Roma Hotel, she'sa half block from my shop. I see things. I say nothing, but I see what'sa go on."

"What do you see?"

"I see somebody, she'sa got red hair."

Mama slapped the table.

"Clito, you make me so tired! You're a tattletale."

Clito pressed his heart with both hands. "Is it for tattletale I want my brother to marry a *puttana?* Is it for tattletale, she is same womans who run the Flamingo Rooms? Ah, no! It is for love of my little brother Mingo. I am barber. They come for haircut: four girl, one womans. I say nothing. I cut the hair, they give da money. But when this womans want to marry my little brother Mingo, is not for tattletale, I talk. I'ma protect Mingo."

"Mingo wouldn't marry that kind of a woman," Papa said. "He's got better sense."

"Mingo, he'sa crazy. He'sa great artiste."

"Not that crazy," Papa answered. "Mingo's a young man. He fools around. It's his own business."

The cunning returned to Clito's smile. "Nobody buy diamond ring, for fool around with redhead."

"What!" Mama said.

Clito folded his arms and grinned like a cat.

"Maybe the ring belongs to somebody else," Papa

ventured. The skepticism injured Clito.

"I am talk with Frank Palladino," he said. "Frank tell everything. The ring, she's redhead ring."

They couldn't dispute that. Palladino owned the jewelry store a few doors from the barber shop.

"He can't marry that kind of a woman," Mama said. "I won't let him!"

"Too late," Clito smiled. "Bird like a feather ..."

Clito left our house and made his report to the rest of our clan. Next day Mama sat at the telephone, making and getting calls. At dinner she gave my father the details. Aunt Rosa, Attilio's wife, was prostrate with grief. Aunt Philomena was too revolted to even talk about it—an ironic thing, for she and Mama actually talked over the phone for nearly an hour. Aunt Teresa wanted to know why Mingo didn't marry a nice, clean Italian girl like the rest of his brothers. Aunt Louisa threatened to tear out the eyes of Mingo's woman the moment she saw her.

For the next three days our people were in a state of mass hysteria. Aunt Teresa came to the house and wept on Mama's shoulder. Mama and Aunt Louisa visited the church and said prayers for Mingo's guidance. Aunt Philomena came to our house, fell on the couch, and wailed. Mama took her hand, both of them crying. Papa suggested going to the Flamingo Rooms for a talk with the woman who had caused all this chaos, but Mama grabbed him by the suspenders and screamed,

"Don't you dare!" And, "Over my dead body!"

Three nights after the news broke, Clito was back at our house. He had gone to the police and checked the redheaded woman's record. Here were the awful facts: the woman's name was Joan Cavanough; she was thirty-two years old. She had been a bad woman for years, and had been arrested twice. But her real name was not Joan Cavanough; it was Mercedes Lopez.

"Mexican, eh?" Papa said.

"No," Clito said. "Portuguese."

"Portuguese," Papa said. "Hmm. That's bad."

"The Church won't allow it," Mama said. "He'll have to get married by a Protestant."

"If she's Portuguese, she's probably Catholic too," Papa said.

"That kind of woman a Catholic?" Mama said. "Never!"

Suddenly Papa was furious. Maybe it was because he had always disliked his brothers-in-law; maybe it was because he loathed Uncle Clito; maybe it was because he was so fond of Uncle Mingo, who went fishing with him; whatever it was, Papa stood there and shouted his defiance, banging the table until the dishes danced.

"Makes no difference! Mexican, American, Portuguese, Catholic, Protestant—makes no difference. A man's got his own life to lead. Leave a man alone. Maybe he loves this woman. Maybe he don't care who she is. Maybe he can take her out of the Flamingo Rooms and give her a home. Did you ever think of that?"

Clito looked at Mama with a sad smile. At last Papa had been trapped; at last he had revealed the sordid liberalism of his credo. Exhausted, Papa sat down and gulped wine. Clito stared wistfully at Mama, pity on his face. As he left nobody spoke or moved.

Papa remained at the table. Mama cleared the dishes, clattering them to indicate she was ashamed of her husband. For three hours Papa sat and drank. He was very quiet, turning the glass in his hand. Twice he went down to the cellar to refill the wine jug. He staggered when he rose to go to bed. But only his legs were drunk. The rest of him was weary with a deep melancholy.

Clito came in a hurry the following night. Holding his hat, he stood in the dining room and made the following report. That afternoon Uncle Mingo had come to the barber shop. He had wanted a shave. There was a three-day growth on his chin. He had looked sallow and dissipated. Asked where he had been, he had said, "Here and there." Asked what he had been doing, he had said, "This and that." And when Uncle Clito asked if Mingo planned to marry, he had answered, "Sometimes, yes, and sometimes, no."

As Uncle Mingo dozed under hot towels, Uncle Clito had tiptoed to the back room and phoned Uncle Julio, the butcher. In two minutes Julio was at the shop. Mingo was still in the chair.

"We don't see you much these days," Uncle Julio had said.

"Here I am," Mingo had smiled.

"Tomorrow's my wedding anniversary," Uncle Julio had said. "Ravioli dinner. You coming?"

"I'll be there."

And after congratulating Julio on his anniversary, he had hurried away. And that was the end of Uncle Clito's report.

"Tomorrow isn't Julio's anniversary," Mama said, "He was married in November, two days after Attilio had his teeth pulled."

"One o'clock tomorrow," Clito said. "Julio's house. Everybody come." He smiled mysteriously and left.

Papa didn't want to go to Uncle Julio's house. At noon the next day Mama was rushing from room to room, her face smudged with powder, her mouth full of hairpins, her breath coming in gasps from the pressure of her corset. Papa sat in the kitchen, wearing his new pants, drinking claret and shouting that it was a trap, that he wouldn't go. But why had he shaved? And why was he wearing his new pants? Though his protests grew louder, he was dressed and ready before Mama.

In single file we trooped through the path cut into the deep snow of the back yard to the shed where Papa kept his truck. Mama sat with him up front, and we three boys settled into the truck bed.

Uncle Julio's flat, one-story house was a mile away. When we arrived everyone was there except Uncle Mingo. Mama panted as she went up the porch stairs. Suddenly she burst into tears. Uncle Julio opened the door and embraced her.

"There, there, Coletta," he said. "Now don't you worry about a thing."

We followed them into a parlor filled with cigar smoke, the pungency of strong wine, and men—hot, sweating men. With respectful silence they watched Mama hurry sobbing into the kitchen, and you could see Uncle Tony's eyes fill abruptly as he bit his lip to control himself. In the kitchen Mama collapsed into the arms of my four aunts. At once they were crying and wailing as Louisa choked out little reminiscences of Mingo's life—how sweet he had looked as an acolyte, how beautiful as an infant, how elegantly he played the piano, and how Ma and Pa (my grandparents) would roll over in their graves if Mingo married this redhead. Then there was the sharp sound of water boiling over and sizzling on the stove. At once the women stopped crying and sprang into action. As soon as the sizzling died down and the cooking was in order, they began again, this time with passionate anger.

"I say, hang a woman like that," Philomena said. "Hang her and let her stay right there till she rots."

"Hanging's too good," Teresa said. "Put a mark on her breast, like in that picture, and drag her through the streets. And spit on her." She spat.

"I'll tear her to pieces," Aunt Louisa said, warming up slowly. "When I see that woman, I'll put these fingernails in her eyes, and tear them out by the roots. I'll fix that woman so that no man will ever look at her again."

In the parlor Papa found a seat on the sofa, first removing with virile contempt a number of pink and green pillows upon which were engraved pictures of the State Capitol, Pikes Peak, and the ruins of Pompeii. Other pillows had poetry on their bright faces. One was a poem called "Mother," and the other "Home Sweet Home." The walls and the piano were weighted down with pictures of relatives, living and dead. And there was that frightfully unforgettable picture of Aunt Teresa's first baby, who died at six months The picture was taken after the baby was dead.

They sat around, the men of our family. Uncle Julio, the butcher; this was his house. Uncle Clito, the barber. Uncle Pasquale, the stonecutter. Uncle Tony, the truck driver. Uncle Attilio, the laborer. My father, the bricklayer. Squashed into that ornate little parlor, they drank wine and smoked cigars, and beneath their tight Sunday clothes their short square bodies chafed and sweated.

They didn't speak of why they were here. Cautiously they grunted about the weather, the hard times. Their feuds were frequent and ever ready to burst anew. My father, the bricklayer, had only contempt for the work of Pasquale, the stonecutter. Uncle Tony, the truck driver, made it a rule never to haul for relatives. For this he was roundly detested. All of them considered Julio, the butcher, a bully and a hypocrite. Uncle Attilio, the laborer, resented the great care the others took to always complain of debts, thereby cutting short any hope Attilio had of borrowing money. Two things these men had in common. They worshiped Uncle Mingo because he was an artist, a bird in flight, a free-wheeling, unshackled bachelor; and they hated Uncle Clito because of his evil tongue. There was no knowing what Uncle Clito felt, for he lived in the lives of others.

Uncle Tony forced a break in the conversation.

"Ah, boy!" he said. "That ravioli smells good."

"What do you *mean*—ravioli?" Uncle Julio said. "You think I'm made of gold? That's spaghetti."

"But I thought..."

"Never mind what you thought. You know why we're here. What we going to do about that woman?"

"I'll talk to Mingo myself," Pasquale said. "I know how to handle him."

"You!" Julio scoffed, the butcher addressing the laborer. "Don't make me laugh."

"I want nothing to do with it," said Uncle Tony, who never hauled for his relatives.

"Maybe he's right," Papa said. "Maybe we should-n't interfere."

"A fine way to talk," Pasquale said. "I suppose you'd like that kind of a sister-in-law."

Papa's voice boiled. "I'd like her better than some I got."

Pasquale leaped to his feet. So did Papa. They rushed one another, their heavy bodies colliding harm-lessly. The others tore them apart while they yelled at one another.

Papa: "He's no stonecutter, that bum!"

Pasquale: "And I suppose *you're* a bricklayer!"

The women rushed from the kitchen, hurrying to their men, pleading with them not to fight, fluttering about like fat hummingbirds. The fight ended without blows. The men ordered the women out of the parlor.

Their united stand against the women forged a better understanding among the men. They sat down again, and the tension was gone. Papa loosened his tie, Pasquale took off his coat, Tony put his feet on the tea table, and Uncle Attilio pulled off his shoes. A powerful odor of feet filled the room. The wine glasses were re-filled. The discussion began again

Cousin Della, Uncle Tony's little girl, staggered into the room on uncertain feet and put her head in Julio's lap.

"Is the bad, bad woman coming?" she asked.

"No," Julio said.

"Why isn't she?"

Aunt Louisa rushed in, pulled Della to a chair, laid the child across her knee, and spanked her sharply. Della's screams filled the house. "I'll teach you to talk about bad women," Louisa gasped. "I'll teach you!"

"You're bad too!" Della bawled. "You're awful."

I took Della by the hand and led her downstairs to the long basement, where my brothers and cousins were gathered. It was a hostile camp, the girls pitted against the boys. The girls were haughty and too proud to fight, and the boys made nasty remarks.

Upstairs in the kitchen the women were impatient. The spaghetti was done, spread into two huge platters, seasoned with sauce and sprinkled with cheese.

Tables were set in the dining room for adults and the kitchen for the children. It was one-thirty.

"He's ashamed to come," Louisa said.

"And no wonder," Rosa answered.

The men folks, their bellies splashing with wine, were in a sour mood. Only Uncle Clito kept up his careful appearance. He sat by the window, not drinking, delicately licking his finger as he turned the pages of a woman's magazine. My father had fallen asleep on the sofa, his mouth wide open.

At two o'clock Uncle Julio said, "Let's eat."

The men rose, their joints popping like broken sticks. Restless and hungry they fell into chairs around one section of the dining room table, grouped together in a tight half-circle. The wives objected. They felt that each man should sit beside his mate. The men scowled and refused to budge. The kids in the kitchen were seated around the table and at bridge tables set up in the middle of the room. The spaghetti was hot but pasty; the tomato sauce had dried, there wasn't enough cheese. When we learned there would be nothing more than winter apples for dessert, everything tasted worse. Quarrels broke out at the bridge tables. Shins were kicked.

In the dining room Uncle Julio complained bitterly. This was the worst meal he had ever eaten. He asked the men their opinion. Their mouths crammed with food, they made it clear that he was right. Aunt Teresa broke into tears, and the women consoled her. It was that redhead's fault: she was the cause of it all. Then everyone quieted down, and all you heard was sucking, chewing, gulping and belching as we ate our spaghetti.

The front door opened. There stood Uncle Mingo and a woman. Mingo was tall, with the golden eyes of a rooster. He had corn silk hair, and his long hands were dangling masses of bones and blue veins. He resembled my great-grandfather, whose mother had been Russian. Mingo was the only one of our people who was not dark-skinned, dark-eyed and thickly built. He was a carrot among potatoes.

The woman at his side was small, her face brightly rouged with the quality of a pressed rose. Mingo pulled her close to him, reassuringly. She was about thirty-two, with high cheekbones and slanting dark mestizo eyes in a pretty face that had once been beautiful.

"Don't be afraid," Mingo smiled.

The women around the table exchanged glances of disgust, but you could see a kind of terror in the faces of the men. Uncle Mingo removed a red fox cape from the woman's shoulders. Beneath it was a loose green blouse tucked into an orange skirt. She was slender, round-hipped, with thin legs. She rubbed her hands together, for they were pink with cold. Uncle Mingo took her hands and massaged them briefly.

This was too much for the women. They got up, lifted their chins, and walked single-file into the bedroom, slamming the door after them. Uncle Mingo laughed.

"What did I tell you?" he said.

The woman looked at him with frightened eyes.

Then the bedroom door opened. Aunt Rosa peered out. "Attilio," she said. "Come in here this minute. I won't have you out there, Attilio. You hear me?"

Attilio half rose in his chair, but Uncle Mingo caught his glance, and he sat down again. The woman smiled, her teeth as white as a dog's. Aunt Rosa slammed the door closed. Uncle Mingo put his arm around the woman and brought her close to the table. He introduced each man to her. They avoided her eyes, nodding coldly. To each she smiled and said, "Pleased to meet you." To Uncle Clito she exclaimed, "Why I know you! My barber!" Clito blinked, said nothing.

Uncle Mingo turned to us kids, crowded at the kitchen door. "Kids. This is Miss Cavanough."

With that, the bedroom door burst open and the women poured out, swooping down on their broods, gathering them like wandering kittens, some by the neck and hair, dragging them into the bedroom. I escaped with my cousin Albert. Mama appealed to my father, and Aunt Philomena ordered Pasquale to remove Albert. The men shrugged, afraid to offend Uncle Mingo.

From the bedroom came the noise of kicking and screaming, of slaps being administered, the women shrilling their rage, their epithets penetrating the walls like a cold wind: that harlot, that home-breaker, that woman of the streets.

The men squirmed and coughed, but Mingo and Miss Cavanough seemed oblivious. Even while Aunt

Teresa shouted, "I'll break every dish she touches," they sat down at the table.

"I'll tear her eyes out!" Louisa shrieked.

Then there was a stamping of feet and the fury of physical violence, punctuated by screams. Once more the door was flung open and Louisa, her hair disheveled, her blouse almost ripped from her, broke loose from the other women and charged across the room toward Miss Cavanough, a hairbrush in her hand.

"I'll kill you if you don't get out of here!" she shrieked. "I'll beat your brains out."

The woman got behind Uncle Mingo in terror as Papa and Uncle Julio carried Louisa back to the bedroom, the hairbrush crashing clack clack against Julio's skull. They closed the door and came back, Uncle Julio rubbing his scalp painfully. Uncle Mingo's jaw was set, his eyes full of indignation, yet he grinned steadily.

"Don't worry, dear," he told the woman.

"Let's go," she said. "They hate me."

"You're welcome here," Mingo said. "Everybody's welcome in my brother's house. Isn't that right, Julio?"

"Yeah," Julio said. "I guess so, Mingo."

"You're not welcome!" Philomena screamed from the bedroom.

Miss Cavanough's lips trembled, her fingers at her throat. She seemed about to cry. She saw a glass of wine before her and drained it in one breath. Then she sat down, put her elbows on the table, churned her hands, glancing at the men, at the walls, at her lap. Suddenly she stood up.

"I can't!" she sobbed "Oh, Mingo, I can't! I can't."
She ran into the parlor, picked up her coat and dashed
out the front door. Mingo went after her, calling her to
come back. He caught up with her as she was getting
behind the wheel of her car, half his body inside the car
door, his hands waving, pleading to her. Then he withdrew, and the car pulled away and started down the
street in a sudden burst of speed.

He came back to the house with his hands in his
pockets. On the porch he lit a cigarette. For two or
three minutes he leaned against the porch rail, smoke
tumbling from his mouth. Then he flipped the cigarette
and came inside.

The men around the table stared at their plates.
There was silence in the bedroom. Mingo sat down
and poured a glass of wine. Uncle Julio touched his
shoulder.

"Sorry this happened, Mingo."

"Shut up," Mingo said.

He looked into each face, bitterness and suffering
pouring from his hard eyes. They left him alone, drinking by himself at the large table, and retreated into the
parlor, where they spoke in whispers. Mingo drank
steadily, thoughtfully. In a little while the bedroom door
creaked open and the silent women emerged. They
stood around the table for a few moments, their anger
gone, waves of tenderness and pity flowing from them
and covering Mingo. Aunt Teresa went downstairs and
returned with a bottle of brandy.

"Try this, Mingo. I've been saving it."

He poured and drank. Aunt Louisa braved his despair to stand beside him, her fingers stroking his bright hair. "It's hard, Mingo," she said. "It's very hard—I know."

He kept drinking, never speaking, the women holding their vigil over a dead love. Soon most of the brandy was gone and his head dropped to the table. They gathered him up, his feet dragging, and carried him into the bedroom. They removed his shoes and clothing and put him to bed. He slept heavily, moaning through troubled dreams. Aunt Louisa stroked his forehead.

"He's young," she said. "He'll get over it."

Suddenly he sat up in bed, his eyes reddened and wild, in a last siege of torment, his fists clenched. We were all present, the women around the bed, the men and children peering through the door

"Clito!" he gasped. "Ah, Clito! Mother of God, why did you do this to me?"

Then he sank back and fell into a heavy sleep. The women pulled down the curtains, darkening the room. They tiptoed out and the door was closed. The heartbreaking sound of Mingo's voice was still with us. Everyone looked at Uncle Clito, who stood white-faced and alone. Aunt Rosa, hands on hips, stood before Clito, glaring at him. Suddenly she spat in his face. At once the women went wild, backing him into a corner.

"Hypocrite!" Mama said.

"Scandal-monger!" Philomena said.

"I'll tear his eyes out!" Louisa said.

The men came to his rescue, dragging him out of the women's clutches and pulling him to the front door. "Go on," Papa told him. "Beat it, Clito, before you get hurt." He pushed Uncle Clito through the front door with such force that the barber lost his balance, fell from the porch, and lay a moment in the snow. Then he got to his feet and walked down the street.

After that, we were no longer afraid of Uncle Clito—none of us. Next time we needed haircuts, Mama told us to go to Joe's Place, right across the street from Clito's Shop.

To Be a Monstrous Clever Fellow

"To think of it," Jurgen reflected,
"that the world I inhabit is ordered
by beings who are not one-tenth so
clever as I am. I have often suspected
as much, and it is decidedly unfair.
Now let me see if I cannot make
something out of being such a
monstrous clever fellow."

—James Branch Cabell
Jurgen: A Comedy of Justice (1919)

ON SATURDAY NIGHT, Eddie Aiken and I sat on
the beach smoking cigarettes. The lights of Wilmington
behind us were carelessly bright and varicolored, re-
flecting under them the moods of people hurrying
nowhere in particular. Up the beach a hundred feet, in

an open pavilion, a jazz orchestra was playing "Tiger Rag," wild. The song reminded me of a Ben Hecht story about a famous anthropologist who searched remotely for primitive ways and customs; but lo, after a life gone grey and in his own home town the great professor found music and alleged dancing as unique as the ceremonial antics of any antediluvian clan of Fiji wild men. Then and there the savant's researches terminated in a blaze of happiness, and forthwith he wrote the book which he had been contemplating for eight years.

I told Eddie the story. He laughed with muzzled curiosity, saying, "Pretty good. Pretty good. But I don't see the point. Let's go up to the Majestic and stag some dances."

I was not a facile dancer. I was always too conscious of my partner, and too sensitive of my contortions before strange eyes.

"I can't," I said. "I have to be on the docks early tomorrow."

"Just dance one or two," Eddie said. "It's only nine o'clock."

"Okay," I agreed reluctantly. "But only one or two."

We arose and brushed the white sand from our pants.

Eddie pinched his sweater. "God, we're both dressed like hell, though."

He was dressed in a white shirt with a black tie, a white sweater and black pants, much nicer than I was. I wore a white shirt and a dark red tie, my brown leather lumberjack, and brown pants.

"What the hell," I said, "are we mannequins?"

"What're they?"

"People who walk in fashion parades."

We advanced on the Majestic. Across the harbor twinkled the lights of San Pedro. Between the lights and us the plane carriers *Lexington* and *Saratoga* lounged at anchor. They looked monstrous, black and cold. I thought of a story.

The dance hall was packed. Colored lights flashed against wall mirrors. Crepe paper strips hung and waved in twisted loops from rafter to rafter. It was the usual type of hall, where admission was free and you paid ten cents a dance, the floor being vacated after each number. A white wicker fence two feet high surrounded the marble floor. Sailors, stevedores and their women, laborers and their wives, and wealthy tourists all struggled on the floor. We greeted a few friends and bored our way to the fence, where we watched the dancers, especially the women, clump past. The orchestra still blazed away at "Tiger Rag." Spasmodically, one fellow howled, "Yippeee! Wahooo!"

Eddie nudged me "A native-born Californian from Texas."

I felt tight and dry-mouthed; dance halls were places where women managed to be the suaver. I tried to think of a suitable descriptive adjective. Instead, my thought supplied me with a feeling of uselessness for descriptive adjectives, and I began to wish I had stayed home and done my thousand words. A girl in black satin, flaunting sleek hips, raced down the floor pulling her sweating partner after her. I followed her with my eyes, wondering what she did for a living and if she read Nietzsche. With such hips, I rambled, she had certainly not had children; but I would bet she was no virgin.

"Come on," Eddie said. "Let's get goin'."

The stags were numerous. We fought our way through them to a small aisle that circled the floor, and walking along this aisle we watched the seated spectators at our right for unescorted women.

"Oh boy," Eddie said.

Before us were two girls, solitary, and one was attractive, with red-brown hair; the other one was ugly. They smiled an invitation as we approached. Eddie beat me to the fairer one.

"I'll see you later," he said. Eddie was a slick one, and an excellent dancer.

I walked on. The ugly girl watched me pass by. Ten feet away I turned around. Our eyes clashed.

"Oh God."

I walked on, faster. I tried to spin words explaining why I had looked back: "There was a fascination about her uncomeliness that, perforce, reverted my eyes in her direction." And I thought the sentence well done indeed for such a short time in which to compose it.

I walked down the aisle to the other side, where I saw two girls seated, one blonde, the other brunette. They leaned forward so that their heads were almost in each other's laps, and both talked breathlessly. They were about twenty-five, probably married, I guessed.

I straightened my tie and walked to them. I was too aware of my size, my smallness, to be suave, and I knew it, a mere physiological disadvantage but impossible to ignore. The girls looked at me through their eyebrows, scarcely lifting their heads. Their jaws, chewing gum, chugged like pistons.

I decided to ask the blonde, called myself a boob, and spoke.

"May I have this dance?"

The music was a slow fox trot.

They stopped chewing simultaneously and stared at one another. The blonde examined her fingernails. They were very long.

"I never dance with no strangers," she said.

She spoke to her friend as she polished her nails on her thigh.

"Go ahead and dance with him, Elsie. He looks like a nice fella."

Elsie screwed her lips so that they pouted, and shook her head slowly.

"Uh, uh," she said. She made me angry.

"You mean, 'No, sir,' don't you?"

She looked up at me.

"Yeah, that's what I mean. 'No, sir.'"

I walked away.

"Hey, you!" the blonde yelled when I had gone ten feet.

I returned to where she sat still polishing her nails.

"I changed my mind. I guess you can have this one with me."

What kind of an egg did she take me for?

"That's very sweet of you," I said, "and since this is a guessing game, I guess you can go to hell."

She bit her lips, squinted at me, and turned a lovely red. I tried to smile but it was hard. As I walked away I heard the blonde say to her friend, "I was never so insulted in all my life," and I congratulated myself on my repartee. I remembered that Voltaire, Huneker, and George Jean Nathan were masters of the business, and I wondered how they would have dealt with her. Maybe not so obtuse, but surely words to the same effect. Then I called myself an ass, but for some time I walked about quoting from memory many things from Mencken's *American Credo*.

The orchestra began a very pretty German song, "Two Hearts in Three-Quarter Time." I went to the floor to watch the dancers swing to the selection. It would be splendid, I thought, if I could sing the words to the song, but since I was wishing, I might as well be thorough and desire to know the whole language. So I reasoned. I told myself that I was an ape for admiring everything Teutonic, for no reason other than that the men I heeded most were German. I wondered what the blonde was saying. I thought of Nietzsche, reminding myself that I was not even sure I was pronouncing his name rightly, though I respected it as much as my own. I recalled Zarathustra: "Bitter is the sweetest woman," and "Thou goest to woman? Do not forget thy whip." I wondered if Nietzsche wrote such acidy words as platitudes. I had to forget Nietzsche if I wanted to have a decent evening. I vigorously told myself that at thirty-three Nietzsche would still influence me. "But," I thought, "suppose Nietzsche should step off the floor and say, 'Hi there, lad. Go outside and blow out your brains.'" I wondered how badly I would take it. The girl in black satin glided by and I forgot him and my mind spurted into a soliloquy on loving her. Sherwood Anderson, I remembered, had written that often to see a woman walk across the floor was a spectacle of pure beauty. He must have meant a woman in black satin; he must have meant something a little off the mark of beauty, the sheer aesthetic quality.

The girl and her partner circled the floor three times. Not for a breath did I flick my eyes from her waist. The waltz ended, she disappeared in a throng at the entrance, and I had not so much as glanced at her face. If I saw her again, wearing a coat, I would not recognize her. And, I thought, according to the religion of my baptism, I had committed a mortal sin, and now I was ticketed for hell more than ever. I cursed all priests.

As the floor cleared, rich bars of blue and gold light shot across the hall. The orchestra struck up a sentimental waltz, an old favorite, "Beautiful Ohio."

I looked for an empty seat where I could listen to the music fully relaxed, appreciating every note. Not far away I saw an empty seat, draped by a woman's coat.

"Is this your coat?" I asked the lady in the next seat.

"Yes."

"Will you move it, please? I want to sit down."

"Why, I guess so."

She was a fat woman. My request vexed her, and I enjoyed her annoyance. I sat down with grand ease, hoping the woman would be the more irritated, but she heaved her broad back before my eyes, and all I saw was the nape of her heavy neck. I rested my head on the back of the seat, staring at the ceiling while the waves of song came across the hall.

I thought: Sister Mary Ethelbert loved this song. She used to play it on the organ when I was in the fourth grade. She's in a convent in Wyoming. She prays for me every night. This song always reminds me of her. Right at this moment she's probably praying for me. And God, what a paradox, every time I think of her, I think of going to bed with her. What did Jurgen say? Now the tale tells—no. Not that. Oh yes. "There is no memory with less satisfaction in it than the memory of some temptation we resisted." But that's kind of vicious, with Sister Ethelbert. And she prays for me. And my mother's home right now praying for me. And so is Father Benson in St. Louis, and so is Paul Reinert, and Dan Campbell. Why should they be priests? If they saw E. Boyd Barrett's books, they'd burn them, but not read them. I should be home reading and writing. I'll have to be up late tonight if I expect to write seven hundred words. I've got to write, write, write. I ought to get to bed early. The steel boats tomorrow. I hate the damn steel. It cuts my hands to ribbons. What the hell. I should feel lucky I have a job. Lucky? What the hell? Concepts of good and evil are merely means to an end. They are expedients for acquiring power. It takes a lot of guts to do what Nietzsche says, but by God, he's right, and I'll do it. Sister Mary Ethelbert was pretty. She thought I'd be a priest. So did my mother. Naked alone would I like to see them, for beauty alone should teach penitence. Now what does he mean by that? I don't know. Like that kid in Sherwood Anderson who said, "I don't know why, but I want to know why." Anderson writes like an old muscle-bound farmer. Cabell writes the pretty lines, O Cabell, O Jurgen, Jurgen. A monstrous clever fellow. Right. For so the tale tells. Hah, Jurgen. I'm only young once. Now, why the hell did Nietzsche chase all over Europe for that Salomé? Why not. He was only young once. I could still be a priest. I wonder if I'll yelp for a priest on my death bed. Me. A coward? No. I'm a monstrous clever fellow I should be home now, instead of sitting here listening to this song. I've got to write and write and write. The song is pretty. Sister Ethelbert liked it.

The song was ended and I sat erect. There was a girl at my right whom I had not noticed until now. Her legs were cased in serpentine gun powder hose, and they were of seductive curve, but the knees were bony and cadaverous. Her dress was of a dark felt material, and she wore a white waist with a dark sport jacket. Her teeth were big, sparkling with vigor, but not small enough for the lips to naturally conceal. Her hair was the color of copper wire stripped of its insulation.

Imitation topaz beads hung from her neck, blending beautifully with her hair and brown eyes.

Rising, I inclined toward her slightly. I tried to look amiable.

"Will you dance this one with me?"

"Why not?" she said. "It's a keen tune." The song was a slow fox trot.

"Just a minute," I said.

She was standing when I returned from the ticket office.

Her eyes were level with my forehead. We entered the gate, I gave the keeper a ticket, and we moved down the floor. She owned hard, sinewy legs, and they followed my floundering steps meticulously. My fingers, at the small of her back, moved like automatic piano keys as her muscles rose and fell. Her powder and rouge gave off a luscious odor. I sniffed it eagerly

"Haven't I seen you before? At Stanford?"

She was a collegian. I would not tell her I was a longshoreman. I hoped she would not feel the calluses on my hands, and I relaxed the fingers of my left hand.

"No doubt," I lied, "for erudition is poured into me at that glorious institute."

She laughed.

"You dance just like a Stanford man."

"Is that a compliment?"

"Indeed!"

You're a damn liar, I thought.

"Aye," I said. "We sons of Leland are proficient with the nether limbs."

"You talk just like a prof."

"Indeed, and that is my position at Stanford." I said this in an obviously joking tone.

"Really, but you're awfully young."

My God, she believes me. Indeed, I am a monstrous clever fellow, or better, she is a monstrous stupid wench.

"I graduated last year. This is my first at teaching."

"What do you teach?"

"Communism."

I was certain that I knew more about communism than she.

"Oh, you old meanie. Communism's against the law."

"What law?" I spoke, amazed. "Haven't you heard of the Bill of Rights?"

"Why, you know," she said, timidly. "I always thought it was against the law."

"Preposterous! Incredible!"

"You must think I'm terribly dumb."

She was on the defensive. I could see Jurgen smiling.

"Oh no. That's not a serious mistake." Then I spoke softly. "But you know, baby, Jehovah made no mistakes when He created you, did He?"

We danced five successive numbers, and when we left the floor, she was calling me Professor. My name, I said, was Professor Cabell.

We drank malted milks and sat in a darkened corner of the hall, almost behind the orchestra stand. Her

95

name was Nina Gregg, and she attended a local junior college. But I soon grew tired of her stupidity, because there was no one to whom I could demonstrate it.

I kissed her many, many times. It was great sport to kiss her. She had lips that were soft red masses, and they were sweet and sticky, clinging to mine as kisses should. She tossed her body carelessly and quite willingly, and I liked it very much, for I had never kissed a college girl before, and having sneered at the legendary ardor of coeds in books, I found this reality most delightful and surprising. When our lips cleaved, her arms were around my neck, and the fingers dug into the loose skin of my back.

After a half hour of this, I asked her to stroll along the beach with me, but she positively refused with a succinct "Never!"

I got mad and almost forgot I was a professor.

Next, I pleaded with her.

"No. I won't leave this hall."

"Why not?"

Arguing with her would do no good. She had so excited me that my temples throbbed. I leaned back and closed my eyes and tried to think of better inducements.

She too relaxed, tossing her head over the back of the seat.

I looked down at her thighs. A red garter peeped from under the hem of her dress.

Unnoticed, I reached over, seized the elastic with my fingers, tugged on it, and let go.

The garter snapped into place, stinging her. Astonished, she seized my hand exclaiming, "Why, professor!"

"Ten million apologies."

"You should be ashamed," she said.

"You shouldn't have displayed your thighs. I was only cautioning you."

She still held my hand, and presently her palm was within mine. Her fingertips moved gently over the calluses, and her hand became tight, as though recoiling from something disgusting. That morning before work I had split the broken blisters open and applied iodine to keep the inner skin from blistering. I could not work with gloves. The splitting left the mounds sharp and jagged, like an animal's paw, so that rubbing my hand across my forearm left white scratch marks.

The girl opened the hand and held it on her knee.

"Heavens," she said. "What horrid hands. What on earth did you do to them?"

The iodine stains looked like dried blood. I could not think of an evasion.

"Oh, it's nothing," I said.

"Sure it's something."

She jumped to her feet and slapped her hands to her sides.

"Say, you've been lying to me."

She was very angry. The cords in her neck bulged.

"Lying?" I had not risen.

"You're no professor. You're nothing but a ditch digger, or a truck driver, or something."

"Well, what of it?"

"What of it? Look at your hands. Look at your dirty old lumber jacket. You're no professor. You're a liar. That's what you are. A dirty liar."

She was almost yelling. Her eyes began to tear. I remained tongue-tied, but if we had been alone, I surely would have mauled her. I stared foolishly at my broken palms and tried to smile. Many people were watching us. I saw an old woman wearing glasses, who smiled. What are you giggling about, I thought, you archaic bag of bones. Then I tried to fashion words to shape my predicament into literature, but all I thought of was profanity, and my fist against the girl's mouth. I thought of an idea for a story, wherein the man kills the woman, and I wondered if my notebook was about so that I could take note of the idea. I thought that if I ever wanted to remember the incident with complacency I should stand up and slap the girl's face, at least. Instead I said, "I'm sorry. I'm truly sorry."

"Oh, you are, are you? You dirty liar."

God, I thought, is that the only denunciation she knows?

Her right hand left her hip, and the back of it thumped across my face. The blow tickled and smarted.

I jumped to my feet. I wanted to knock her down. Instead, I scribbled mentally, "Her hand shot out, and he felt a sharp pain under his eyes, and he leaped to his feet."

Mumbling curses, I sat down again, casting hostile leers at the gaping audience. The girl had disappeared in the crowd.

98

Suddenly I thought of Nietzsche and Cabell and Nathan and Lewis and Anderson and many more. God damn Nietzsche. God damn the great Mencken. God damn Cabell. God damn the whole God damn outfit. I should have torn the virago to shreds. What's wrong with my hands. God damn my father. God damn my mother. God damn myself. Why didn't I hit her? Why didn't I knock her for a roll? Be hard—Oh Nietzsche, get away, will you? For Christ's sake, leave me alone for a minute. Concepts of good and evil are merely means to an end. All is good which proceeds from strength, power, health, happiness and awfulness. What does he mean by awfulness? Not horror. No, he means full of awe. I should have killed her. Jurgen is indeed a monstrous clever fellow. At least she thought I was a professor. I should have called her a poltroon, or an ignoramus, at least. Everett Dean Martin's definition of an educated man is just fine. Sex equality should continue—but what the hell could I do. Nietzsche says that at bottom the sexes are antagonistic. I'd like to have my hands on her for about two minutes. I should be home. I must write seven hundred words and read fifty pages.

I went to the fountain at the entrance of the hall and ordered a cup of coffee, then a second. The waitress stood near me as I put the usual three spoons of sugar into my cup.

"The next time," she said, "I'll pour your coffee in the sugar bowl. It'll save energy."

"Your knowledge of physics is abominable," I said. "Don't you know that no energy can be lost?"

"Smart egg, aren't you?"

"I'm a monstrous clever fellow."

Kiss a man, and kiss a man, and then, because his hands are calloused, be insulted. Because he works hard, think he's a scoundrel. There's one for *The American Credo*. She's a poltroon, a Christian. She belongs in a nunnery. Sister Ethelbert is in a convent in Wyoming praying for me. Paul Reinert and Dan Campbell are in a novitiate in St. Louis. Jesuitism. Damn all religion. I must strengthen my irreligion. They should legislate against religion. William J. Bryan was a scoundrel. And what awful books he wrote. I must go home and write. I should have killed her. What did Jurgen say? Didn't he have a parallel case? I'll never be able to write like Cabell. Wistful, shy, sweet writer. My mother's up, waiting for me. What the hell, can't I take care of myself? Some day, I'll blow up this myth around women. Maybe, as a gentleman, I might have gotten her to walk with me. Maybe, as a gentleman, I could have had her down on the cool sand. Hah! There I go, arguing like Jurgen. Marvelous. I must go home and write.

I turned and saw Eddie. His brow was dewy. The sparkle of his eye was of one who was having a great evening.

"For Christ sake!" Eddie said. "Where have you been? I been looking all over for you."

"Oh, here and there."

"I been every place."

"Ready to go home?"

"Home? God no. I got something. Something swell!"

"No more vixens for me."

"What're vixens?"

"Women."

"Oh. But can the book talk, will you?"

"I came very close to a successful evening," I said.

"Yeah?"

I told him about my professorial interlude.

"You're a sap. I woulda ruined a dame like that."

He was impatient "Come on! Let's get going."

I paid for my coffee.

"Where?"

"Places, boy. Places."

"No, I have to go home. Hard day tomorrow."

"All you ever want to do is stick your nose in books. It don't do no good."

"Sez you."

"They're swell girls." He smiled, outlining the form of a woman with his hands.

I winked a question.

"A cinch," he drawled, snapping his fingers. "They're down in the car now. I thought you'd be waitin' there. I been looking all over for you "

"Let's go."

I decided to write only three hundred words. My reading could be dismissed for the night.

We stepped out of the dance hall.

"They're a blonde and a brunette," Eddie said. "You take the brunette."

"Is she easy to look at?"

"Wait!"

Eddie's car was a block away. It was a yellow-wheeled Ford roadster. The girls' heads were visible through the small back window.

Eddie placed one foot on the running board.

"Well, Elsie," he said, "here's your boyfriend."

The blonde-headed one put her head out and examined me.

Great was our mutual astonishment, for it was the same girl who earlier in the evening had guessed that I could dance with her. Her companion was Elsie, the same girl who was with her then.

"Oh," she said, "so it's you?"

"Correct." I was laughing.

"Oh," Elsie said.

"You know them?" Eddie asked.

"Intimately. Verily, but I consigned her to flaming perdition, but an hour past."

"Aw, can the book talk and talk United States."

"May you, too, suffer the eternal pains of hell," I said.

The brunette, Elsie, deliberately looked away.

"What's he done?" Eddie asked.

"He insulted me," the blonde said.

"Me too," Elsie said.

"Jesus," Eddie said. "You're a fine egg. You think you know too much. You busted up a swell party."

"I won't ride with him," Elsie said.

"Me neither," the blonde said. Her name was Sarah.

102

No one spoke for two minutes. I gazed at my shoes. Sarah leered through the windshield, her chin projected with some exertion. Elsie still looked out the other side. Eddie drew pictures with his finger on the side wing.

"Aw hell, " he said. "Let's forget it."

"No."

"I should say not."

"If he apologizes," Eddie exclaimed, as though he were suggesting something brilliant, "will it be okay?"

Apologies were really unnecessary. The girls would come around, for they were anxious for a good time,

They looked at one another and smiled.

Elsie said, "He has to be real, real sorry."

"Apologize," Eddie said.

"Elsie," I said, "I am so prostrate with grief that I wouldst kiss thy feet, if thou but findeth my sorrow sincere."

She clapped her hands. "Wasn't that sweet, Sarah?"

"Swell."

"Boy, that's the way to do it."

"I would have you know that I am a monstrous clever fellow."

Eddie spat.

"And I'll have you know that you sure love yourself," he said.

"You're forgiven," Elsie said. "You can ride with me now."

"Sure," Sarah said. "You're forgiven."

Elsie got out of the front seat and climbed into the

rumble. In performing this movement, she gave me to understand that her legs were stockingless, and that she wore sky-blue step-ins.

I started after her.

"Wait a minute," the blonde said. "Haven't you forgotten something?"

"My perception is a-quiver to the minutest details," I said, looking at Elsie's legs.

"Aw, talk United States," Eddie said.

"What did he forget?" Elsie said.

"He said he'd kiss your feet," Sarah said, giggling.

"Like hell, I will."

"You said you would," Elsie said.

"Go on," Eddie said, "do it. Let's get started before sun up ."

I denounced the idea with gusto, albeit mightily pretentious gusto; and then I kissed her feet.

I climbed in beside her, the motor sputtered, and we were off.

The night was lovely. There was a yellow moon.

Elsie's breath was putrid, smelling of wine and garlic.

I reached into my pocket for a package of gum.

"Chew?"

"Oh, I never touch gum."

Earlier in the evening, when I first saw her, her mouth was full of it.

"You should. It exercises the gums in these days of Hoover prosperity and soft foods."

"Well, I'll chew one, if you will."

104

After a while I showed her the calluses on my hands. She pressed a kiss in each palm, and I cursed the college girl. But I would have preferred her to Elsie with me, in the rumble seat.

"My brother has them worse than that," she said.

"These calluses are unequivocally the worst in the world. I challenge comparison, even your brother's."

"My! But you are a monstrous clever guy."

"You mean, a monstrous clever fellow," I said.

Elsie and Sarah never drank, they swore, and we were not surprised at their oaths, so Eddie steered the car to a dark section of the harbor, where we pooled our money and purchased a case of beer. The bootlegger gave us four additional bottles, gratis.

We decided not to guzzle the beer until after midnight. But when Sarah and Elsie insisted they were not hungry, each of us consumed a bottle and then we went to a restaurant and ate a delicious supper. Never had I seen such gormandizers as Sarah and Elsie.

When we left the restaurant, it was almost midnight. Elsie and Sarah suggested that we take them home. They didn't like to stay out late since those San Diego murders, and you never knew who you might meet.

Eddie and I roared.

Then Eddie drove to a hotel, where we rented a suite. The night clerk allowed us to transport the beer through the lounge room, so we gave him a dollar tip and two bottles of the stuff.

At five o'clock the car leaped the curbing before my place, and I got out. The blonde was driving. Eddie slept at her side. Elsie too was asleep, in the rumble seat. For an hour we had driven over the surrounding beach territory fruitlessly searching for the girl who had slapped me at the dance hall, but at that hour we saw no one, least of all a precise girl. Very angry, Elsie had suggested the search after I related the incident, though finally, in tears, she had fallen asleep.

Riding in the morning air, now whitening with fog, had sobered me. The hour was too late to go to bed, and too early for work, and yet I was not tired. I determined to write until morning. I knew that my mother was waiting for me inside, her rage bubbling to be released.

I opened the door noiselessly, but my mother, sitting under the lamp, woke up as by instinct. In the same room my brother slept on a davenette; together we shared the bed.

"Well, here you come, you old bum," my mother said.

I closed the door.

"You've been drinking, I can smell the nasty stuff over here."

I sat down on the bed.

"I spent three thousand dollars to give you a good Catholic education. And now look at you. Shame. Shame."

I began untying a shoe.

"Lift up your heart to God and see what you're doing."

My shoe fell with a soft thud.

"Mortal sin after mortal sin. I suppose you were out with some nasty girl, getting yourself full of disease. O God, forgive him. Forgive my son."

My stockings were sweat-soaked. Why did Nietzsche dislike beer so much? The man had an iron will. Asceticism did a man no good, but if concepts of good and evil were purely human products, I suppose it was his privilege.

"And dear God only knows I've slaved to keep this boy of mine right."

I wish I knew somebody who could interpret Nietzsche for me in practical terms.

"Why can't you be a good boy like Paul Reinert? He's studying to be a priest, and there's God in his heart. He never done the things you do. He don't get drunk or read books against God."

But suppose every man accepted Nietzsche's words, and followed them. Why then, I suppose men like myself would soon run to some extreme, like Emerson. Emerson sure likes to show off his vocabulary. He keeps you dizzy thumbing a dictionary. Let's see, his definition of the soul is The Pervading Spirit of the Universe. A hell of a lot of information that gives. Pious hocus-pocus.

"Like father, like son. You're worse than your father. Oh why did I marry him? Why didn't God strike me dead at the altar?"

If I only had time to read all of Emerson, though. Undoubtedly it's excellent vocabulary training.

"You're just a dirty animal without a thought of God or man. Oh, I'm tired of this life."

I could buy all of Emerson in the dollar books. If I had saved my money tonight I could have bought seven books. But thank God I'm a poor working stiff, or I'd never touch a book.

"Almighty God, Blessed Virgin Mary, St. Joseph, take me from this suffering world."

My brother turned over and snarled, "For God's sake, get to bed. I can't sleep with all this noise."

"Unless I'm woefully mistaken, I haven't spoken a word," I said.

"You have plenty of time to give him the dickens tomorrow, Ma," he said.

"And here I work and slave and all you do is read books against God. Don't those nasty books tell about obedience?"

Alas, I'm suffering the same torments as Jurgen after Koshchei brought forth Jurgen's wife.

"Do those nasty books tell you to go to church? Or love your mother? Oh, you dog, you don't love your mother. You'd rather see her dead."

"But I do love you, Ma," I said.

"Love? Love? Is this love? Staying out with dirty, impure women. I know you've been with them. I can see it. You can't fool me."

"I have to have some pleasure," I said.

"Pleasure? Pleasure. You call mortal sin a pleasure?

Oh, my boy, my poor boy. Is that what the books tell you? You never saw Paul Reinert out with dirty women, did you?"

God damn Paul Reinert and all God damn priests in the world.

"You're ruined. Your soul is black. Black as coal!"

I decided not to wear pajamas. I was beginning to tire. I decided not to write. I looked at my hands, and regretted that I had not knocked the girl down. I wished that I could go to school with her opportunity. I could see the girl in black satin, racing down the dance floor. I would read a passage from *Zarathustra* and ponder it in bed before sleep.

"Tomorrow I'm going to tear up all your dirty books," my mother shouted. "I'll burn every one of 'em."

"You do, and by the gods I'll leave home."

"Get to bed!" my brother shouted.

"Yes, please," said my sister from the other room.

I went to my desk and found *Zarathustra*.

At random I opened it, reading "They called God that which opposed and afflicted them, and verily, there was much hero-spirit in their worship."

Kissing mother, I rolled into bed.

She went into her room. I heard her knees crackle as she knelt down; then the rattling of rosary beads.

Washed in the Rain

HAZEL CLIFTON IS George Clifton's sister, and George Clifton is my boss down on the waterfront, at the California Fish Cannery. It was George who first told me about Hazel. I fell in love with her a long time before I saw her. I'm that way. I fall in love with women who don't know it. Like Norma Shearer. I was in love with Norma Shearer my last two years at Santa Barbara High. I know it was love. But she was too far away. I never had the chance or the money to get close to her. Then she married that fellow, and all at once I wasn't in love with her. But while it lasted it was love.

I'm always falling in love with women a million miles away. It's a jinx. It's very strange. It's because I'm really afraid when I get too close to women. I can't talk or even breathe easy. I stammer and act like a fool. My tongue is a ball of glue. It's a hunk of lead. It falls asleep at the bottom of my mouth. After the woman is gone it wakes up and says the things it should have said before the woman went away.

George Clifton, I am going to talk to you now. I am going to ask you something. Do you remember that afternoon on the dock when we were sitting there and the two Mexican women were in the launch under us? They were laughing at us, and making wisecracks. They wanted us to jump into the launch and go for a sail. I wanted to go. I said I didn't, but cripes! I did. I couldn't say it, though. My tongue fell asleep, and as long as the two Mexican women smiled and made wisecracks, my tongue went on sleeping. That was all. The two women were disappointed and rowed away alone. And there we sat.

Why didn't you go with them? If you had jumped into the launch I would have too. But no, you didn't. Then you gave me the raspberry. I mean about women. I had to say something. I had to defend myself. I mean about women. If I told you the truth, I couldn't tell you anything, because I've never had anything to do with real women.

So I told a lot of lies. They weren't so bad. I could have told worse. I guess every fellow tells a few about women. Still, the lies I told you weren't really lies at all. Those things never happened to me, but I told myself they did, and if I thought them the truth, they *were* the truth.

I'll show you what I mean. I told you I was a

football star at Santa Barbara High last year. That was an awful lie. I went out for the Santa Barbara team four straight years, but I never did make the first team. I never even made the second team. As a matter of fact, I was only quarterback on the third team. When I told you Pop Warner came down and asked me to go to Stanford, that was another lie. But George, you don't know me. I'm that way. Things like that *did* happen to me. I *did* make the first team. I *was* a star quarterback. Pop Warner *did* come down from Palo Alto and ask me to go to Stanford. He came every Saturday for four football seasons. I sat on the bench, and he used to whisper to me. He used to say:

"Come to Stanford, Jordan. We need you up there. You'll be on the first team, Jordan. I promise you that."

And listen, George Clifton. I told you I had a lot of girl friends at Santa Barbara High. I did. So help me, I did. But they weren't the real McCoy. My father only made eighteen a week at the drugstore before he died, and you can't have the real McCoy on that much money. I used to fake my girlfriends. It wasn't so bad. It was just one jump behind the truth. When I told you I took a girl named Helen Purcell to the Santa Barbara Biltmore, it was the truth, but there isn't any Helen Purcell that I know about. Oh, listen. I took hundreds of girls to the Santa Barbara Biltmore. This may sound like applesauce, but I took Norma Shearer to the Santa Barbara Biltmore. Almost every night in the week. I've danced a hundred dances with Norma Shearer, a hundred times on that Biltmore floor. Oh, it's hooey. It's fake. But it's fake because I wanted to show you I am good enough for Hazel.

It started the day I saw Hazel Clifton's picture. That day I went to George's office and asked him to give me a lift home. The minute I stepped inside, I saw that picture. It was the whole room. It was small, it stood up like a book end, but it was the whole room. That was Hazel Clifton. She was standing under a palm tree, holding a bouquet of gladiolas. Phew! She was a beauty. She was perfect. I fell hard for her. I didn't know who she was, and I didn't care. But I was in love with her. Like my crush on Norma Shearer. I only saw Norma Shearer in pictures, but I was in love with her. That sounds like hooey, but it's true. When I saw Hazel Clifton standing in the picture holding the bouquet of gladiolas, I fell for her like a ton of bricks.

I picked up the picture and looked at it. George came in and saw me. I said:

"Say George! You sure know how to pick them!"

He laughed.

"Frank," he said. "That's not my girl. That's my sister."

I said, "Your sister! Boy! She's sure swell!"

I could hardly believe it. The two didn't look very much alike. George Clifton is about thirty-eight. The girl in the picture was about nineteen. She was slender and not very tall. George is a big fellow. He weighs two hundred and stands six feet high. The only resemblance was the hair. The picture was multi-colored, and Hazel's hair was blonde, like George's.

I wanted to ask him if the girl in the picture was married, but I didn't have to ask. George must have read my mind, because when he said it, I turned as red as a beet. I mean, when he said:

"No, Frank. She's not married."

A fellow always asks a lot of questions about a pretty girl. Well, I wanted to. But I couldn't. He was her brother, and I didn't want to be snoopy. I put the picture down as if I was through with it, but I got another look at it over my shoulder when we went out the door. I was in love with that girl. I know it was love. I had a million questions buzzing in my brain like a million hornets, and when that happens, you're in love. Like the time with Norma Shearer. I had a million questions then, too. I bought all the movie magazines I could afford, and I even wrote in and asked questions about her.

But I didn't have to ask many questions this time. George opened up about his sister Hazel while he was driving me home. She was in Los Angeles, studying at USC. She was studying music. She was twenty. This was her second year in college. Her mother and father were dead, so George was putting her through school.

Oh, I found out everything. She must have been a wonder in high school. She went to high school here in the harbor. In her last year she was president of the student body. She was a swell tennis player—captain of the girls' team. But the big thing was her music. She was so fine that in summer she gave lessons, and George said that last summer she made two hundred and fifty bucks.

She was popular in college, too. In her freshman year, seven sororities bid for her. Finally she picked Zeta Alpha Nu. And that November when I first saw her picture, she was vice president of her sorority and president of the sophomore class.

I couldn't hear enough about that Hazel Clifton. It tickled me pink that she was getting along so swell. George said some day she would be a great musician. I knew he was right. I felt it. Once I had the same feeling about Norma Shearer. Norma Shearer was not a star then, but I knew she'd be one some day. I was right.

Then George said Hazel was almost engaged to marry Phil Mannix. It practically spoiled everything for me. I mean, Phil Mannix is the star Trojan quarterback, and football stars have always been my jinx. This may not make sense, but if it hadn't been for football stars at Santa Barbara High, things wouldn't have been so tough for me. I hate the big shots—the stars. For four years they made me sit on the bench. This Phil Mannix is more than a star. He's a whole football team. He made a ninety-five-yard run against Notre Dame last year, and was picked on the All-American team because of it. When George told me about Mannix, it hurt. It was an old hurt, and it hurt in the same place, with that same queer ache I got the day I read that Norma Shearer married that fellow. It hurt right in the middle of my throat, as if somebody punched me on the Adam's apple.

George drove up in front of my place, and we talked about the big game two weeks away. Southern

California was playing Stanford. It was the last game of the season. I hadn't thought much about it, but now I wanted Stanford to win.

George asked me how I thought it would come out.

I said, "I hope Stanford wins by a thousand touchdowns."

George, he laughed. I stood on the curb and watched his car turn the corner. He was a block away. I could still hear him laughing. It made me so mad I couldn't eat any supper that night, and my mother thought I was sick.

Hazel Clifton, you will never know how much I love you! There is no way of telling you. I can't tell you. But if we were married, I could tell you.

Maybe you'd say I was a fool the night I put on my hat and coat and went up the street to the high school. I'd never been there before, but since you went to school there, I wanted to see what it was like. I was in love all right. I could smell it in the air. It was a swell night and the street lamps were bright. I thought of you all the time. The smell of the grass on the high school lawn made me think of you. I went up the stairs to the main entrance and thought of how you used to walk in and out of those big doors. Then I pretended I was a big football star leaving the stadium. As soon as you saw me, you hollered and came running.

"Oh Frank!" you said. "I love you!"

I said, "Hazel, I love you."

I picked you up and let you feel my shoulder pads.

You said, "Oh Frank! I love you!"

I said, "Kiss me, Hazel. I love you."

Just then the coach came out of the stadium. I was a big star and he thought a lot of me.

"Here! Here!" he said, winking at you. "What do you mean by stealing the heart of the greatest young quarterback in California?"

I got red and said, "Aw, coach. Roll over and die, will you?"

"Frank," he said. "If I catch you breaking training rules, I'll make you warm the bench in Saturday's game."

I said, "Horse collar! Put me on the bench, and you'll lose that game."

He said, "Quit your kidding, Frank. You don't know how true that is."

Then you said again, "Oh Frank, I love you so much."

And I said, "Hazel, I'll always love you."

Those are the things I said to Hazel Clifton the night I sat on the high school steps. I must have sat there for two hours. Finally the janitor came by on one of his rounds. He saw me and kicked me out of the yard.

Things got to be different at the cannery between me and George Clifton. He started acting strange. He was willing to talk about the football game, but he wouldn't talk about Hazel. He knew I was in love with

Hazel. I gave it away by the way I looked at him when he talked. He wouldn't speak about her. All he talked about was Phil Mannix,

I hated that Mannix. George knew why. He kept talking about him. He kept saying Phil Mannix could beat the whole Stanford team, all by himself. I thought Stanford was going to lose, but I didn't let on. I gave it away, though. I mean, about Mannix. I let George find out I hated him because of Hazel.

I said, "If somebody kicks Phil Mannix below the belt, it'll suit me fine."

Another time I said, "I think Phil Mannix is yellow. The only reason he gets away for long runs is on account of the interference he gets."

But one day George called my bluff. I was trucking some boxes past the office. He was in there. He called me. I put down my truck and went in.

"Say," he said. "If you're so sure Stanford is going to win Saturday's game, why don't you bet some money on them?"

I couldn't bet much. I only made fifteen a week. George, he made sixty. He had me on the spot. I wasn't going to back out, though. I had to pay rent and grocery bills, but I wasn't going to back out.

"Okay," I said. "How much do you want to bet?"

George said, "I'm not betting. How much do *you* want to bet?"

I said, "How about four bits, even money?"

He broke out laughing.

"Four bits!" he said. "My God! I thought you

wanted to bet some *real* money!"

"Well," I said. "Just what do you call real money?"

He said, "How about fifty bucks?"

He didn't bat an eye. Oh, he had me on the spot that time.

I said, "How can I bet fifty? I only make fifteen a week."

"Well," he said. "If you lose, you can pay me off each week. That's fair enough, isn't it?"

I told him I would think about it. I went back to work, trucking the boxes. The bet worried me all afternoon. I almost went nuts. Finally, I couldn't stand it. At two o'clock I went back to his office. He was writing on the typewriter. He didn't hear me come in. Hazel's picture was on the desk. He didn't see me staring at it, but he must have felt me staring at it, because he turned around. It must have made him mad, my staring at the picture.

"What do you want?" he said.

"I'll take that bet," I said.

"You'll do what?" he said. "You'll do what?"

I said it again. I said, "I'll take that bet."

Ah man! I had him on the spot this time. His mouth dropped open, and he pretended he didn't remember.

"Oh!" he said. "You mean the Stanford game."

Ah man!

I said, "Yeah, George, that's what I mean."

"Okay," he said. "It's a bet."

We shook on it.

120

I may be a crazy fool; I may fall in love with women who don't know it; I may do a lot of crazy things, but I got a conscience. I had my mother to support and rent to pay and groceries to buy, and there I was with a whole month's wages bet on a football game.

That was Wednesday. I didn't sleep Wednesday night. Thursday night I didn't sleep either. I got up at two o'clock and took a walk to the high school. There was a white fog that night, and the fog suited me. It covered me up. I went behind the high school and sat on the bench in the tennis court. That made me feel better. I was making this bet for Hazel Clifton. She was like the fog. She suited me. As long as I sat there, I was glad I made the bet. But as soon as I was out of the fog and inside my room and under the covers I got nervous again. I heard my mother snoring in the next room. It nearly drove me crazy.

Stanford won that game. They pulled the biggest upset in years. They beat the holy living hell out of those Trojans. I listened to the game over the radio in the barber shop. I nearly passed out from the excitement. Oh, you Stanford! Oh, you red and white Cardinals! It was an avalanche. The Trojans were three to one favorites, but they were smashed. The Stanford line stopped Phil Mannix in his tracks, and the Stanford backfield went on a rampage with trick plays and end runs and forward passes, and at the final gun there wasn't anything left. The Trojans were mopped up. The final score was Southern California 3, Stanford 21.

After the game, I stopped in front of the Harbor Haberdashery and looked at the men's suits in the window. I was rich now. I was fifty bucks in the clear. I wanted to buy some clothes. But I saw a sign in the window that gave me an idea.

I went inside and talked prices with the clerk. The prices were high, but I ordered what I've always wanted to have, ever since I was a kid, and that was a letterman's sweater from Stanford University. I knew I could never go to school and earn one because my father was dead and I had to support my mother. School days were over. I ordered a white, wool-knitted, v-necked sweater with the big "S" of Stanford right on the chest. The clerk said the sweater wouldn't be ready for two weeks. That was all right with me. Any time was all right with me.

The night I got my sweater something happened. Hazel Clifton came home for Christmas vacation. Phil Mannix came with her. I read about it in the harbor paper. I couldn't miss it, because it was all over the front page.

ALL-AMERICAN TROJAN IN WILMINGTON

Phil Mannix, Trojan warhorse, and two-time All-American quarterback, is in Wilmington. The famous football star arrived by automobile this morning with Hazel Clifton, popular former Wilmington High School girl now attending the University of Southern California. Mannix will be the week-end guest of the Cliftons at their home, 234 Tower Street.

It made me so mad I couldn't see straight, because all week I'd been asking George Clifton when Hazel would be home, and he kept telling me he didn't know. But there it was, all over the front page. I never felt so lousy in my life.

I put on my new sweater and looked in the mirror. And there I was ... I wasn't so hot. I was just a fifteen-dollar-a-week cannery stiff trying to hide it. No wonder George Clifton didn't want me to meet his sister.

I couldn't stand it. I hung around the house for a while, but everything got on my nerves. Finally I grabbed my cap and went outside. It was raining, the first rain of the first rain of that winter. Man! How it came down! I was ruining that white sweater, but I didn't care. And I didn't care if people saw me, either. A lot of people know me in the harbor, and they know I'm not from Stanford, but I didn't care. I didn't give a darn. The rain could drown me, for all I cared. The rain was coming from the north, and I flopped along, right against it, face first. I was soaking wet before I went two blocks.

At the boulevard stop there was a big black lake of rain in the gutter. I was going to wade right through it, shoes and all, but the signal was against me, so I had to wait. The water oozed out of my shoes.

While I was waiting for the signal to change, a yellow sport roadster came alongside the curb. It came to beat the band. It plowed through that lake of water. I got soaked all over.

I yelled, "Hey! What the hell!"

But the side-curtains of the roadster were up, and the driver didn't hear me. The water splashed my face and almost washed my cap off. It was black and greasy and it tasted like asphalt and oil. The whole front of my sweater smeared with a black smudge. I got sore. I stepped off the curb and waded to the side of the car and pushed my face against the side-curtains.

I couldn't see much. But I saw enough. The driver was Phil Mannix. I knew him from pictures in the paper. The girl was Hazel Clifton. I knew her from the picture in George's office. They drove away before I got a chance to say anything. I stood in the street there and shook my fist and cussed a blue streak. But they didn't hear me.

I didn't care any more. I didn't give a damn for anything. When I thought of how Hazel was sitting so close to Phil Mannix, with both her arms around his right arm, and her head on his shoulder, I didn't care. I was through. I was all washed up. And I didn't care about the black splotch across my sweater. I didn't care at all. And while I was walking through the rain toward home, I took out my jackknife, and I cut and hacked that sweater off me. I ripped it off in hunks and strips, and tossed them into the gutter.

I Am a Writer of Truth

THE TRUTH IS often unpleasant, but it must be told. In this case the truth is that Jenny is not a beautiful girl. She makes a lamentable heroine for this story. She is short and fat, with ripples of fat that wash from her. Her stupidity is beyond the power of my pen. Indeed, she disgusts me. No: that is not the truth, for she does not disgust me. But she does something to me which is not good. She saddens me. When I think of her a sense of hopelessness possesses me, a feeling that I can do nothing about the inequality between men and women. I do not hate Jenny, but I certainly despise the things for which she stands. As for what those things are, I am unable to say.

One evening, out of breath, she ran into my room with her arms extended. She was shrieking with delight, her grey eyes laughing and laughing in triumph. I turned from my typewriter and asked for an explanation.

"Look!" she said. "On my wrist! Look! My boyfriend gave it to me!"

It was a wristwatch.

"Jenny," I said. "In the name of God stop saying 'boyfriend.' I loathe that word. I hate it!"

Jenny's boyfriend is a fellow named Mike Schwartz. He is Jewish—a tremendous man. I have seen him many times, a two-hundred pounder, strong and silent, who comes here almost every night to see Jenny in her room. His strong, silent strain does not fool me. I personally am neither one nor the other, but I am aware that the quiet strain in big men is invaluable. When he comes up the stairs in his quiet way I can easily understand what he desires from Jenny. Of course I can understand it! I am aware that the quiet strain has its uses.

About the wristwatch. Jenny is a stenographer in a downtown Los Angeles office. On that very afternoon, she said, Mike Schwartz had come there. Quietly he came, a big man carrying the wristwatch in a tiny box. There he stood, strong and silent. I could visualize the whole thing clearly. I think it monstrous; the truth is, I have to laugh when I think about it. Mike Schwartz asked her what she thought of the watch.

"It's cute," Jenny said.

Cute! Oh Lord! What a ghastly description. Cute! What a loathsome word! A wristwatch can be interesting, or charming, or even beautiful. But never cute. Never! Only a person of limited intelligence, such as Jenny, would ever call a wristwatch cute.

Mike said, "It's for a friend of mine—a girl about to be married. It's a wedding present."

This disappointed Jenny, who thought the watch was for her. Without another word she handed the watch back to him. It was cute, and that was enough. I can see the whole thing. With her nose tilted, she returned the watch.

Mike Schwartz started to leave the office. He turned his back and walked toward the door. I am telling you exactly what Jenny told me. I am a writer: I see it all very clearly. At the door he turned and there were tears in his eyes. Tears in his eyes! Imagine that! A strong, silent man, a giant of a man, with tears in his eyes. I wish to be truthful, and to me a man of forty with tears in his eyes is a jackass. He turned and there were tears in his eyes, and no doubt tears on his shirt and tie, and he came back, fell on his knees before Jenny, who is fat and twenty, and crushed her in his arms.

"Keep it, Jenny!" he gasped. "Keep it. I was lying. It's not a wedding present. It's for you. Keep it— forever!"

Forever! Tears in his eyes! What a spectacle! I can visualize it, and I have to laugh and laugh. There he was, a man of forty, strong and silent, sobbing on his knees before a girl twenty years younger than himself! Lord, it's funny. I laugh and laugh. The fool! Such tears would not have fetched me. I should have laughed in his face.

Nor did they fetch Jenny. But Jenny is clever, grasping, shrewd. Now the watch became more than cute. It was now a wonderful watch, and she cried too. And there they were, two people crying over a mere wristwatch. And that night Jenny brought the watch to my room and told me about it, annoyed me with all this nonsense, telling me that Mike Schwartz touched her soul and that she cried for the sweetness of him.

"I couldn't help it, Mr. Bandini," she said to me—a writer, an interpreter of human psychology.

I refuse to believe Jenny. Furthermore, I refuse to believe she cried for that reason. She is too shrewd, too grasping, too fat for sorrow and tenderness. My theory is that if she wept at all, her tears were tears of joy, of possession, because now she owned the watch, it belonged to her now, and she wept in triumph.

"Let me see this watch," I said.

I examined it indifferently. It was a Bulova Bagette, or some such folderol. A tiny silver watch, with a bit of silver chain clinging to it—a really absurd watch, a mere toy, for one could scarcely see the watch-face, let alone the hands: a joke of a watch, preposterous, and no good at all for seeing the time of day. I turned it over in my palm. There were scratches on the case, wounds made by a pen knife, as if someone had rubbed away a monogram. A second-hand watch. Unquestionably a second-hand watch.

"Ha!" I said. "Old merchandise! A second-hand

watch! Precisely what I suspected. The man is a fraud. A hounder. A cheap charlatan."

Jenny knew it was second-hand for she was shrewd indeed. She knew more than that. She had gone to the jeweler and priced the watch. Trust Jenny to do that!

"Well," I said. "What did the jeweler say?"

She refused to answer me.

"Rather expensive," she said.

"Be honest, please," I said. "I am a writer—a man of truth. Hypocrisy is foreign to my nature. How much did the jeweler say it was worth?"

"Quite a bit," she smiled.

"Well," I said. "Far be it from me to pry into your prosaic activities. But if you must know the truth, I tell you here and now that I can get a better watch than that for three dollars and fifty cents. A much better watch."

I handed the watch back to her.

"There's little purpose in defending the man before me," I said. "Without question he's a fraud. An unmitigated fakir. He's brummagem. He amuses me to the nth degree. When you leave this room I shall start laughing about him."

She chained the watch to her wrist without a word, and then she went away. She was hurt. She does not wear the watch now. She hasn't worn it since then. It lies in her dresser-drawer, in a little box which I discovered one night when I went through her things in search of cigarettes.

The wristwatch is of no significance. True, it was an inexpensive watch and Mike Schwartz could have afforded better. But Jenny coming to my room and asking me what I thought of it—ah! Now there you have something most significant! It reveals her own suspicions. The common run of writer would have praised the watch elaborately, distorting the truth. But not I. My words stabbed like a hot knife. For in her heart she knows what Mike Schwartz really wants, and I know too. The watch was a pitiful subterfuge, an insult. But for all that, it is no affair of mine, nor am I greatly interested.

There is nothing between Jenny and me. I live on one side of the hall and she lives on the other, upstairs in the second story of a two-story house. The other room up here is the bathroom. When first I came here I thought there might be something to it all. I heard clicking high heels in the hall and in the next room, and in the bathroom I saw pale blue things hanging out to dry. I touched these, for they pleased me, and their softness and fragrance brought pleasant little things to my imagination. But nothing happened.

When I heard the click of high heels I sat in my room, always in the evening, and pounded violently on the typewriter, hammered it for all I was worth, writing anything that came to mind, just anything, the Gettysburg Address, or a Shakespearean sonnet, or anything, only hitting the keys with great force so that the sound carried, for there are some who will know a writer is in a room by the noise of his typewriter, and they will like the sound and come to the door and ask him if he writes, and what he writes—I mean women—for so it has happened to me many times, for I have lived here and there in this great city, in houses, apartments, and hotels, and I know the business of violently whanging a typewriter is invariably successful, invariably bringing someone, a man or woman, often enough a woman who is lonely and curious; and sometimes, oftener than not, a man, a man in a rage who tells you to cut out the racket so he can get some sleep.

I lived in this house three days before I saw Jenny. The noise of my big machine never lured her, never once caused her to pause at my door and wonder, and perhaps investigate. This surprised me, and I thought of other methods. But in one way or another all things come from my typewriter, and I could do nothing more, so I hit the keys even harder. This was at night, after I heard her get into bed. But the noise never disturbed her. Apparently she slept without interruption. Finally it was she who lured me.

It was the telephone. Every evening it rang continuously at the bottom of the stairs, and it was always for her. At length I weakened, took my aching fingertips away from the keyboard, stood at the door and listened to the telephone conversation. This time she spoke to a person called Jimmie.

"Why Jimmie, you darling!"

"Oh Jimmie, you bad boy!"

"Why Jimmie, you bad bad boy!"

"Jimmie! You naughty thing!"

I listened to this sort of thing for a long time, stunned by the stupidity of such banal dialogue. As soon as she hung up I rushed back to my typewriter and began pounding again. But it was no use. Her feet mounted the stairs and crossed the hall without pause, and then her door closed.

Later I met this Jimmie. He was a stupid clod, a dandy who wore checkered coats and the neckties of a savage, a bounder who was not impressed by the daring simplicity of my bare feet in house slippers, even though my feet were on Jenny's table and I smoked a pipe larger and longer than any other pipe in the city of Los Angeles. Jimmie was a magazine subscription agent.

"I sell to all the big shots," he said. "Anne Harding is one of my customers."

No doubt he expected me to fall out of my chair at this. I smoked in silence, while he and Jenny waited for my comment.

"Who?" I said. "Not the cinema actress? Very tragic. Very tragic indeed."

Later Jenny told me even more of this Anne Harding pishposh. "She buys all her magazines from Jimmie. Dozens of them."

"That," I said, "is curiously unimpressive. Even the fact that no doubt stories of mine were printed in those magazines fails to arouse my enthusiasm."

Here again the clever urbanity of my remark was

scattered on yokel soil. But it didn't matter, for I was not greatly interested and her friendship with Jimmie was no affair of mine.

I will tell the truth about my first conversation with Jenny. It was the night the landlady introduced us. I invited Jenny to my room for a glass of wine. In truth, I tried to shock her. She was smoking a cigarette, leaning against the dresser while I poured the wine. I looked at her squarely.

"Do you mind if I call you Jenny?" I asked. "The name has an amusing bucolic flavor."

"Not at all!" she smiled, because she didn't know the meaning of bucolic. I handed her a glass of wine.

"Ummm!" she said. "Thanks!"

I was studying her face closely, studying it as a student of mankind, a writer, would study it. This made her a bit uneasy. She raised her glass.

"To you!" she said, "I know you must be a great writer."

I touched her glass and laughed. For the moment I became aware that, after all, the girl was not completely hopeless.

"The matter rests with History," I said. "I live only in the past and future."

We drained the wine glasses. I poured two more.

"Jenny," I said. "I am a man of Truth. Permit me to make an observation about you."

She lifted her glass.

"Fire away, Mr. Charles Dickens! Give me both barrels!"

"Jenny," I said. "I'm like my great predecessor, Huneker. Nothing on the face of the earth annoys me more than a teasing demirep."

"Demirep?" she said. "What's a demirep?"

"A doxy." I smiled.

"Doxy?" she said. "I'll bite, professor. What's that?"

I shook my head sadly.

"A doxy," I said, "is a harridan."

"What's a harridan?"

"A harridan," I said, "is a mopsy."

"You've got me again, professor. What's a mopsy?"

"A mopsy is a trull."

"A trull?" She frowned, then laughed. "It sounds good, but I'm still at sea."

"A Delilah," I said. "A Thaïs. A Messalina. A Jezebel."

"Come again," she said. "Try once more."

"The dictionary is right there. Look it up."

She put down her glass and sprang for the dictionary.

"Sure enough!" she said. "Which one?"

"You'd better try trull," I said.

And she did. Then she closed the dictionary.

"But what's this got to do with me?"

I am not sure what I answered is true. But no one will deny that it had the sound and force of a startling analysis, a bombshell, and true or false, one worth exploding, simply for the effect.

"Jenny," I said. "All womankind is an embryonic trull. The tendency is powerful, and from puberty women must fight it as they would typhus."

She put down her wine glass, snuffed out her cigarette, and walked out of the room.

"You're horrible," she said. "Just awful."

But as time went on nothing I said shocked her. Every night we talked, I doing most of the talking, and she paying no attention to what I said. If you were to ask, there is no word or phrase of mine which Jenny could remember. This is a tragedy. I have said some fine things, sometimes even surprising myself. I am unable to recall them now, but I remember that at the time they were spectacular, exquisitely phrased and worth remembering.

I have said that I wish to tell the truth. I must pause now I to admit that I have failed. I have said that Jenny is fat and not beautiful. That is rather inaccurate, for Jenny is none of those things. No. Jenny is a beauty. She is slender and supple. Her poise is as arrogant as a rose. It is a joy to live near her. The hair on her head is a wonderful thing. It is neither red nor gold, but both, and she combs it with mysterious intricacy, knobbing it at her neck in the manner of Slavic women. She has been married, but now she is divorced. Her husband was a poultry man. This amused me.

"Jenny," I said. "What does a poultry man look like?"

There was no reason for this. As a matter of fact, I know perfectly well what a poultry man looks like. My uncle in Colorado Springs is in the poultry business, and I worked all one summer on his ranch.

Mike Schwartz is a widower. I would classify him as handsome. He has a son, a fine boy, six years old. Sometimes Mike brings the boy here to see Jenny. The boy calls her Aunt Jenny. He has a wonderfully strong little body, with legs like burnished ivory, and curly hair. A fine boy—a son such as I would proudly claim as my own. He is very noisy. Sometimes he wanders into my room and I sit him before my typewriter and allow him to hammer the keys like a monkey. He enjoys this. A fine boy. It is a tragedy that his father is such a dumb cluck. The boy has pronounced literary talent. If he were mine I would make a literary genius out of him. At twelve I would see to it that he wrote and published an autobiography. It would be a sheer masterpiece, I would see to that too. As it is, the boy will unquestionably grow up to be a boob like his father, a man without poetry who falls on his knees and bawls like a calf as he presents a girl a lump of metal.

Jenny grows excited when Schwartz brings the boy. It begins to look as though Schwartz is going to marry her. She has the boy's photograph on her dresser and she worships it. I for one am pretty sick of that boy's photograph. Every time I enter her room to borrow a cigarette I must tolerate it shoved under my nose, together with a collection of the lad's bright sayings. They are no doubt very fine, but I am not interested. I like the boy, he is a fine fellow, but his puerile epigrams bore me. I am really not interested at all.

138

Mike Schwartz comes regularly to see Jenny. Every night before he arrives Jenny dashes into my room and asks if her dress is fitted correctly, if her hair looks nice, if I like this or that pair of shoes. Mike Schwartz has money, great stacks of it in the bank. He is the owner of a brickyard. Nor is that all. He owns a house in Los Angeles, a mansion in Bel Air, to say nothing of two Packards and a Pontiac.

"Jenny," I said, "he may own a brickyard and a castle in Bel Air, but does he have a soul? Has he any depth? I personally have observed him closely, and I fail to discover any beauty in his nature. He is a cold, bloodless, money-grubbing Babbitt."

"He's awfully sweet," Jenny said.

"A perfectly meaningless judgment. Has he any perception of the finer things of life? The deep, enduring things?"

"He's just sweet. And big as he is, he's gentle as a lamb."

I raised my eyes to the ceiling.

"Ah, Jenny. Your naïveté saddens me. It makes me want to go blindly into the night and weep on a high lonely hill for the sorrows of women. The mere fact that Schwartz is gentle proves nothing. A cow is gentle too. What I mean is, does he have any poetry in his blood?"

"He's never written me any."

"The man is a fraud. He amuses me. He has no more poetry than a stomach pump."

"I think he's awfully sweet."

139

"That's because he owns two Packards, a Pontiac, and a house in Bel Air."

She only smiled, for she was not even listening to my appraisal of the whole situation.

To tell the truth, I am no materialist. But I should like to tell Jenny a few things. I should like to tell her that in my time I have been an automobile owner. It was a wonderful car, all-steel body, with high compression oil pump, shatter-proof glass, side-wings, spotlight, and huge blowout-proof tires.

Do not misunderstand me. I tell of the Plymouth because I would have you know I have lived, more or less, the life of that blockhead Mike Schwartz. It didn't last long, for the finance company soon put an end to it. But I didn't mind, for I had already tired of it, and there were a flock of new stories I wanted to write. Yet I wish I had that car now. For one reason. Jenny is continually relating to me long accounts of the wealth of Mike Schwartz. I am not really interested. I am simply philosophic, a little amused, and a little sad.

And yet, in spite of it all, I wish I had my Plymouth. For only an hour I wish I had it to call my own. I know how it is done. I would take Jenny for a ride in it some evening. As supercilious as possible I would sit beside her, my hands on the wheel, and saying nothing, not a word. I would let the Plymouth do all the talking. We would drive to Santa Monica and park the car on a hill where the sea meets the stars. With an indifferent flip of my fingers I would throw the switch on the dashboard, and out of the belly of the machine the radio would respond, emitting the frog-croakings of Bing Crosby. I would remain strong and silent, and doing nothing. No need to tell Jenny her hair dizzied me, that the look in her grey eyes was enough to make me forget, for a little while, prose and plots and such wearisome stuff. The whole thing would be machine-made; but for a little while, for only an hour, it would be enough. The Plymouth and Bing Crosby would move Jenny to the depths of her soul, and for a little while it would be all right. Soon enough I would grow tired of it, in an hour perhaps, and we would drive back to the city. Later Jenny would tell others she knew a writer with a Plymouth. Not a mere writer, but a writer with a Plymouth. It wouldn't matter though.

Prologue to Ask the Dust

ASK THE DUST ON THE ROAD! Ask the Joshua trees standing alone where the Mojave begins. Ask them about Camilla Lopez, and they will whisper her name. Yes, for the last one who ever saw my girl Camilla Lopez was a tubercular living on the edge of the Mojave, and she was heading East with a dog I gave her, and the dog was named Pancho, and nobody has ever seen Pancho again either. You will not believe that. You will not believe that a girl would start across the Mojave desert in October with no companion save a young police dog named Pancho, but it happened. I saw the dog prints in the sand, and I saw Camilla's footprints alongside the dog's, and she has never come back to Los Angeles, her mother has never seen her again, and unless a miracle happened she is dead out there on the Mojave tonight, and so is Pancho. I do not have to weave a plot for this, my second book. It happened to me. The girl is gone, I was in love with her and she hated me, and that is my story.

Ask the dust on the road. Ask old Junipero Serra down on the Plaza, his statue is there, and so are the streaks across it where I lit matches, smoked cigarettes, and watched humanity pass by, I, John Fante and Arturo Bandini, two in one, friend of man and beast alike. Those were the days! I wandered these streets and sucked them up and the people in them like a man made of blotter fiber. Arturo Bandini, with one short story sold, great writer dreaming big plans. I can still see that guy, that Bandini guy, with a green-covered magazine under his arm, perpetually under his arm, walking this town with gentle tolerance for man and beast alike, a philosopher he was, a young one, the plain tale of a writer who fell in love with a bar girl and was told to go.

But look, let me try to tell my story. I fell in love with a girl named Camilla Lopez. I went into a café one night, and there she was, and ever after, even to now, tonight, when I write about it I choke when I think of the beauty of that girl. She was there, beside me, she was a waitress in a beer hall, she brought me coffee and I thought it was bum coffee and we talked. Then I came back again and again, and soon I was so crazy in love I behaved like a fool, and all the time she loved somebody else, she loved a bartender in the Liberty Buffet where she worked, and the bartender couldn't stand her. So she went out with me, to forget him, she went everywhere with me, and I was insane about her, and I got worse, and she got worse about the bartender. She began to smoke marijuana. She taught me to smoke it. She cracked up. She was put into an insane asylum. She was there a month. She came out and I saw her again. She was still in love with Sammy the bartender. He couldn't bear her. He couldn't bear her because she was simply a Mexican to him and he was an American and she was beneath him, and that is the story—that is the Ramona theme, only this time it is an Italian-American telling it, and he, Bandini, is sympathetic with the girl because he understands how it is with this business of social prejudice, and he loves her madly and she can't understand him. He is a writer. He is alone in Los Angeles. He writes sonnets to this girl. She reads the sonnets and tosses them in the street. Ask the dust on the street, ask the sawdust in the Liberty Buffet, ask the goddamn dirty sawdust in that place and it will say that it received little pieces of paper and they were my sonnets, because she didn't care for me, I only amused her, she was mad about the American Sammy.

You don't think I have a novel? Listen goddamnit, I met Camilla and the first night we went to the beach and swam naked, and she swam far out, far beyond the breakwater in Santa Monica Bay, we drove out there in her car, and she swam away, out there in the moonlight, beautiful girl, beautiful Camilla, oh hell how I loved that girl, and oh hell what a dirty hand she dealt me, she thought I was a lunatic, that I said funny things, she swam out, far too much swimming for a normal girl, and in that cold ocean at two in the morning, and when I saw her in the moonlight I had a hunch, that very first night I had a hunch that she was the sort of girl who cracks under social pressure, there was something sensitive and beautiful about her even then and always, gorgeous girl, black hair, cream skin, swimming in the moonlight, daring me to come out as far as she had swum, and I didn't, I swam out a distance and got tired and then she came in and we rolled up in a blanket on the beach and went to sleep—a couple of naked kids, but I felt it lying beside her then—that feeling that I would never possess this girl, felt that somehow she was poison and that it would never happen, felt passion without desire, felt the strangeness of her, felt it within me with the sureness of my mother's breast, this thing devouring a beautiful Mexican girl who *belonged* in that land, under that sky, and was not welcome. And I, the sympathetic one, the lover of man and beast alike, ask the sand along the Santa Monica Bay if the great Arturo Bandini was so great a lover that night, no no no, because I was sorry for her like a man sorry for his little girl and it wasn't passion I felt but only desire, and that's all it ever was. And then at five in the morning, with the sun coming up in the East, we drove down Wilshire and she was so pleased that I had not touched her, she was driving the car, and she said a strange and significant thing, I remember the words exactly, she said, "This was such a beautiful night. It won't ever happen again." But always there was with me the suspicion that I had acted like a fool, not that night alone but every night I was with her, as we visited many strange and fascinating places in this great city. Do I speak of Hollywood with its tinsel blah? of the movies? do I speak of Bel Air and Lakeside? do I speak of Pasadena and the hot spots hereabouts?—no and no a thousand times. I tell you this is a book about a girl and a boy in a different civilization: this is about Main Street and Spring Street and Bunker Hill, about this town no farther west than Figueroa, and nobody famous is in this book and nothing notorious or famous will be mentioned because none of that belongs here in this book, or will be here much longer. This is Ramona in reverse. It's good. It's myself.

So I call my book *Ask the Dust* because the dust of the East and Middle West is in these streets, and it is a dust where nothing will grow, a culture without roots, a frantic grasping for entrenchment, the empty fury of lost hopeless people frenzied to reach an earth that cannot ever belong to them. And a misguided girl who thought the frenzied ones were the happy ones, and who tried to be one of them.

Arturo Bandini, myself, great writer, with one story sold to *The American Mercury*, the story ever in my pocket just to prove my success as I hung around the Opera House and watched the richies going in, sometimes slipping out of the crowd to accidentally touch an ermine wrap, just a fellow passing by, excuse me, lady, and through long hours of the night I'd think of her, wondering who she was—perhaps even the heroine of my great novel, talking to her while the lights of the St. Paul Hotel blinked red and green and threw colors across my bed.

Those were the days. Ask the dust on the road, ask the cobwebs in my room in the St. Paul, go to the mice coming out of the corner of the room, ah such friendly mice, I had them for pets, why I used to talk to those mice. "Hello mouse, how are you tonight, where's your pals?" Sure, a friend of man and beast alike, feeding the mice to make them my friends, a great man, a kindly soul, reader of Thoreau and Emerson, big coming writer who had to be tolerant, spreading crumbs for my mice to eat in the night with the lights of the St. Paul going on and off and I lay watching them scamper to and fro, until it had to end, they got too affectionate, they climbed up on my bed and sat at the foot, we were great friends, but hell they multiplied like Chinese and the room was too small.

Do I speak like a lunatic? Then give me lunacy, give me those days again. Give me a whimsical novel of one who pitied mankind, great person Bandini, maker of magnificent exits, the pity of it all, the absurd city around me, fortunate foster parent of my genius, and up Angel's Flight, up two hundred stairs to Bunker Hill in the middle of town, consecrated steps, Sir, Bandini trod upon them to immortality! Some day, ye people, ye yea-sayers, these steps shall ring with my memory, and over yonder on that high wall shall be a plaque of gold, and upon it a bas-relief—the image of my face. Am I

148

alone now? Poof! My loneliness bears fruit, and there shall be a Los Angeles of tomorrow to remember that a Voice trod these stairs, and Benny the Gouge down on the corner of Third and Hill will weep for joy as he telleth his grandchild that he once spoke with a man of the ages. And so to my room, to have a conversation with myself in the mirror. Or maybe to practice a bit for the days of my fame, to set the mirror at an angle, to see how I look sitting at my typewriter, the great one at work, answering questions for the press, blinking patiently while the flashbulbs explode. "Gentlemen, gentlemen! If you please! My eyes, gentlemen—after all, I too have my work, you know." Laughter from the gentlemen of the press. "Jesus, that guy Bandini, a swell fella, fame didn't get to him. Just like any of us, common newspaper guys—a real swell fella."

Ask the dusty halls, ask the dusty lobby, ask the dusty people in the dusty lobby of the St. Paul, the tired dusty people themselves old and soon to be dust, here to die, the old folks, the dust of Indiana and Ohio and Illinois and Iowa in their blood, to dust and die in a rootless dusty land. Six years ago and so many are already dust, but some there are who remember the great writer, no dust in his mouth, nay, nay, no dust in his mouth, big liar writer talking about big stories in *The Saturday Evening Post* and proving it with a story in a green magazine. Great writer, frequenter of dusty bookshops, lifting dusty magazines and blowing the dust from his beloved story, buying them up, his story, that it should not become dust. Yea, ask the dust on the road.

Ho hie ho, big writer writing letters home to Mamma, big writer finding it tough, but look Mamma, I got a story coming out in *The Atlantic*, in the Pacific, so send five dollars, Mamma, send me five dollars. And so with five dollars, with ten dollars, big writer with green magazine in clip joint talking to dusty blonde telling big blonde of a greater day. Had she read "Carissima Mia," by Arturo Bandini? No, then too bad. Had she read "Mea Culpa," by Arturo Bandini? Yes, she had. Strange. Because it was never written. But five dollars and ten dollars, out of the dust of Colorado, to help Mamma's boy—mea culpa, mea culpa, mea maxima culpa.

A book teeming with people, dusty savage people. The real Los Angeles, Bunker Hill, that part of town below Figueroa, and Arturo Bandini dreaming of great days. The people who crossed his path: Marcus, the wineseller, who gave me a job as busboy because he thought I wrote serials for the *SatEvePost*. Mrs. Adolph Lang with her pink fat breasts which she offered me, I lived next door to her at the St. Paul, her pink fat breasts she offered me because she was the mother of God and I should partake of the milk of life. Dave Myers the Communist on the corner of Third and Hill with his crippled leg out of which he sold marijuana cigarettes. The old ladies who were God's Chosen People and had to make sacrifices with the Blood of the Lamb, but they had no lamb, so they killed a beautiful Siamese cat. The fat Negro who took Camilla and me down a long black sinister alley to Central Avenue and up some rickety stairs to a room in a deserted hotel where men and women lay about like dead people, and the fat Negro throwing them off the bed, splitting the mattress open and selling us marijuana out of the slit. Later in my own room we smoke the marijuana. One cigarette, no effect. Two. The room dims. Arturo's body lifts. He is off the floor, one inch, two. Up and up and oh absurd world, absurd Camilla, and Arturo laughed and laughed, but not Camilla, her mouth softening, white saliva like threads of silk clinging to her wanton mouth, opening tenderly to say his name, Arturo, Arturo. Yea and amen. Big stuff. Jesus what a novel! The two lesbian women playing the piano at the Embassy, playing Strauss waltzes for Camilla while Arturo turns black and spits beer over the piano and into the violinist's hair. The drunken painters in the studio above, the sad painters, the hopeless painters, school of S. McDonald Wright, last vestige of a painting movement to unite the east and west. The hundreds of crummy lower Fifth Street nightclubs crammed with beautiful women, girls writing home to Iowa and Indiana that they were clicking, clicking in the big town, fooey, they were not clicking, they were fucking anybody and anything, Filipino and Jap and Negro in a place glutted with a plethora of beauty. Ah, those nightclubs, where I learned to wander and idle, sometimes with money from another short story sold, sometimes broke, often borrowing money from the girls.

The poor box at the old Plaza church, from which I stole sixty cents because I was poor wasn't I? The

Filipino dance hall the cops raided for drugs, the cops rushing in, the lights going out, the cops screaming and fighting madly in the blackness, and the calm little Filipinos off in dark corners, flipping safety razor blades off their index fingers with the speed of machine gun bullets, cutting the faces of the cops to ribbons.

The quaint and the strange and the beautiful: one night a woman too beautiful for this world came along and on wings of perfume, I could not bear it, could not resist following her, who she was I never knew, woman in a red fox and pert little hat, trailing after her because she was better than a dream, watching her enter Bernstein's Fish Grotto, watching her in a trance through a window swimming with frogs and trout as she ate, and when she was through the boy enters the Grotto, seats himself at the very seat she used, fingers the very napkin she used, because she was so beautiful and—just a cup of soup, waiter, not hungry, just a cup of soup for fifteen cents. Love on a budget, a heroine free and for nothing, to be remembered through a window swimming with trout and frogs.

Hamsun's *Hunger*, but this is a hunger for living in a land of dust, hunger for seeing and doing. Yes, Hamsun's *Hunger*. Clarence Melville the drunken Spanish-American War veteran, he lived across the hall. He had a light housekeeping room. He was tired of oranges, too. He had a car. We got in it one night. He knew where to get meat. We drove to San Fernando. We parked the car. We crawled through barbed wire fences into the pasture. We tiptoed to the barn. There

152

was the calf. Clarence hit it over the head with a sledgehammer. We dragged the bloody thing to the car and drove back to Los Angeles. We dragged it through the back way to his room. God what a night that was! The calf wouldn't die, no matter how hard we hit it. Then the blood on the floor, the carpet, the walls, the bathtub. I was sick. I couldn't eat any of it. Blood in the hall, and the police came. They found Clarence in the bathroom, butchering the calf. He got sixty days, and all the time he was on trial and in jail I stayed in my room, spent a great part of it praying, not to Hamsun or to Heine, but to Our Blessed Lord and Savior, Jesus Christ. Save me Lord, I am innocent.

Ask Camilla Lopez. Ask her. Tell him, Camilla. Tell this hardheaded publisher about us. "Well, you see: my name is Camilla and Arturo loved me, and I thought he was so silly, he wrote me sonnets and they didn't make sense. I passed them around to the drunken lawyers in the Liberty Buffet, and they laughed, so you see he was silly because even lawyers laughed. Once I told him, I said, Arturo, I want to be smart like you. So he bought me a speller, this was right after we met, and he bought me a speller, and he said to learn five words a day, and I did—the first day—but he wasn't like Sammy, the bartender. Oh that Sammy! Such eyes in the head of Sammy, and Sammy was a man, not a silly writer guy, not a sissy, and I loved that Sammy, and he hated me, oh God he hated me. Because I was a Mexican, he called me Spick, he called me Greaser, he hurt me so. But him! This Arturo, he told me to be proud I was a

Mexican, he even said the meek shall inherit the earth, Jesus, I didn't want the earth, I only wanted Sammy, and I threw the speller in his face, because I like a man to be like a man, I don't like a man who is only words, words, words, that's all he was, this Arturo, ask the bed in which we slept, five times I gave him his chance, five times and he talked to me like a doll, but he never touched me and I tossed my hair and laughed and told him, Arturo, you're not a man, there's something wrong with you, because you're not a man. But I didn't want him anyway, I didn't care, I wanted to forget Sammy, and there was Arturo in the bed and he was crying, saying he didn't know why but he couldn't do it, he loved me so, he loved me so. I used to go to his room in the St. Paul Hotel, toss pebbles at his window, and he'd pull me in, and I'd stay, because I knew he wouldn't touch me, and then I hated him because he kept saying I should be proud I was a Mexican, and then I dared him to touch me, I lifted my dress and threw it over his face and he who knew so much and was so clever with all his words, he blushed and said please don't do things like that, Camilla. And when we went down on Main Street to the shooting gallery and shot clay pigeons, how many did I knock down? All of them! Every one of them. And him? He missed them all! Not one did he hit—but Sammy was not like that, Sammy knocked them all down, too. We used to go riding at night, Arturo and me. Riding out to Terminal Island, to San Pedro, and I liked crazy things, like straddling an oiltank truck, but would Arturo do it? No he wouldn't, no he

154

said it was absurd, that's what he called it, but the truck driver didn't think so, no the truck driver laughed, and I left Arturo out there and came back with the truck driver. And then he'd come into the Liberty after that, whining to see me and giving me a poem but he made me so mad because he wasn't like Sammy, even if Sammy beat me, even if Sammy called me a Spick. But sometimes he was cute, sometimes he gave me flowers, he bought me one flower at a time, he called it a camellia, like my name, so I guess I learned something after all out of him, because I didn't know those white and pink flowers were named like my name. But I didn't care much for them, they didn't smell half as good as gardenias."

And I, Bandini, was grief-stricken and crawling in the dust, myself so soon to die. So write a suicide note, Bandini, write a good one—a long one for Camilla. And it was done, a long suicide note written with a broken heart, the tears falling on the keys through the long night as he wrote, then fell asleep in his chair, then crawled to bed, too tired to commit suicide. And in the morning over coffee he read his suicide note, and oh boy was it sweet! Oh boy all he needed was a title, and he gave it one and mailed it off and in a few days there was a check and a note from the editor of the green magazine: "Dear Bandini—this is one of the most amusing pieces we have ever read. We are glad to have it and hope you'll send us more like it. Our check is enclosed."

Bandini, great humorist, rushing down Angel's

Flight to bring his story to Camilla: look, it's marvelous, very funny. A new side of my talent: I'm a humorist! And she read it and laughed, and then he died the death he forgot to die that night, for he hoped that she would see the tragedy, but no, even she thought it was funny.

Dust in my mouth, dust in my soul, so away from the dusty ones to the green sea, off with a green-dressed girl to Long Beach to a little room in Long Beach overlooking the sea, and all night a bottle of gin and the green-dressed one, calling her Camilla by mistake, until she screamed; "Stop calling me Camilla! My name's Doris—not Camilla." Asleep with the green-dressed one, pretending it was Camilla, all that night and all next day by the green sea—two hundred for another story and I'll get my Camilla in my own fashion, for I have had you Camilla in my fashion. All that day and in the evening a paralysis of death over the earth, a whispered silence of angry dust, and suddenly the room is reeling, the house is falling apart, the walls groan, the dust rises, the women everywhere scream and when we reach the street no bird is in flight, no twilight fills that March evening, only dust from the earthquake, and in the dust and ruins the dead everywhere, and I panic-stricken, the earth convulsing in hatred for my sins, because the earth hated me and all of us, the dead under bloody sheets on the lawns, the birds gone, and dust upon the world. Then hurrying back to Los Angeles, hoping she is dead, hoping Camilla is among those gone back to the dust.

But a great man must forgive, and so the great man sat in his room and pondered the twisted soul of his love and condemned himself for her shame—she was not at fault any more than any nice American girl would be at fault for screaming her hatred at the vulgarity and grossness of lower Main Street. A letter of apology was necessary, to be written in well-chosen words and in pen and ink upon simple white paper and signed with the full flourish of a carefully practiced signature. No sooner said than done, a careful letter not admitting his great love and closing with "Cordially yours."

A few nights more and again the sounds of pebbles on my window pane, and she was below smiling, she had forgiven and forgotten, and to prove her generosity she slept with me while I tossed and shuddered at this desire without passion.

Then the days that brought Camilla's change, the wasting away of her flesh, the cloudy eyes, the lassitude, the lies, lies, lies. A night when she appeared with a blackened eye: an automobile accident, she said. Then Sammy got tuberculosis and had to go to the desert, and she followed him out there and he drove her away, told her to get away from him, that he wanted to be alone and die alone in an adobe he built at the edge of the desert.

Sammy, my enemy, and he too became a writer and she brought his flimsy stupid stories to me, "because you're smart, Arturo, you can help Sammy become a writer." And I read them and I laughed at the fun I'd have tearing them to pieces, and I did it: three stories he sent me and sentence for sentence I tore them to pieces, told him he had best stick to bartending, but a great man must be friend of man and beast alike, so I tore up the letters and wrote them over, doing my best, giving him what I thought sound advice, and he began to write me from the desert, that stupid Sammy, but he was a good man at heart, a trifle cold-blooded, always referring to Camilla as "the little Spick," advising me she was a sweet lay and that she was mine if I handled it right. "Treat her rough, Bandini, treat her like she was dirt under your feet, like the dust on the road, kick her around and she'll wrap herself around your cock and die there." And this was the man Camilla loved—this was my competition.

So why not? I tried Sammy's advice. She came one night and Bandini was waiting. "Hello, you little moron, from what alley have you come this time?" Her eyes widened, her lips smiled and she was strangely quiet as Bandini carried on: I'm busy here; if you've come to waste my time, get out. And it worked! Then I knew she didn't want to be treated as a queen, as a true love, as a Cabell dream of fair woman. She was used to harshness and afraid of admiration. And it made me sick, it nauseated me, and I threw her out, took her by the arm to the door and told her to go away and never come back. She walked away delirious with desire, ready to fall in the dust at my feet. God what a pitiful Bandini that night, his queen preferring to be a slave.

Then the night we smoked marijuana. Down feet,

stay down my feet, but they rose and I was a foot off the floor, two feet, and I couldn't come down, and she was so absurd, her body so fantastic, her beauty something to laugh about—and that was the night there was passion without desire and a seduction from Baudelaire and DeQuincey. But it ended everything for us, she went away and I lay on the bed and my body would not come down but as the effect wore off my head ached vaguely and I felt something I had not felt since childhood, that need for confession, for retribution, for punishment, because I had spoiled a dream and broken a law of God and man. Still my feet would not come down, still that feeling of being off the earth, longing to return, and I reached for a water pitcher, broke it on the floor and walked in the broken glass until the ecstasy of retribution was sharpened to faintness and I thought to stop ere I collapse. That was the night I limped to a little Catholic church in the Mexican quarter and spent long hours sitting in the quiet, trying to reorganize my life, making plans and vows to be a better man. Always to be a better man, that was the idea with Arturo Bandini, to be the great man, up from the dust on the road, lover of man and beast alike. To go and sin no more.

The days went by and I worked hard, and as it always happened with me, when I worked hard there was success. No more Camilla, I stayed away and she did not come back to throw pebbles against my window. Three months passed and luck and work combined to suddenly change matters and a play I'd written was bought by the movies and I'd got almost $10,000.

So the great man gets himself tailored and perfumed and in a fancy chariot goes back to the scenes of his early struggles, to chat good-naturedly with Benny the Gouge and slip him five dollars for his kids. "Regards to your wife, Benny. Tell her I remember her well." Over to see Marcus, insisting I owe him ten, he insisting I don't, forcing him to take it, admonishing him for his bad memory, glad to pay ten dollars for such a triumph, an honest man, a great man, squaring up old accounts.

Then the last stop. But she is not there, another girl is in her place and the world is suddenly lonely and the success of Bandini is hollow and incomplete. But she must know. If SHE does not know, then it has not happened. But everyone is taciturn and nobody knows what has happened to her. A bribe to the new waitress and I got her address. I go there, meet her mother—a woman like my mother, sweet woman with a broken heart living in a shanty in the Mexican quarter, tragic-faced woman telling me Camilla had been taken to Patton, the asylum. We weep about it and I go away and out to Patton, but they won't let me see her. A month later she was released and I saw a ghost girl, terror in her eyes and loneliness hurting her. She wanted one thing from me—would I buy her a dog? So it was done. We called him Pancho, and she was happy with him and nothing more, sleeping with him, talking with him, ghost girl whose ghostliness was like a disease and with the passing of days Pancho too became a ghost, a strange dog with a hungry lonely look like his mistress's. Always she cried, we sat under a eucalyptus tree in her backyard and unaccountably the tears would start, Pancho would howl and his eyes too would smart, and I knew she was still in love with Sammy. Then one day a letter came from him in the desert, he wanted me to come out and get her and her goddamn dog, she hung around his adobe like a beggar asking for crumbs of love, he couldn't stand her, and would I come out and get her. I drove a hundred miles out there. She was gone. Her battered yellow Ford, the tires flat, was parked off the dusty road in a grove of Joshua trees. Where was she? Sammy didn't know. He had ordered her away, thrown stones at the dog, he was sick of her and didn't give a goddamn. And so it is, nobody knows. Her car is still out there, the tires stripped from it, everything movable stolen from it. She is gone, swallowed up by the desert. Maybe someone picked her up and took her to Mexico. Maybe she got back to Los Angeles and died in a dusty room. All I know is that she is gone, the dog is gone, and there is nothing left but her story which I want to tell.

Bus Ride

HE SAT IN THE REAR of the bus, did Julio Sal. Always back there for the Pinoy. A couple of Mexicans back there with him. A Mexican and his wife and child, Mamacita changing the baby's diaper. The bus was loaded now. Julio Sal had a full seat to himself.

Goodbye, Los Angeles! All aboard for the mighty San Joaquin. Bakersfield. Merced. Turlock. Modesto. Lodi. Stockton. Sacramento. A bit of Julio Sal in all those towns, fragments of his life, grains of his years, oozing from his pores in the days that were dusty, in the days that were rainy, in the cold and heat. The stoop-worker: tons of tomatoes, asparagus, onions, lettuce, melons, rice, carrots. This was his country. This earth had covered him, fed him, hurt him, sheltered him.

Aye, he knew it better than his beloved Luzon, his

sperm fruitless in a hundred rumpled beds, up and down the fabulous hot valley, the soil so rich a broomstick blossomed, where the cattle were fat and bright-eyed, where the cherries were as big as walnuts, walnuts as big as plums, plums as big as pears, pears as big as melons, melons as big as Filipinos. Where everything grew except the sperm of the Pinoy.

The Danceland in Sacramento. The Linda Ballroom in Stockton. The Teapot in Bakersfield. Manuel's Place in Lodi. Steve and Mary's in Modesto.

Peggy, Martha, Connie, Alice, Babe, Opal, Jenny, Jean, Virginia, Oklahoma Mary—what's in a name? But la! The fragrance of their arms, the fruit of their loins, the greedy little dreams in their eyes when the crop was done and the perfumed Island Boy came bounding up the stairs, his pockets jingling with stoop-money.

Julio dozed. The Mexican baby wailed. The driver turned off the interior lights and the bus rumbled through the night toward Hollywood and Cahuenga Pass. Up front two American girls chatted with the driver. Julio listened vaguely. They were undergraduates of the College of the Pacific. Their voices floated a thousand miles down the length of the bus. Incomprehensible, something about Delta Gamma and Tri Delt. About Professor so-and-so in Zoology, what a darling he was, not caring if they cut classes ... and the weary mind of Julio Sal conjured up a pruning knife hacking away at he knew not what. Sleep captured Julio Sal. He awakened when the bus pulled into the San Fernando Station. He watched the Mexican family get off.

Without the baby's sobbing the cavernous bus seemed empty. Three new passengers boarded the bus. A man and woman stumbled down the aisle and took the seat vacated by the Mexicans. Sticky-eyed, his hat tilted over his forehead, Julio Sal watched them. He could not see their faces. The man sat next to the window. He made a nest with his arm. The woman snuggled into it, quiet and content.

Behind them came the third passenger, a girl. She looked about for a seat. Julio Sal glanced at the empty section of his own chair, then at the girl. Thought Julio Sal: high class. Now she was making her way down the aisle, carrying a small overnight bag. She wore a camel's hair topcoat and a white tam-o'-shanter. She saw the empty place beside Julio. Quickly she groped her way toward it. The bus jerked forward and the girl caught herself on an overhead strap. She was about to throw herself into the seat when she saw Julio Sal.

"Oh."

She did not sit down.

"It's okay," said Julio. "Sit."

"No, thank you."

Her smile was full of gratitude, but she did not sit down. Instead, she clung to the overhanging strap and placed her overnight bag beside Julio on the seat. Julio looked at the bag, at the girl. Again she smiled.

"Do you mind?"

"Is okay for you to sit too," he said.

In front of Julio sat a young man in a yellow leather jacket. He had neat blonde hair, neatly parted.

He turned to look up at the girl, then he swung around and glared at Julio Sal, who pushed himself closer to the window to make way for her. A most polite girl.

"No, thank you," she said. "I'd rather stand."

It was not a new experience. In his time, Julio Sal had frightened countless American girls on streetcars and buses and at store counters. He had seen them standing beside him and quaking on San Francisco cable-cars, and he had seen them shudder and wince on San Jose buses. He had scared them out of their wits in San Diego, and he had made them clammy with fear in Long Beach.

Bravely the girl stood in the aisle, her lithe body racked in anguish to the overhanging strap, her lips uncomplaining, the tassel of her tam-o'-shanter bouncing with the movement of the bus. Again the blonde young man swung around to glower accusingly at Julio Sal. But Julio Sal was very tired, his eyelids fluttering, fumes of cigarette smoke and champagne mumbling in his body.

Once in the state of Washington. One time, one summer up there in Washington, a beautiful girl had once shared a bus seat with Julio Sal all the way from Seattle to the apple country around Yakima. A priceless memory. True, the citizens of Yakima later ran Julio Sal and fifty other Filipino apple-pickers out of town. But that had nothing to do with the sweet girl who had shared the seat with him, shared it in rich, beautiful silence. A golden memory. He slept.

When he awakened, the bus was forty miles from

Bakersfield on the Grapevine over the somber fog-drenched Tehachapi Mountains. His sticky eyes sought the tam-o'-shanter girl. She was no longer in the aisle. Instead, the blonde young man in the leather jacket stood there, clinging gallantly to the strap. With fierce stamina he looked down at Julio Sal, then disdainfully at the empty seat beside him. The girl had taken the young man's place in front of Julio Sal. She turned to smile gratefully at the young man. It seemed to give him renewed strength. His body tightened. His eyes shone with determination. He was her hero.

The bus came to a stop before a combined café and filling station, and the driver announced a five-minute stopover. Outside the cold fog half-smothered the lights of the café, The groggy passengers rose and staggered down the aisle and out the door.

Julio Sal's dry mouth said: water.

He followed the others, stepping down upon a graveled path beside the gasoline pumps. Bending over, he drank water from a short length of rubber hose. From inside the café came juke-box music and the voice of Bing Crosby. It was Julio's first clear view of his fellow-travelers. The tam-o'-shanter girl and the proud young man sat at the counter, talking shyly as they drank hot coffee that steamed up before their faces. The college girl's mouth was wide with laughter at something the bus driver was saying. The others sat around the counter sipping hot coffee, blowing into their cups with tired breaths.

Then he saw the other Pinoy.

Yes—another Filipino was among the passengers. He sat in the only booth in the café. The person with him was an American girl. The girl was holding a fragment of doughnut to the Filipino's mouth. He snatched it with glistening teeth. The girl laughed and kissed his lips quickly.

Julio Sal frowned. Trouble ahead for that Pinoy. Nobody knew it better than Julio Sal. Shivering with the cold, he pulled the lapels of his topcoat tight around his neck and groped for a proverb: experience is a dear school but a rolling stone saves time. Once more he felt the knife of a dancer named Helen twisting within a wide expanse of his soul marked Los Angeles. The memory brought pain to his entire face. He turned from the window and went back to the water hydrant. As he drank, Julio Sal made up his mind: he would foil the girl in the café; he would warn his fellow Pinoy before it was too late.

One passenger got off at the Grapevine stop. When the journey was resumed there were seats for all. In the seat ahead of Julio, the tassel of the tam-o'-shanter bounced happily on a leather-jacketed shoulder. Across the aisle sat the Filipino and his American girl. She half-lay upon him, her cheek against his neck.

It kept Julio Sal awake. Out of the corner of his eye he watched the twitch of the other Filipino's shoulder, the restless sleepy searching of the girl's head. In the rear, one of the Negroes began to snore. It was as effective as a lullaby, deep and soothing. Except for the driver and Julio Sal, everyone seemed asleep.

At Bakersfield the driver announced a twenty-minute stopover. The lights came on and the mangled passengers yawned and gasped. The Filipino across the aisle wakened his girl companion and said something Julio could not hear. The girl smiled sleepily, crushing herself against him. The Filipino's brown hand stroked her hair. It was a gesture of tenderness, and when he bent down to dip his lips into the girl's blonde curls a pitying sneer tore the lips of Julio Sal.

He watched the couple stretch to their feet, the Filipino straightening his rumpled coat, the girl yawning and straightening her hair. There was a moment of indecisiveness as the Filipino deliberated about his topcoat which was slung over the seat. He glanced about, as though wondering for its safety.

Then he saw Julio Sal, and Julio sensed in the young man the swagger of a bantam cock. The smile of recognition on Julio's face was also the smile of a warrior from the battlefield of love who had experienced much and profited thereby. Pushing a small black cigar into his mouth, the Filipino made way for his American girl and followed her down the aisle.

Through the window Julio Sal watched them move with the others toward the station restaurant, tattered ribbons of fog flapping in the cold morning air. At the doorway they seemed in doubt. The Filipino talked rapidly. The girl shook her head. Then the Filipino pointed with his cigar at something across the street. Julio sat up in surprise as the two almost ran in that direction. Quickly Julio Sal stepped down from the bus and peered across the street.

He was just in time to see the Filipino and the girl enter a hotel called The Valley Inn. So. At the desk they were registering. So. Now the clerk was leading them upstairs. So.

Julio Sal leaned against a lamp post and lit a cigarette as one of the darkened windows of the two-story hotel suddenly blossomed with light. Then the curtain came down. So. Julio Sal inhaled deeply and shook his head.

Said he, "Poor Filipino boy."

Poor Filipino boy. Julio Sal entered the restaurant and ordered a cup of coffee. He had seen it happen before. El Dorado Street in Stockton. California Street in San Francisco. Temple Street in Los Angeles. And now, a small hotel in Bakersfield. Everywhere, up and down the whole Pacific coast, at all hours of the day and night, the Filipino boy getting trapped by disease, running in and out of hotels, hurrying to the doctors, hurrying back to the girls. Helen too. Maybe it had all been for the best. Maybe what had happened between him and Helen was God's way of sparing Julio Sal from the ravages of the clap.

He drank his coffee and ordered a second cup. Some of the passengers were moving back to the bus. It was ten minutes to four o'clock in the morning. Julio kept glancing from the clock to the hotel across the street. The moments sped by.

By now all the passengers except Julio and the couple across the street were aboard. With one minute to go, the stationmaster and the driver stood at the bus door and checked the time. Smoking a cigarette, Julio paced up and down. He was no longer alarmed about his fellow Filipino's danger from the clap. He was more concerned that the Pinoy would miss the bus.

Said the driver, "Ain't you one of the passengers?"

Said Julio, "Yes."

"Then what the hell you doing out here?"

On tiptoe Julio peered over the hood of the bus for one last glance at the hotel. They were coming. Hand in hand, the Filipino and the girl were running across the street toward the station.

Julio tossed away his cigarette and got aboard. He watched the panting couple come down the aisle and throw themselves into their seat. The doors closed, and the bus began to move out of the Bakersfield station. The tam-o'-shanter girl resumed her position on the shoulder of the blonde young man. Across the aisle, the American girl breathed heavily in the Filipino's arms.

The lights inside the bus went out. Then there was a flash of light as the Filipino struck a match and lit his cigar. The flame exposed a triumphant brown face that smiled with satanic majesty. It exasperated Julio Sal. More than ever he was determined to talk to this wayward countryman before matters got out of hand.

Four hours later the bus reached the Fresno depot. Fresno, slightly more than the halfway point to Sacramento. Daylight now, hot valley daylight, the bus reeking of human smells.

The Filipino and his girl companion gathered their belongings. It was the end of their journey. Julio watched the couple step down and enter the station. So they were gone. It was just as well. He could do nothing for the boy. Let him learn the hard, brutal American way, as he, Julio Sal, had done.

Meanwhile, twenty minutes for breakfast. He was hot and sticky, sweat fastening the underclothes to his skin like an adhesive. In six hours he would be in Sacramento. For what? Julio Sal knew not. At any rate he would see his paesano Goldberg in Sacramento. He would stay with Goldberg a few days, for old times' sake.

He stepped from the bus and walked into the men's washroom. He pulled off his coat and necktie, filled a washbowl with water, and soaped his bristled face. It worked a miracle in his soul. Scratching the cold water from his face with a paper towel, he felt his spirit rise like a flexed biceps. He felt stronger, and he was grateful for a sense of hunger in his tight little belly. With a pocket comb in his hand, he turned to the mirror that ran the length of the wall.

In the mirror he saw another Filipino beside himself. It was his fellow-passenger. He too was combing his hair.

The man nodded.

"Hello," said Julio Sal.

172

"Ya."

"Long ride," said Julio. "Tired."

"Ya."

Each parted his hair at the same moment. Julio smiled.

"For you, is most pleasant trip," he said.

"Ya."

"You have most beautiful wife."

The Pinoy's comb stopped in mid-air.

"Wife?" He shook his head. "Not wife."

"Alla same, better," said Julio Sal. "No?"

The stranger resumed his coiffure abruptly.

"Is my business."

He shoved the comb into the upper pocket of his coat and brushed off his trousers with quick angry slaps. He seemed to wait for Julio Sal to say more.

Said Julio, "Sometime, American woman is good for Pinoy. Other time, she is bad."

The stranger looked at Julio Sal contemptuously.

"You talk like damn fool," he said. "Is no such thing as good woman. American, Chinee, Mexican, New York, San Francisco, Reno. Is all the same thing. No good."

It was good to hear a man talk like that. Julio Sal put his comb away and stretched out his hand. "Name of Julio Sal," he said.

"Name of Nick Fabria, Pismo Beach."

They shook hands.

"You smart man, Nick."

Fabria grinned. "Damn toot. Nobody make a monkey from Nick Fabria."

"American woman also smart too," said Julio "Maybe already she catch without you know it."

Said Nick Fabria, "Is not possible. Nobody catch Nick Fabria."

"Maybe."

"No maybe. This girl, I catch myself. She is my sister-in-law."

"Sister-in-law? That is good?"

"Good?" said Fabria. "Is perfect. Here—" He dug into his coat pocket. "Have cigar. Compliments, Nick Fabria."

They shook hands again.

"I give you advice," Nick said. "Free. When you marry, catch 'um wife with sister. Kill both stones with same bird. Goo'bye."

He tossed his hand in a salute and was gone through the swinging doors.

A moment later Julio Sal followed. At the other end of the waiting room he saw Nick Fabria and his sister-in-law moving toward the street entrance. The girl clung tightly to Nick's arm. He walked gallantly on high-heeled oxfords, a camel's hair polo coat flung dramatically over his shoulder, his hat tipped over the back of his head, bosky puffs of blue cigar smoke tumbling in his wake.

Julio Sal walked to the restaurant counter and ordered a cup of coffee Long after the coffee had cooled before him, he sat there studying the cigar Nick had given him, turning it in his fingers. In six hours he would be in Sacramento.

Mary Osaka, I Love You

IT HAPPENED IN Los Angeles, in the fall of that breathless year. It happened in the kitchen of the Yokohama Café, and it happened during the dinner hour, when Segu Osaka, her ferocious father, was up front minding the customers and the cash register. It happened very quickly. Mary Osaka, her arms full of dishes, came into the kitchen and laid the dishes on the sink board. Mingo Mateo was washing dishes at the sink. He was slushing out a batch of soup bowls.

Said he, "Mary Osaka, I love you very much."

Mary Osaka reached up with two firm brown hands and held the face of Mingo Mateo to the light. "And I love you, too, Mingo. Didn't you know?"

She kissed him. Mingo Mateo felt the blood and bones melting out of his shoes, and they were very expensive shoes, the very best, with square toes, made of pigskin, costing twelve dollars a pair, three days' wages. "I've loved you since you came here three months ago," she said. "But—oh, Mingo! we can't. We mustn't. It's impossible!"

Mingo dried his hands on a dish towel and got his breath. "Is possible," he said. "Is absolutely possible. Everything is possible!"

There wasn't time to answer. The swinging doors crashed open, and Segu Osaka rushed into the kitchen waving thick fingers and shouting: "Helly up, helly up. Bling 'em chop suey two times, bling 'em tea one time, alla same, helly up, yes!"

On the other side of the kitchen Vincente Toletano dug out two orders of chop suey from the big cauldron on the stove and threw them on the serving tray. Vincente Toletano was a proud Filipino, a somber, brooding man, who, but for the scarcity of work during those times, would have spat upon a Japanese rather than work for him. After Mary hurried away with the orders, Vincente Toletano was alone with his country- man, Mingo Mateo.

Said Vincente: "Mingo, my friend, I see you make passionate love with this Japanese girl. You are a crazy man, Mingo. Also, you are a disgrace to the whole Filipino nation."

Mingo Mateo turned around. He folded his arms and glared, chin jutting, at Vincente Toletano. Said he: "Toletano, thank you ever so much if you mind your own business. For why you peek like a sneak, if you see

I make love with this wonderful girl?"

Said Vincente: "I have right to peek. This girl, she is Japanese woman. Is not good for you to make kiss with this kind of woman. Better for you to wash your mouth with soap."

Mingo smiled. "She is very beautiful, eh, Vincente? You are jealous little bit, maybe?"

Vincente turned his lips as though an evil taste fell upon them. "You are a fool, Mingo. You make sickness in my stomach. I make challenge. If you kiss some more with Mary Osaka, I quit this job."

"Quit," Mingo shrugged. "I no care when you quit. But me—ah, I never quit making kiss with Mary Osaka."

Vincente's voice changed. It was threatening now, soft and menacing, as he leaned forward with his hands gripping the table that separated them.

"How you like if I tell Filipino Federated Brotherhood? How you like that, Mingo? How you like when I stand before Brotherhood and point finger and say to Federated Brotherhood, 'This man, this Mingo Mateo, he is make love with Japanese girl!' How you like that, Mingo?"

"I no care," said Mingo. "Tell whole world. It only make me more happy."

Vincente Toletano had more to say, but Mary was back in the kitchen again. "Pork chow mein on two," she called, crossing to Mingo.

Vincente threw two platters on the table and spooned out the order. Mary was talking, and what she

177

said made Vincente splash chow mein crazily.

"It can't happen, Mingo. You know how Papa feels about you. About Vincente. About all Filipinos." She was standing very close to Mingo, a small, snug girl, whose black hair reached, sleek and lovely, to his nostrils.

"Smell good," he said, sniffing the bright blackness. "It make no difference about your papa. I no love your papa. I love you, Mary Osaka."

"You don't know Papa," she smiled.

"I know," said Mingo. "We have little talk."

Here was his opportunity, for the swinging doors flew open and Segu Osaka charged into the kitchen waving his short arms. "Helly up, quick. Bling 'em chow mein two times, chasso, chasso!" His quick black eyes lashed at Mary, at Mingo, at Vincente. Popping himself on the forehead with his open palm, he rushed back to the dining room. They could hear him muttering in Japanese something about Filipinos.

Suddenly without shame Mingo Mateo dropped to his knees and threw his arms around the slim waist of Mary Osaka. He clung to her, his face tight against her.

"Oh, Mary Osaka," he panted, "please, you be my wife?"

"Mingo, be careful!"

She tore herself away, dragging him so that he walked a little on his knees after her before letting go. When she had disappeared with the two orders of chow mein, there was Mingo Mateo on his knees,

178

sitting on his heels, and across the room with lips curled in disgust stood Vincente Toletano. His face said, "Finished." His cold eyes said much more than that.

Grabbing his high-crowned chef's hat, Toletano flung it to the floor. He stood upon it, wiped his feet upon it, while his fingers fought and burst the strings of his apron, which he ripped away.

"Already I am quit," he said. "Is too much for one Filipino to see."

But the eyes of Mingo Mateo were on the swinging doors. Half-kneeling, half-sitting, he watched them go thump-thump, thump-thump, before coming to a stop. His hands hung loosely at his sides. His chin lay like a heavy stone against his chest.

Vincente Toletano crossed to him. "My countryman!" he sneered, and he seized the head of Mingo Mateo by the hair, turning the face upward toward him. Deliberately he slapped Mingo first across one cheek, then the other. Now he held the face toward him again. Calmly he spat upon it.

"Fooey!" he said, pushing Mingo. "Disgrace to the good name of the Filipino people."

Mingo did not resist, did not speak. The tears fell from his eyes and slithered down his brown cheeks. Vincente was gone; the alley door slammed loudly behind him. Mingo staggered to his feet. He washed his face with cold water, pulling the flesh at his cheeks with long fingers, running his hands through his hair,

179

clenching his teeth against a surge of grief that shook his body like a fit of coughing. When Mary Osaka returned to the kitchen, she found him that way, his head bent down and smothered in his hands, his sobs louder than the sound of the running water that was coming from the faucet.

She put down a trayful of dishes and took him in her arms. The curve of her neck fitted his forehead like a nest as he leaned heavily upon her. She stroked his wet hair with spread fingers; she smoothed his thin shoulders with small, eager palms.

"You mustn't. Mingo, you mustn't."

"Nothing good in this world but you," he choked. "Is better to die without my Mary. Make no difference what Vincente say, or your papa, or anybody."

Vincente? She looked about and realized the cook was gone. All at once Mingo was erect, tense, his eyes aflame, his two hands on her shoulders, the fingers hurting her flesh as he held her at arms' length.

"Mary! Why we care? Filipino, he say is disgrace to marry Japanese. Japanese, he say is disgrace to marry Filipino. Is lie, big lie, whole thing. For in the heart is what count, and the heart of Mingo Mateo say alla time, boom boom boom for Mary Osaka."

The face of Mary Osaka brightened, and the eyes of Mary Osaka were drenched with delight. "Oh, Mingo!"

Eagerly he spoke. "We marry, yes? No?"

"Yes!"

He caught his breath, held back a giddy laugh, and

180

fell at her feet, his knees booming on the floor. He kissed her hands and pulled them across his lips. He was pecking quick kisses on the tips of her fingers when Segu Osaka bounced into the kitchen.

"Helly up, helly up!"

There was Mingo Mateo at his daughter's feet.

Said Mingo Mateo, "Mr. Osaka, if you please——"

Said Osaka; "No no no. Get 'em out. Fire. Go. Out!"

Not tall, Osaka, but squat and powerful. His fists were quickly inside Mingo's collar. There was a tearing of cloth, with Mingo's face a thickish blue as Osaka dragged him sacklike across the floor and out the kitchen door.

"But Mr. Osaka! Is love! Is marriage!"

"No no no. No no no."

Sprawled in the alley, Mingo saw the stumpy little man slam the door, heard it bolted. Inside, Osaka spluttered violent Japanese, and Mary answered with equal vehemence. Mingo jumped to his feet and rushed the door, kicking it, drumming it with knuckles.

"Don't hurt her," he shouted. "Don't touch!"

The voices inside grew louder. Desperately he flung himself against the door. The wood panel splintered, the bolt and hinges creaked. For a moment the voices were silent.

Then a piercing cry cut the night as Segu Osaka shrieked: "Help, police! Help!"

Mingo paused, glanced up and down the alley. The moonlight illumined a canyon of fire escapes and garbage tins leading to a bright street fifty yards away. Osaka still screamed. Now there were other voices and the sound of running feet inside the kitchen.

Mary's voice rose above the noise. "Run, Mingo, run!"

Pulling off his apron, Mingo threw it into a garbage can. Upstairs a window howled, opened. The frail head and shoulders of Mary Osaka's mother peered out. She did not speak, only looked down at him nervously, her hands clutching her mouth. He backed into the darkness and ran toward the street, his feet filling the alley with tiny echoes.

He slowed to a walk when he reached the street. Little Tokyo was crowded with Saturday-night strollers. Coatless, he lost himself among the shoppers, making his way past the toy stores and cafés, the clean, bright shops. The windows always shone in Little Tokyo, there was less refuse in the gutters, the street lamps were brighter, and incense from a hundred doors filled the air with sweetness. Like the others, Mingo Mateo sauntered unhurried and at ease in the warm December night.

The brightness of the street gradually ended. Now there were blackened warehouses, and beyond them the Filipino Quarter began. Flophouses and wine shops, burned hamburgers and strong perfume, barbershops and massage parlors, juke-box music and chippies, and everywhere his countrymen, the little brown brothers, exquisitely tailored, exquisitely lonely, leaning against poolroom doorways, smoking cigars and staring alternately at the stars overhead and the clicking high heels passing by.

At the fountain of the Bataan Poolhall Mingo ordered a glass of orange juice. As he raised it to his lips, someone touched his shoulder and spoke his name. He gulped the drink and turned around.

Vincente Toletano stood there. The two men with him were Julio Gonzales and Aurelio Lazario. Without glancing at Toletano, Mingo understood why they were there. These men were officers of the Filipino Federated Brotherhood. Vincente Toletano had gone to them with the name of Mary Osaka on his lips .

Julio Gonzales spoke first. "Come into back room, Mateo. We wish to have little talk." He was the largest of the three, a middleweight prize fighter with mauled ears and a crushed nose.

"Talk with Toletano!" Mingo sneered. "He is stool pigeon. He tell everything."

Said Toletano: "You lie, Mingo. I do this for good of the Filipino Federated Brotherhood. You make the oath. You must keep."

Said Mingo: "Cannot keep the oath. I am in love with Mary Osaka. I resign from Brotherhood."

"Not so easy to resign," said Gonzales. "Better to come and have little talk."

Said Mingo: "I love Mary Osaka. Go to hell."

Said Gonzales, "How you like when I put best right on whole Pacific Coast inside your mouth, bust out the teeth?" He lifted a heavy brown fist into Mingo's view.

"Is make no difference. Still I love Mary Osaka."

Aurelio Lazario got between them. An educated man, Aurelio. Bachelor of Arts, Pomona College; Doctor of Law, University of California; now a dishwasher in Jason's cafeteria. Aurelio laid his thin, soap-softened hand on Mingo's shoulder, and friendship was in his voice. "Come with us, Mingo. There won't be any trouble. I promise you that."

Mingo looked into the warm eyes of Aurelio Lazario, and he knew that Lazario was his friend, the friend of all Pinoys. Twelve years he had known this man, twelve years in America, and the fame of Aurelio Lazario had spread to every Filipino community on the Pacific Coast. Lazario, the fighter for Filipino rights, a leader in the asparagus country, with gunshot wounds to prove it; Lazario, who got them better housing in the Imperial Valley. Aurelio Lazario, an old man of thirty-five, his head still high and unbroken despite the clubs of the vigilantes; prunes in Santa Clara, rice in Solano, salmon in Alaska, tuna in San Diego—side by side with his brother Filipinos, Lazario had worked and suffered; and though he had gone on to the university and become a great man among his people, yet his face, like Mingo's, was forever marked by the hot sunlight of the San Joaquin, and his brown eyes were soft and womanlike with compassion for all men.

"I come," said Mingo. "We talk."

184

He got off the stool and followed them past the pool tables to a door that led to the back room. Gonzales opened the door and switched on a plain light bulb hanging from the ceiling. The room was dusty, empty, with newspapers spread over the floor. Gonzales stood at the door, waiting for them to enter. After they filed in, he closed the door and stood before it with folded arms. Mingo crossed to the far corner, leaned against the wall, biting his lip, opening and closing his fists. Lazario stood directly under the light, Toletano beside him.

"So you're in love, Mingo," Lazario smiled.

"Whole lots," said Mingo. "I no care what happen."

Toletano spat on the floor. "Japanese girl! Ugh. Is terrible."

Said Mingo: "Not Japanese. American. Born in Los Angeles. American citizen."

Said Toletano: "And her papa, her mama?" He spat again. "Japanese."

Said Mingo: "I no love her papa, her mama. I love Mary Osaka. Crazy for her."

Abruptly Gonzales crossed from the door and pushed Mingo against the wall. He held him there with his right hand. Drawing back his left, he held it on a line with Mingo's nose. "Say one more time you love this Japanese woman, and I give you best left hook on whole Pacific Coast."

The eyes of Mingo bulged; his face turned bloated and purple; still he blubbered stubbornly, "Mary Osaka, I love you."

Lazario raised his hand. "Wait, Gonzales. Violence won't help matters. He has his rights like the rest of us."

Gonzales shook his right fist between Mingo's eyes. "I have right, too, best right on whole Pacific Coast. I think maybe I let him have it."

Lazario waved him away. "Let's get down to the facts. We founded the Federated Brotherhood of Filipinos in protest against the Japanese invasion of China. We've pledged ourselves to boycott Japanese goods, to have as little as possible to do with all Japanese elements. Unfortunately, some of us can't carry out this pledge. We need jobs. Sometimes we have to work for Japanese employers."

It was Lazario, the man of learning who spoke now, and they listened respectfully. Gonzales pulled a cigar from his checkered sports coat and bit off the end.

"Boycotting Japanese goods is one thing," Lazario went on, "but falling in love with a Japanese girl who isn't Japanese at all, but an American of Japanese descent—well, I don't know. The Federation perhaps might be overstepping itself here."

Gonzales lit his cigar and puffed contentedly. Aurelio Lazario, the smartest Filipino on the whole Pacific Coast, was talking, and what he said was gospel, even though he, Gonzales, understood not one word of it. Slumped in the corner, Mingo rubbed his bruised neck and stared at the floor. Toletano shoved his hands in his pockets. Plainly he had no patience with Lazario's argument.

Lazario turned to him. "Vincente, have you ever been in love?"

Toletano considered this. "Yah. Two times." Melancholy softened his face. "Two times," he repeated. "Is wonderful, sad. It hurt so—" he touched his heart— "here."

"Were you in love with American women?"

"Beautiful American girl. In Stockton. Blonde."

"And did you ask her to marry you?"

"Alla time. Every few minutes."

"And why wouldn't she?"

"She was American. I was Filipino."

Said Lazario: "You see, Vincente? The same is true of Mingo. She is of Japanese descent. He is Filipino. We mustn't be prejudiced. A man's heart knows nothing of race or creed or color."

Toletano shook his head doubtfully. "Good Filipino can always smell Japanese." He went on shaking his head. "Is different. American girl is one thing, Japanese something else."

But Lazario wouldn't have it. "Love is very democratic, Vincente. Nationality is an accident. You say you were in love twice. What about the other girl?"

Vincente sighed. "Was same blonde American girl. She move to San Francisco. I follow her. Fall in love in San Francisco, too."

Lazario gestured with both palms. "There. You see?"

Gonzales took the cigar from his mouth and flipped the ash. "Maybe better," he said, "if Mingo fall in love with American girl."

"Mary Osaka is American girl," said Mingo. "Hundred percent. Graduate, Manual Arts High School."

Lazario crossed to the prize fighter, laid a hand on his shoulder. "Look, my friend Gonzales. Put yourself in Mingo's place. We are all Filipinos. We all know the life of a Filipino in the United States is hard. How can we expect justice if we interfere in the life of one of our brothers? He loves this girl, this Mary Osaka. You, Julio. Have you ever been in love?"

Gonzales filled his great chest proudly. "Four times," he said. "All American girls, finest on whole Pacific Coast."

"And what happened?"

"Was wonderful. I marry with all of them. Then divorce."

Lazario blinked thoughtfully. He placed his arm around the pugilist's shoulder and turned him toward Mingo, slumped in the corner. "Look at him, Julio. There he is, a small, insignificant little Filipino. He's your countryman, Julio, brother of your brothers. But you're a strong man, Julio, a great middleweight, with a deadly left hook. You're successful, handsome, exciting. Women fall at your feet. You have to fight them off with your fists. But look at him! Timid, scared. He needs the support of a tiger like you. Why shouldn't he marry this girl? After all, she's probably the best he can find."

Gonzales pouted, the cigar in the middle of his mouth. He rolled it thoughtfully. "Sure," he said finally. "Is okay by Julio Gonzales."

In the corner Mingo hung limp and tear-sodden, his arms like broken branches at his sides.

Gonzales stepped forward. Said he, "Mingo, you want to marry this woman?"

"Mary Osaka," Mingo groaned, "I love you."

Gonzales pulled a bunch of keys from his pocket. "Here. I have Packard roadster, white tire, red leather upholster, go hundred-ten mile an hour. You take, Mingo. Go to Las Vegas. Get marry tonight."

Mingo lifted his sodden, grateful eyes. Slowly he sank to his knees. He took the hand that held the keys and kissed it, wet it considerably with his lips and his tears. Gonzales tried to pull his hand away.

Said Mingo: "God bless you, Julio."

Gonzales dropped the keys to the floor, jerked his hand free, and hurried from the room. Lazario and Toletano stood with dry mouths. Quietly they tiptoed away.

A new Mingo Mateo stalked out of the back room of the Bataan Poolhall. Sunlight in his face, stars in his eyes, and lips grinning like a crescent moon. Twirling a ring of keys, he stood at the tobacco counter and ordered a cigar. Removing the gold band, he fitted it around his small finger. Said he: "Mrs. Mingo Mateo."

There was a wall telephone, and he dug for a nickel. Six times he spun the dial, then listened to a soft humming. Her "hello" filled him with fine music.

"Mary."

"Are you all right?"

"Everything okay. Meet me tonight. City Hall steps. Twelve o'clock."

"But, Mingo—"

"Goodbye, Mary."

In the street he found Gonzales's car. It was a rust-colored job, a roadster with fender lights, spotlights, fog lights. It crouched with white-walled paws, like an animal ready to spring. He circled it breathlessly. When he touched the horn the first bars of "Tiger Rag" snarled forth. He slipped under the steering wheel, gripped it tightly in both hands.

Probing the switches and dials on the dashboard, he finally got the radio started. It was a news broadcast; something about two special Japanese envoys talking hopefully of peace with the State Department in Washington. Mingo scowled and pushed another button. It brought forth music: steel guitars, a Hawaiian voice singing of a certain island princess with plenty of papaya to give away. He leaned back and listened, his eyes sailing through the blue-black dome of the sky freckled with white stars.

"Mingo, my friend, hello."

Standing at the curb was Vincente Toletano. A girl clung to his arm. She was Chinese, not more than twenty, her black hair in bangs. She lowered her bright, delicate face and stared at the sidewalk. She wore a long smock buttoning to the chin, slit from hem to knees. Her cheeks were rouged, and her lips were wet scarlet.

Vincente slipped his arm around her waist, patting her with considerable affection.

"Look what I got, Mingo. Pretty good, no?"

"Pleased to meet," said Mingo.

"Name of Lily Chin," said Toletano, introducing her. "Lily, my friend Mingo Mateo."

"Please to meet."

Toletano rolled his eyes over her. "How you like, Mingo?"

Said Mingo, "Is pretty." He dropped his eyes.

Said Toletano, "What you think, Lily?"

"He's cute," she said.

Toletano motioned her to move away, to leave him alone with Mingo. They watched her glide to the corner. Toletano opened the car door and got in.

Said he, "How you like this girl, Mingo?"

"Fine. Pretty. Chinese, no?"

"Yah, Chinese. Not Japanese, Chinese."

Said Mingo "Mary Osaka is not Japanese. She is American, hundred percent."

Toletano waved it aside. "Is better to talk about Lily Chin. You like, no?"

"Sure, I like."

Said Toletano, "She is pretty, no?"

"Wonderful pretty."

"Make fine wife?"

"You betcha."

Toletano offered him a cigar. "Special Havana."

Mingo bit off the end and put it in his mouth. Toletano had a light ready immediately. Mingo puffed, tasted the smoke. "Good cigar," he said.

Said Toletano: "I am your friend, Mingo. Tonight you make me lose job, but I say nothing."

"No, Vincente. You quit job. Is not my to blame."

"For you I quit, Mingo. For you, for whole Filipino nation. To make big sacrifice, to show you lesson, so you don't disgrace Filipino people."

Mingo took the cigar from his mouth and looked at Toletano's face. It was a cold, hard face. Toletano leaned back, his eyes to the sky. It was like a fist, his face, tensed and threatening like a closed fist.

Said Mingo: "Vincente, what you want from me? For why we talk like this? Is already settled. Lazario, he say get married. Gonzales, he give me the car. But you, Vincente, you fight with me. Why?"

Toletano swung round and shook him. "Because I am great Filipino. Because I have fire of love in my heart for my country, but not for Japanese girl, enemy of my people. To marry Japanese girl is like dirt in the face of whole Filipino nation."

Panting, Mingo tore the hands from his throat. "Is nothing I can do, Vincente. The mind, she is made up."

He was not a fighting man, this Mingo Mateo. He was too small and gentle for that. But when rage took him, it was with the fury of a mad dog. At that moment it got hold of him, and in a deluge of fists and teeth he was punching and tearing the man beside him.

Somehow the car door opened, and they were on the sidewalk, rolling over and over among the legs of a crowd that quickly gathered. He neither saw nor felt what he did, this Mingo Mateo, and it was not until a dozen hands had jerked him to his feet and held him that he realized what he had done to the figure sprawled face down on the sidewalk.

He picked out certain faces in the crowd, faces of his countrymen, the face of Lily Chin. Then he heard a police siren and an old voice, a good voice that calmed the kicking of his heart.

Said Aurelio Lazario: "Go, Mingo. Hurry. The police are coming."

Mingo looked down at Toletano.

"He's all right. We'll take care of him."

Brown hands led him to the big car. Someone slammed the door. He felt the keys. Their coldness gave him strength. Around him the faces of his countrymen, begging him to escape. He started the car. The power of the engine entered his arms and legs like a hypodermic shot. He saw clearly now, even turning to look back and wave to Aurelio. A block away he swung into Los Angeles Street and passed a black squad car with blood-red lights, its siren howling as it sped to the place he had just left.

Mingo lived on Bunker Hill, that high island of Mexicans and Filipinos not far from the City Hall. It was his most intimate fraction of American earth. He had gone there the first time twelve years before, an immigrant boy from a village in Luzon, with two straw suitcases and a thousand dreams. Now he was twenty-nine. He had learned to love the sad ruin of Bunker Hill, the smoke-licked rooming houses, the paint-bloated apartments. Each spring, going away to follow the crops, to work in the canneries, he remembered it as home, and in the fall he was back again.

Bunker Hill: sacred soil. A block away from his rooming house was a park, no more than fifty feet square. Around it grew five palm trees. Beneath them was a bench. Holy ground: the feet of Mary Osaka had trod it. The bench had felt the weight of her body. It was here they had met for snatched hours the past three months. She had come in spite of everything, even the wrath of her father, because he had asked it. Vincente Toletano could call her Japanese; but Mingo Mateo had seen the dream of America through the eyes of Mary.

Those were the nights—the moon throwing yellow arms through the five palms, the great city below, and the soft voice of a girl beside him, speaking of this bright land of American youth. She had told him that Artie Shaw's was the best American band, that Benny Goodman played the best clarinet. For twenty minutes she had expounded the cool nostalgia of Bing Crosby. She had picked Oregon in the Rose Bowl, Minnesota in the Big Ten. She entranced him with thoughts on boogie-woogie, Joe DiMaggio, and the Micromatic shift. She loved Clark Gable. He held her hand and was pleased to listen, the warm breeze picking up her scent and wafting it over the city. She liked automobiles and cigarettes, Joe Louis and scented face powder, nylon hose and Ginger Rogers; she liked Fred Allen and Bob Hope. She liked Rhett Butler and Scarlett O'Hara. She talked of Wendell Willkie, the Okies, John Gunther,

194

Cab Calloway, slacks, *Harper's Bazaar*, President Roosevelt. America the wild and wonderful, out of the sweet lips of a small girl who loved it deeply, spoke of it intimately, as though it were her brother, her house, her life—this girl whom he was meeting tonight.

A few minutes before midnight he was coasting down the steep incline of Bunker Hill toward City Hall. He had bathed and shaved, flung a palmful of lilac perfume into his dark hair, changed to a light-brown suit. When the massive white tower of the City Hall came into view, dismay squeezed his heart: all at once he was sure she would not be there, that he had been a fool, that his dream had run amuck.

He parked the car beneath a sign warning him that parking was at all times forbidden. The street was deserted. The moon had crossed town and disappeared behind the skyline to the north. A few lights shone in the City Hall; but the façade was dark and empty. Like a torrent of white stone the broad stairway poured from the high, pillared main entrance and flowed to the street. She was nowhere, not in the street, on the stairs, or among the pillars. A trolley approached. He sat up, watching. A tall woman in slacks got out. With loose hands he sighed and sat back; Mary Osaka didn't wear slacks, nor was she tall. Ai, he had made a big mistake, hoped for too much.

He pushed a button on the radio. "The Star Spangled Banner" filled the night. He listened, hearing only the roar of his own mind calling him foolish. Over the music came the tolling of a bell. It was midnight, the station was going off the air.

A small figure came from behind one of the pillars and descended the stairs. It was she, no bigger than a doll; but she came like an army of ten thousand that swept him into ecstasy. On quick feet that laughed in the night she hurried toward him, and when he saw that she carried an overnight bag, he knew her thought had been his own, his dream melting into hers, and suddenly he was hearing "The Star Spangled Banner," humming it fervently, because there were no words in his throat to equal his joy and because she was upon him now, opening the door and leaping in beside him, deluging him with her perfume and her bright smile. He clung transfixed to the steering wheel, his face rigid and bloodless with terrible joy. She knelt in the seat, dropped her coat and bag to the floor, put her warm hands over his ears, and kissed him with a cool mouth like fresh lettuce.

"Oh, Mingo. Crazy Mingo!"

He was still without words.

"We're mad, Mingo. Both of us. Isn't it wonderful?"

His tongue moved. It was his thought to speak endlessly of his gratitude and adoration, of love and life eternal; but his mouth trembled so, and his hands, too, that he might have been merely chilled and shivering a little.

He managed one small word. "Mary—"

"Of course I'll marry you, silly!"

196

It left him demented, hypnotized. He started the car and swung to the center of the street, following the streetcar tracks. She curled beside him, her knees like golden oranges close to her chin, her hands clasping his arm. It was a long time before the spell was broken and he noticed a traffic sign. They were on the road to Santa Barbara. Las Vegas was in the opposite direction. He went around the block and found the boulevard to Pasadena. Now he could speak a little.

He said: "Good car. I borrow him."

He said: "Pretty night. Stars."

He said: "I try hard, make you good husband."

He said: "Mary Osaka, I love you."

She pulled some bobby pins from her hair, and the warm night made it fly like blackbirds. Her eyes wandered among the spilled stars. Beneath them the tires crooned on concrete. By one o'clock they were under the orange groves beyond Glendora. They stopped for coffee in Barstow, where it was cold and their breaths were misty in the chill. She was asleep in the frozen dawn when they crossed the California line below Death Valley. They reached Las Vegas at eight-thirty. By nine o'clock in the morning he had got a marriage license. Across the street was the office of the justice of the peace. Man and wife, they emerged from it at nine-twenty. He tried to walk as though he had done this every day of his life; but it was Mary who was calm. When he opened the car door, she paused to look into his face and smile. He looked down at his shoes, swallowed, and glanced around furtively.

"Kiss me, Mingo."

"Here? For all the people to see?"

"I don't see any people."

He pecked at her cheek. She flung her arms around his neck and crushed her lips to his mouth, holding him passionately. His eyes widened, the whites showing as he rolled them in fright and joy.

A mile from town they found an auto court with small white cottages built in a semicircle. The shirtless manager greeted them with winks and sly smiles. Mary stood at Mingo's side while he dipped a matted pen-point into the inkwell and wrote on the guest register:

Mr. and Mrs. Mingo Mateo, Dec. 7, 1941.

Driving back to Los Angeles in the Sunday twilight, Mr. and Mrs. Mingo Mateo sat without speaking In the west the bloody sunset was fast disappearing. Something had happened. Something had gone wrong. It was everywhere. Why had they stared, those people? The manager of the auto court and his wife, their cold eyes upon them as they drove away; the waitress and the cashier at the restaurant, the truck drivers at the counter, the wordless hush during the meal, with only the sound of clattering dishes to disturb it; the state trooper climbing off his motorcycle to ask them questions as they bought gasoline; the white-clad service attendant staring at Mary until she dropped her eyes. Too much rouge on her cheeks? Too much lipstick? She adjusted the rear-vision mirror to her reflection, turning her face right and left, examining her chin, patting her hair.

"Mingo, what's the matter with me?" she asked.

He knew her thought. "You are beautiful. No wonder they look."

"No. Something's wrong. I feel it."

She flipped the radio control, pushed a button. It burst out like an explosion, the war, springing to life. Pearl Harbor, Wake, Guam, Midway, the Philippines. They listened with racked mouths.

"It's a stupid joke," she said.

"Must be."

She buttoned another station, another voice. Pearl Harbor, dive bombers, the *Arizona*. Words like bullets, piercing their flesh, not pain but a sense of bleeding to death. Her hands at her throat jerked with the panic of her heart. The nausea sweeping her face made it grey and ugly. In his belly Mingo felt the cut of bullets, piercing his life, painless, like bleeding to death.

"Is not possible. Cannot be."

She sat back with her grey face and her lost hands. They were in desert country, the night's first stars coming cold and quiet, and they both felt it—the surge of power, the vast invincibility of all that surrounded them. Still the words came, slugging them with incredible change. The car plunged forward, sucking up the white road.

Luzon. Dive bombers.

Mingo winced because that hurt, blood spilled on memories of his childhood, rage expanding his bones as he gripped the wheel and bit the edges of his teeth. Dirty dogs. Dirty Japanese rats. And he shouted it, screamed it into the onrushing night.

"Mingo—" He touched her knee. "We are Americans, you and me."

They were drugged with war, sick and slugged with it, when they got back to Los Angeles. Little Tokyo was quiet, its streets all but deserted. They passed a barbershop with smashed windows, police standing about. An army lorry full of soldiers rumbled across an intersection. Here and there pathetic little shops had American flags flying bravely over them.

It was almost two o'clock when they pulled up in front of the Yokohama Café. Upstairs a lamp glowed behind a yellow shade. The café itself was in darkness. Mingo wet his lips. His world had suddenly somersaulted. Last night Segu Osaka was a man to he feared. Tonight the fear was gone and the daughter of Segu Osaka was his bride.

He followed Mary to the door. She found a key an her purse and turned the lock. They stepped into the darkness. She faced him then and threw her arms around him.

"Don't blame my parents, Mingo. Please. They're so good."

He bent down and kissed her, tasted the salt of her grief. "No, no. Is not their fault."

She led him by the hand through the darkness to a door that opened on the stairs. They ascended on tiptoe. At the head of the stairs a board creaked, a shadow fell upon them. In a kimono and straw sandals Segu Osaka stood looking down. For a moment Mary hesitated. She locked arms in Mingo's, and they climbed the stairs together.

"Hello, Papa."

He was wild-eyed, trembling. Even the stubby hair on his head was disheveled, plowed up and crushed about by frantic hands. He was staring at Mingo.

"He's my husband now. We were married this morning in Las Vegas."

Osaka exploded like a string of firecrackers, all over the room, his stiff fingers plucking nothingness out of the air. He paced and champed, zigzagging up and down the room, his slippers swishing, his thick bowlegs showing under his flapping kimono. For a long time he shouted, biting words and spitting them out, circling the two of them as they stood in the middle of the room. Abruptly he stopped and threw himself against the wall, his back to the wall, the back of his head bumping it monotonously.

"He says this is terrible," Mary translated. "He says you're probably a good boy but you're Filipino, and the war will wreck our lives. He says congratulations anyhow, and he hopes we will be happy "

Osaka sprang across the room, grabbed Mingo's hand, and pumped it violently. The same wild expression wrung his face. "So," he said. "So so. So so."

A door creaked, and Mary's mother came out. She was stooped, frightened, whimpering. Quickly Mary spoke. The old lady examined Mingo uncertainly. She looked at his feet, his legs, his loins, his waist, his chest, his face. Then she smiled, bowed, and backed quietly out of the room, closing the door after her. Osaka was shouting again. He kept moving in a circle, waving his arms and making wild gestures with his fists: punching, tearing, pulling, choking.

Mary translated: "He says the war is not his fault. He says he is loyal to America. He says he is richer and happier in this country than he ever was in Japan. He says the twenty-five years he has been in Los Angeles are the happiest of his life. He says the Japanese have gone mad. He says they will lose the war. He says he is glad, too. He says it is the end of Japan. He says this makes him happy. He says he is ashamed of Japan. He says it is not the common people of Japan, it is the ruling class. He blames a man named Yamamoto, Admiral Yamamoto. He says the common people of Japan are peaceful. He says in the name of the Filipino people, you must forgive him."

Mingo nodded. "Sure. I forgive you. You bet."

Osaka seized his hand, pumped it violently. "So," he said. "So so. So so. " He was off again, sputtering words and tearing up and down the room.

When he had quieted, Mary translated. "He wants to know why you're here, why you don't join the army and fight for your country."

Mingo had made that decision a long time before. "I go," he said. "Tomorrow."

Osaka was pumping his hand again. Said he: "So. So so. So so."

Said Mingo, "So so."

The old man was off again, sputtering a torrent of words into his face.

Said Mary: "He says you must fight bravely, because our children will be Americans, because we must win the war for them. He says when the war is over he will make you his partner in the restaurant. He says he'll teach you the business, and you'll make money to raise our children and give them a good education."

It was Mingo who reached now, shaking Osaka's hand in both of his. Said he: "Thank you, so so."

Said Osaka: "So. So so. So so."

Again he exploded, his gutturals jumping from his excited lips as he pointed to the stairs, to the ceiling, to himself and Mary, until he had stopped in front of Mingo, shaking him violently with both hands.

Said Mary; "He says you have to go now. He says tomorrow may be too late."

Said Mingo: "Not now. Everything closed up."

Said Osaka: "Go! Alla same, go—"The rest of what he said was in Japanese.

Said Mary: "He says go now, find the place, be the first in line."

Said Mingo: "What do you think?"

"I think yes." Her eyes were wet.

Said Mingo: "Then I go."

He wanted to kiss her goodbye as they walked those few steps to the stairway; but Segu Osaka was pounding his back and spluttering endlessly. At the bottom of the stairs Mingo turned and looked up at her. She was crying, trying to wave with a feeble wrist.

Said he: "Mary Mateo, I love you. I come back. You wait for me."

She sobbed, broke suddenly from his view.

Said Osaka: "So. So so. So so."

Said Mingo, "So so."

The Taming of Valenti

I WAS IN BED when Valenti telephoned.

"Come over. Hurry."

"What's up?"

"You come over."

It was almost two in the morning. I called Leon at the desk and told him to get me a cab. Valenti and Linda lived in a single apartment in the Wilshire district. Fifteen minutes after his call I was walking down the hall toward their apartment. Before I had a chance to knock, he said, "Come in, Jim." I could see him in the kitchen, sitting at the table, clutching his black hair with both hands. Every light in the place was turned on. Valenti was crying, sobbing quietly. As I crossed the living room I heard throaty sounds from the bathroom. That was Linda; she was crying too.

"What's the matter?" I said.

"That trull," he said. "That low wench."

"Who—Linda?"

"That two-timer. That piece."

Valenti and I were old friends. A lot of things made Valenti cry. He cried the night he came to my hotel and told me Linda would marry him. Three weeks ago we had driven to Las Vegas. I was his best man. Valenti was so moved by the ceremony that the old preacher had to stop while Valenti sobbed on my shoulder.

"She's been unfaithful again," Valenti said.

"Again?"

He held up three fingers.

"Three times in three weeks."

"Liar!" That was Linda. She rushed out of the bathroom, a blue negligée fluttering after her, a long-necked, round-bellied perfume bottle in her hand. Before I could react, she let it fly across the kitchen. Valenti ducked, but he ducked right into it, and the bottle bounced with a thud off his chest and fell to the floor. He coughed, jumped to his feet, and charged for her.

"You lousy trull!"

"You evil-minded devil!"

I got between them. Over my shoulder Valenti grabbed Linda's blonde hair and pulled. She put an arm under mine and reached for his face. Her long nails came away, leaving three red marks down his cheek. Finally I quieted them. They stood like fighting cocks, poised, ready to start again. Then Linda stamped her foot and wailed.

"My nice perfume. It was a present from my sister. Just look at it now."

The bottle still rocked dismally back and forth, its contents spread over the blue linoleum. The kitchen smelled of Vol de Nuit. With a cry of agony Linda stomped back to the bathroom. Valenti touched his face and stared at his bloodtipped fingers. His lips trembled, his tears dripped like wax from a candle.

"And now she attacks me. My own wife."

"Forget it."

He laughed dramatically, whirling around as though staggered by a blow, both hands appealing to the ceiling "Forget it. How can I forget it? What have I done to deserve this? Me—Alfredo Valenti?"

"Forget it."

"Stop telling me to forget it. Who asked you for your advice?"

"You phoned me. You got me out of bed at two in the morning."

"I shoulda' known better."

I went to the bathroom door and knocked.

"It's me, Linda."

"Don't come near me," she said. "You'll be accused too."

I went back to the kitchen and almost fell when my heel hit the spilled perfume. Valenti had his head under the faucet, letting cold water wash his scratched face.

"Valenti," I said. "You're just jealous."

He stood erect, water dripping down his shirt-front. "Me—jealous?" His thumb jerked toward the bathroom. "Of *that?*" He laughed viciously. "Don't make me laugh." And he laughed again.

"Linda's straight. She loves you."

Valenti made his tongue and lips flap. "Love—plplplplp! This afternoon I come home, and who do I find sitting in this kitchen like he owned the place? My own brother Mike."

"And so?"

"You don't know that guy, Mike. You don't know what a lowdown, two-timing gigolo he is. Every girl I had, he took her from me. Now he's after Linda."

"Nonsense. You're married now."

"That suits Mike just fine. It makes it all the easier. Him sitting in my kitchen with his coat off!"

"It's been hot. I had my coat off too."

"You should see those silk shirts of his, those red fireman's suspenders! I know why he took off his coat. How do I know what else he did?"

"Forget it."

"Stop saying that!"

"You're crazy."

"And yesterday. Here I am, working like a dog to make her happy, and when I come home, where do I find her?"

I didn't say anything.

"Standing downstairs. Talking to that no-good Walters, a lousy shoe salesman."

"So?"

"I wouldn't trust a salesman from here to that stove. You know how they are."

"You're very unreasonable. She's got to talk to somebody."

"You don't know her. The way she walks. The way she wiggles that tail of her. It's a come-on. Why does she wear her skirts so short, and so tight? If I fell for her, why shouldn't somebody else?"

"Forget it, Valenti."

He pounded the table slowly with his fist. "If she'd only *admit* it! I got to know where I stand."

"Admit what?"

"Those others."

"You're crazy. You're insane, mad."

"I got to know. I can't stand it."

"You said three times. What about the other time?"

"Ah," he said. "That slimy little rat!"

"Who?"

"The grocery kid. He's always hanging around. One of those high school kids with a lot of pimples. Always hanging around, chewing his fingernails."

"Hanging around?"

"Yeah. He brings groceries and stuff. He's always hanging around, looking at her legs. I've seen the little sneak."

"I don't blame him. Her legs are beautiful."

I shouldn't have said that. He bit his lower lip and stared at me, his hands opening and shutting. Then he pulled himself together and spoke with a great deal of dignity. "Jim, you're my friend. But please remember that this is my house, and we're discussing the woman I married."

I apologized, slapped him on the shoulder. The gesture brought tears to his eyes. He dried them with a knuckle. I had never seen him so upset.

"This grocery kid," I said. "I'm sure he means no harm. I wouldn't worry about him just because he stares at Linda's legs."

"But what's going on in that dirty little mind of his? *That's* what I'd like to know! And how do I know what happens when I'm downtown, slaving my life away?"

I crossed to the bathroom and knocked. "Come out, Linda," I said. "Let's get this straightened out."

She opened the door and stood there, impishly lovely, her lips pouted. Valenti walked past her to the medicine cabinet. She lowered her face and studied his cheek from under her brows.

Tilting his head, he poured iodine over the cuts. The brown disinfectant floated down his cheek and splashed his shirt front. He winced and murmured with pain. Then he turned to her.

"Help me!" he said. "Don't just stand there acting cute."

She found a wash towel, dipped it under cold water, and patted his face gently. She was the same height as Valenti. She was one of those women who could wear anything and look good in it, and she knew it. Her body had a way of exhibiting its easy acceptance of perfection.

"Poor darling," she said.

He gritted his teeth, and you could see him make a strong effort to control his eyes, but the tears came anyway, big, pellucid tears that got mixed up with the iodine.

"And I pulled your hair," he sniffed. "Your beautiful, wonderful, golden hair."

That made Linda cry too, and I stood there sleepy and annoyed, but happy that Valenti had come out of it so sensibly. They were holding hands on the divan when I left. It was almost three o'clock. As I closed the door I could hear Valenti begging for forgiveness for being such a fool, and Linda was saying that perhaps, after all, there was some justification for his behavior.

A week later Leon telephoned to say somebody was in the lobby and wanted to come up, but he didn't think she was any friend of mine. "She looks terrible," he said.

"Send her up," I said.

It was Linda. She stood in the doorway, her right eye puffed, her nose and cheek purpled. She limped painfully, and I helped her to the couch. Then I went into my kitchen and poured her a drink. She drank it up, with a lot of her tears.

"That bum!" she said. "That fiend!"

I tried to console her. She threw herself face down on the couch and shook with misery. After a while I got the story. That morning the milkman had stopped to collect. Valenti was still in bed at the time. Linda had stood in the kitchen, talking to the milkman. She liked the milkman. He was a nice fellow, she said. He had three little girls, and he was very proud of them. He told her all about them, and she was delighted. But she couldn't let the poor man stand in the doorway all morning. And besides, he wanted to tell her his wife's recipe for banana-upside-down cake. So she had asked him to sit down and have a cup of coffee And all the time, Valenti had been listening. With a leer, and a "Hah! So that's how it is!" he had burst into the kitchen in his pajamas, thrown the milkman down the stairs, punched Linda half a dozen times, and then dressed and gone to work.

"I'm through," she said. "I'm going to get a divorce."

I thought that was a good idea, and I told her so. Then I remembered my old friend Alfredo Valenti, and school days together, and I remembered the lean days of '32 and '33, slim days for a writer, when Valenti had stuck by me both morally and financially, and when I thought of all those things, and the way he loved her, I knew I would be loyal to him even though I liked Linda very much.

"Let's have another drink and talk it over," I said.

"It's no use," she said. "I'm through."

We had several drinks. We pushed the dispute back and forth, and we always came to the same equation: she thought Valenti was a bum, but she loved him. That was something. I had got that much out of her. As for going back to him, it was impossible. She should have followed her mother's advice. Her mother had once known an Italian, too. The Italian her mother knew had carried a stiletto. She should have listened to her mother in the first place.

She was with me two hours. When I finally got her to agree to go back and try once more, I was pretty happy about it. I had been loyal to my good friend Valenti. I had saved his marriage. I had returned him to his love. To a measure, at least, I had repaid him for his faith and friendship. But one thing she demanded. Valenti had to get down on his hands and knees and say he was sorry.

"And there's something else," she said. "I want a new car. A Chevrolet roadster. The kind with the two-tone body."

"All right," I said. "You go home. I'll see Valenti."

I drove her home. We stopped for some beefsteak for her eye. "He's emotional," I said. "But he loves you."

"The rat," she said. "And he called my mother an old toad."

"That's nothing."

"But she isn't. She's fat, but she's nice."

I let her out in front of their apartment house. Then I drove downtown to the Bureau of Power and Light. Valenti was assistant to the chief engineer. It was a good job, and I knew he would go far. I found him in the blueprint room, studying some plans. A thick bandage covered his right ear.

"How'd that happen?"

He smiled innocently.

"She did it. The water pitcher."

"She didn't tell me about that."

"Did she tell you she chased me out of the place with a butcher knife?"

"She told me you knocked her down."

"I barely pushed her—easy like."

"What about the black eye?"

"That wasn't me," he said. "Maybe it was the milkman. Maybe Walters downstairs. Maybe the grocery clerk. Maybe my brother Mike—he's hot-tempered. Maybe they all got there at once and there was a fight. She's got so many of us, there's bound to be a little friction now and then."

"You've got to apologize," I told him.

"To that little tramp? Never."

"You blacked her eye."

"She had it coming."

But Valenti apologized. When he got home and saw the spread of purple under her nose, he fell on his knees and begged her to have her revenge. "Call the police. Send me to prison. Divorce me, Linda. I don't deserve you."

She didn't argue the point. He kissed her purple eye and she kissed his bandaged ear. They stood in the middle of the room and kissed each other's lips. Then Valenti raised his head and sniffed the air. I could smell it too—the fragrance of spaghetti sauce. He turned from her and walked into the kitchen. She stood smiling awkwardly with the good side of her face. We heard him in the kitchen, fussing with a spoon and a pan. He came back to the living room, his face inscrutable.

214

"How come spaghetti?"

"I thought you'd like it."

"You cooked it for me?"

"Of course, darling."

"Pretty sure of yourself, aren't you?"

She looked at me, frightened a little, and I looked at Valenti. His black eyes sparkled mischief.

"What do you mean?" she said.

"I mean, we had a fight this morning. You assaulted me with a pitcher and a butcher knife. You threw me out. I said I wasn't coming back."

Linda sighed. "But darling, Jim said he'd bring you back. I wanted to surprise you "

"So you cooked enough spaghetti for seven people."

"Is it too much? I didn't know, darling."

Valenti folded his arms.

"Maybe you were going to celebrate the fact that you kicked me out. Maybe Mike and Walters and the milkman and the grocery boy were invited."

I said, "Shut up, Valenti."

Linda said, "I can't stand it! I hate him! I could kill him!"

Valenti smiled.

"You see, Jim? You hear that? Kill me."

I got tired of it. I told him so. I said, "Valenti, you're disgusting. This girl loves you. She's trying to make you happy. She's doing all she can. But you reek with jealousy, Valenti. Your mind is diseased with it. You don't deserve her. I think she ought to leave you. I think she's had more than enough."

Valenti threw himself into an upholstered rocker and stared at his shoes. My words had hit him hard. He would probably start crying. We watched him stare blankly. We watched his eyes. Their brightness began to dim. Two black pools took shape, overflowed, and spilled down his cheek.

"Jim's right," he said. "Linda, you ought to leave me."

Then Linda broke. The sight of him, so wretched and conscience-bitten, was too much for her. "Oh, my poor darling! Dearest, darling Alfredo!" She fell on her knees before him, produced a tiny green handkerchief from some place, and dabbed away his tears. "Jim's wrong, darling. It's none of his damn business, anyway."

"And I slugged you!" he sobbed. "Kill me, Linda. Kill me dead."

They started over again, Linda kissing his bandaged ear, Valenti kissing Linda's swollen eye. I'd had enough. I couldn't keep up with their moods. It was either murder and death, or life and love. I guess they both liked it that way. I didn't. Without a word, I backed toward the door. Valenti saw me as I stepped into the hall. "Jim!"

He came after me, put his arm around my shoulder.

"We both love you, Jim. You got to stay. Linda's spaghetti's wonderful."

I told him I had another engagement. To emphasize it, I looked at my wristwatch and whistled. He walked down the hall with me to the automatic elevator. He had his arm around my shoulder all the way.

"You're my best friend, Jim. You're the only one I can trust."

I saw his wild black eyes and thought of something else. "So long, Valenti."

He put both arms around me and hugged me. Then he kissed my cheek. I could smell the disinfectant from his bandaged ear. "The only man I can trust. Jim, you don't know what that means to me."

"I think I do," I said.

When I got out of there and into the cool street, I felt my lungs expand and I realized I had been suffocating. I was glad for the setting sun and the freedom of the pink and gold of the twilight sky. I was glad to be alone. It seemed the most precious thing in my life. I got into my car and drove back to my hotel.

Leon was at the desk. He handed me some mail.

"Leon," I said. "You remember that girl with the black eye? Next time she comes, I've moved. I've gone to China."

"China," Leon nodded.

China. When you're down the home stretch on a novel, and the prose runs smooth, it's like China, or Africa, or the moon. You're far away from everything, the days tumble by and you lose track of them. I don't remember exactly: it was seven or eight or nine days later. I finished the novel and got sick the same day. It was fever and a slight chill. I called Dr. Atwood. He looked at my chest and found what I hadn't noticed. Spots. I had the measles. By evening I had a lot of them. The hotel management wanted me to go to the hospital, but Atwood talked them out of it. I was isolated in my room on the third floor.

It was the night Valenti came. He arrived unannounced. I don't know how he got by Leon at the desk, but I know what he did when he read the *Keep Out: Sickness* sign on my door. He came in. I looked up when I saw the door opening. There stood Valenti. The last time I'd seen him only his ear was bandaged. Now the top of his head was swathed in a thick turban of cotton and white adhesive. The low desk lamp was on the other side of the room and he couldn't see me very well.

"Jim!" His voice was worried. "What's the matter?"

I was feverish and irritated. I didn't feel like taking on other people's troubles. I wanted to be alone in the semidarkness with my fever and my ugly little spots.

"Your head," I said. "Linda?"

"Yeah. With a claw-hammer. Eight stitches."

"Valenti," I said. "Please go away."

He sat down.

"I need your advice."

"No you don't. I'm sick, Valenti. It's contagious."

He stood up "What's contagious?"

"Measles. I've got the measles."

I remember very little of the next few minutes. I remember that I was too weak to defend myself, and I remember the heavy thud of Valenti's fist against my jaw. I think he knocked me out of the bed, picked me up, and knocked me into bed. Never underestimate the measles. Some time during the barrage I caught a flash of his black eyes, and I felt that he had gone insane, something I had always suspected would happen, something I didn't like to think about. Then I realized that Linda had probably caught the measles too, and Valenti had drawn his own conclusion. But I was too weak to explain, and it wouldn't have done any good. I remember him standing in the open door, shaking his fist and sobbing: "To think that I trusted you—my friend. Nuts!"

The measles left me in two weeks. Valenti's souvenirs hung like fresh figs from my eyes for two months. I insisted my nose was broken, but Atwood disagreed. As for the three missing upper teeth, my dentist had condemned them before Valenti's visit. I said very little about it. I knew nobody would believe me, anyway. Even Atwood doubted it. Both Valenti and Linda phoned a couple of times, but Leon told them China.

It wasn't China, but it had to be New York, because my new book was coming out. I decided to drive there. It took longer, and it would give my face a chance to heal. I was sitting in my car, watching Julio, the Filipino boy, stacking luggage in the back seat.

Across the street a fancy klaxon sounded, and I heard my name called. A new Chevrolet roadster, a two-tone job, slid into the curb. It was Linda. She waved proudly. I thought of driving away; instead, I waved.

She got out and slammed the roadster door. She seemed pleased with the process. But there was something odd about her carriage: it was stiff and robot-like. Then I saw what it was as she crossed the street toward me. She wore some kind of steel and leather brace around her neck, with a leather cushion under her chin. Valenti was getting rougher every day. I looked up and down the street. You never could tell when Valenti would show up.

"Jim!" she said. "Where on earth have you been?"

"China," I said. I nodded at her neck-brace. "How did he do that?"

"I'm sick of China, China all the time. You haven't been to China at all. You don't like us anymore. He pushed me down the stairs."

She was standing in the street, her head inside the car. She looked lovelier than ever. The brace was surprisingly becoming. It held her face like a pedestal.

"How were the measles?" I said.

"Poor Jim," she said. "You poor darling. Valenti told me."

"What did Valenti tell you?"

"That you had the measles. That's why I kept calling, but it was always China," she replied.

"Didn't you have the measles, too?"

"We thought it was the measles. It was something I ate. Strawberries or something."

"So he broke your neck."

"It isn't broken, Jim. It's only fractured. He's changed, Jim. He's different now. Look what he bought me."

We both looked at the new car.

"Nice," I said.

Then I heard my name called. I knew the voice. It was Valenti's. He was double-parked next to Linda's car, across the street. He was leaning on his horn and waving wildly.

"Jim! My old *paesano*, Jim!"

"Linda," I said. "Step back."

"But Jim."

"*Paesano!*"

I let the clutch out and pulled into the light traffic. They were both yelling and waving for me to stop.

"Jim!" Valenti said. "Where are you going?"

"China!" I yelled.

The Case of the Haunted Writer

THREE YEARS AGO we left Los Angeles and bought a home in Roseville, the railroad town near Sacramento. At first, and for reasons which I shall explain, my wife disliked this particular house. But we were weary of house-hunting, the price was within our reach, and I even liked the place.

The question rises: what in Sam Hill were we doing in Roseville in the first place, for Roseville is a jarring town. Eighteen miles from the state capital, it is the principal division point of the Southern Pacific Railroad. There are more boxcars than people in Roseville, and the population is around twelve thousand. The railroad yard is the largest on the Pacific Coast, even larger than the Los Angeles yard. Day and night the town is pounded by the big noise—chugging engines, screeching whistles, and the ceaseless crashing of boxcars being bullied by yard engines.

There were two reasons why we moved to Roseville, and the first is so contradictory that I hesitate to mention it; to wit, we wanted to live in a quiet country town. Roseville was neither quiet nor was it a country town. The second reason was our people. My wife's mother lived there, as did my Old Man and Mama.

Now, here was this house: it was the kind of place a roofing company uses to symbolize the American Way, a snug white bungalow set upon a carpet of green lawn and surrounded by eucalyptus trees. It was a two-story structure with an expansive front porch that exuded Pride of Ownership. Situated in a tract known as Sunshine Heights, the address was 1515 Harmony Lane. It had everything.

Before buying the house, I asked the Old Man to inspect it. Though his trade is bricklaying, this was a mistake. Puffing a cigar, the Old Man made a hasty inspection of the barren rooms. He was not impressed. Then he went down into the big concrete basement. He spent a long time down there, finally emerging draped in cobwebs and enthusiasm. This was only natural, since his own house had no basement at all, and he had need for a deep cool place to age a couple of hundred gallons of Sacramento Valley claret.

"Fine house," he said. "One of the best in town. Good and solid. Very fine basement. Buy it."

My wife held back. In childhood she had known

the tragic family that once lived in the house. Their name was, significantly, Coffin, and she could not forget that two of them had died at 1515 Harmony Lane. Mrs. Coffin had succumbed to a heart attack in the front bedroom, while her son Edward had died of polio in the back bedroom. These depressing events of fifteen years ago had no effect on me. I was surprised that my wife should encourage such melancholy associations.

"You, of all people," I said.

"Are you sure you'll be happy here?"

"All my life I've searched for this place," I told her. "It's as though I've been here before, in a dream."

This was not exactly the truth, but the thought of one more real estate agent put murder in my heart. We went down to the bank and signed the papers. The house was ours. We spent a sickening amount on furniture and moved in.

At the rear of the house was a sun porch which looked out on a few eucalyptus trees and a back fence glutted with variegated ivy. The porch was to be my workroom. My wife hung some curtains, a couple of Van Gogh prints, and the usual props a writer has to stare at. But it was a fine workroom. There was sun and space and fresh air. Here, I thought, is peace: here the words shall come, the pages mount. And I began to believe what I had said in the first place: that I had seen this house in my dreams.

The words did not come, nor the ideas. But the painters came, and the carpenters, for my wife wanted to change the house inside and out, to obliterate every trace of its past.

The house was built in the early twenties. The living room walls were panels of fine walnut covered with a thin coat of varnish to accentuate the grain. They seemed to give the room age and warmth, but my wife insisted they made the room dark and gloomy. She had the woodwork painted white, and the rest of the wall covered with a green fern-patterned wallpaper. The change brought brightness to the room, but now it looked like the Hollywood apartment we had just left. There was a big potbellied stove in the room which made me look forward to cold nights and a roaring fire. After the white paint and green ferns, the poor stove was hustled away and a floor furnace installed. This involved a lot of ripping and pounding and money. It made heavy invasions of my serenity. I did no writing in my workroom. Seated at the desk, I listened to the noise and figured costs.

Meanwhile the painters climbed the house from the outside, scraping and patching in preparation for two coats of battleship grey. Mr. Smitters, the paint contractor, stood on a ladder and kept looking at me as I tried to work. He had big white teeth and was unpleasantly good-humored, with the usual inanities about the soft life of a writer. I thought of going outside and staring at him as he did at me, and making unkind remarks about his profession. All of these interruptions nibbled at the clock, and one sterile day followed another. We had been in the house for a month, and I had nothing on paper except some figures proving we would starve to death that winter.

Then the Old Man arrived in his truck, with four fifty-gallon barrels of red wine. He backed the truck down the driveway to the outside entrance of the basement. For two days he hammered and sawed and sang directly beneath me. He constructed racks for his barrels and he repaired some broken furniture stored in the basement. The lighting arrangement didn't suit him, and for eight hours one day he disconnected the main switch and strung mysterious wires into the basement from the garage. But he knew nothing about electricity, he was only guessing, and his efforts ended in a confusion of wires and complete darkness at the end of the day. We had to call an electrician to untangle the mess.

When the Old Man arrived with his barrels, we assumed he only wanted to store the wine in that cool place, to let it age in a quiet, healthy atmosphere. But we underestimated the Old Man's resourcefulness. The wine had come from the vines of a *paesano* outside of town. He had bought it for twenty cents a gallon, hauling it seven perilous miles in his bumpy truck. The ride had angered the wine, clouding its redness. The old Man sat beside the barrels like a doctor at a deathbed, smoking a cigar and frowning. Occasionally he poured a small amount into a glass and held it up to the light. He tiptoed around and spoke in whispers.

After a breathless, nerve-wracking week in which all of us participated, the Old Man announced that the potion was saved, that it was bright claret and not vinegar.

Having saved the patient's life, he now proceeded to drink it. He came with his *paesanos* from the local wine shops, he brought bricklayers and carpenters and hod carriers. The basement was transformed into a saloon. It was acceptable the first time, even plausible. Here were lovers of the grape who were normally served at bars for a dime a glass. And here was my Old Man, bread and wine his soul and sinew, the prince of hosts. He passed out thick tumblers and told his guests to help themselves. They came in mortar-begrimed trucks, and the less opulent simply walked the ten blocks from town. The uproar in the basement was like the fury of dogs in a kennel.

It had to stop somewhere, but it was not easy to challenge the Old Man. For too many years he had preached the Fourth Commandment. Indeed, that children should honor their mothers and fathers, particularly their fathers, was the very core of his philosophy. But I had to speak out,

"It's got to stop," I told him.

This was after the *paesanos* had departed and he sat happily in the ruins, great splotches of wine on the floor, pieces of glass, and cigar butts.

"What's the matter, son?"

"No more parties. They mustn't come anymore."

"You're talking about my friends," he said. "Your father's friends."

228

"They make too much noise. I can't work."

"Work?" He giggled. "You call that stuff work, the stuff you write?"

A familiar attack. I refused to be diverted.

"No more parties, Papa."

"Son," he said. "You're talking to your father. And your father, he don't like it. Your father's an old man, son. He's seventy years old. Watch your language."

My wife had less patience.

"You're being very unreasonable," she told him. "If those men come again, you'll have to take your wine out of here."

The Old Man rocked in his chair.

"What she said, son. What she said!"

He got to his feet with heavy dignity, his eyes flooded with wine, and floated toward the door. Pausing, he patted my shoulder.

"God help you, son. You're gonna need it."

He never came back to that house again, but he did not forget the wine. Once a week he sent my brother with jugs to keep a supply on hand.

The upstairs bedrooms were in very good shape, clean and roomy, despite a musty odor. For the first time in five years of marriage each of us now had his own bedroom. It saddened my wife, but I welcomed the change, feeling that it could do nought but add zest to the marriage bed.

The bedrooms were beneath a gable, the ceilings

rising to the peak of the roof. In each bedroom was a small trap door opening to a cramped dark attic. Here we found a few relics of the Coffin occupation—a couple of bedpans, a carton of tattered curtains, some dusty blankets, some old light fixtures. My wife insisted that these be taken out and destroyed. I dragged the stuff out and dropped it through the window to the lawn.

Now she requested that the trap doors be nailed shut. This seemed foolhardy, since electricians would have to pry them open in case anything went wrong with the wiring. But the doors were battened down, the painters hauled away their splattered planks and ladders, the Old Man swore he would never darken our door again, and at last the house was quiet and truly our home.

Mine was the back bedroom. My wife informed me that Edward Coffin had died there. I was not impressed. But one day among my wife's books I found Edward's picture in the Roseville High School annual and learned that he had been president of the Senior Class, captain of the basketball team, and chairman of the senior prom. My wife sighed and supplied additional information. She had dated Edward quite often the Spring before he died. She had kissed him a couple of times, too. This, I thought, was extremely significant, even though I realized it had no significance whatever.

At first my wife slept wretchedly through spooky nights filled with dreams of horror. Hers was the bedroom in which poor Mrs. Coffin had expired. The clothes closet and built-in shelves were always turning up some small memento of that sad time: a strand of grey hair, a fragment of thread, a button, a hairpin. My wife stared at these trifles with awful premonitions.

But the house really expressed itself at night, contracting after the great heat of the Sacramento Valley sunlight. It creaked and gasped. It sighed and whimpered. Two or three times a week I woke to find my wife beside me, her eyes streaked from shattered sleep. She insisted that she had heard footsteps all over the place, people walking up and down the stairs, voices in the kitchen, someone crawling in the attic, the rhythmic squeak of a rocking chair. But I had heard nothing and slept well.

"Imagination," I said. "Pure fancy."

Nevertheless I bought a gun. I bought it quite suddenly one afternoon in Sacramento, seeing it in the window of a second-hand store. It was a Smith & Wesson .38 caliber Police Special.

Propped against a box of cartridges, its blue steel leering with evil beauty, the weapon beckoned with frightful blandishments. Excepting an air-rifle, I had never owned a gun, and now I wanted this one. And why not? I owned a house. A man should have a gun to protect his property. I brought it home with a box of cartridges, a can of oil, and a gun-brush, the storekeeper having instructed me on how to clean it.

The gun terrified my wife. She covered her eyes with one hand and motioned me out of the house.

"Get it out. Take it away."

"But it's not loaded."

I broke it open, spun the chamber, and pulled the trigger a few times.

"I don't care. No guns in this house."

We reached a compromise. I could keep the gun in the house if I separated it from the cartridges. She found a remote and futile place for the cartridges on the back porch, in the broom closet, at the bottom of a laundry bag full of discarded silk stockings. I took the gun up to my room and immediately proceeded to clean and oil it.

The revolver filled me with craven fascination. I wanted to take it up into the Sierra foothills and fire it, but my wife resisted so fiercely that I gave up the idea. Instead, I found amusement in other ways. I practiced drawing the gun quickly. I learned to spin it around my trigger finger. I stood before the mirror and practiced dueling. I gave up the old habit of reading before sleep and cleaned the gun instead. Every night I sat propped up in bed with my gun brush, a small can of oil, and a cloth. The gun shone like a black jewel.

Gradually my wife's restlessness disappeared. In the morning she was refreshed from sleep and eager for the new day. She no longer feared the gun. She even picked it up and pulled the trigger.

With writers, sleep and prose are brothers. If the stuff comes, if it moves across the page, the nights are serene. If there are no words, there is no sleep. It was one of those times. I couldn't sleep.

232

It was also the time of Roseville's strangest bandit. Every day the *Tribune* had a fresh report of his crimes. Housewives were furious. The baffled police added an extra car to the night patrol, but the thief struck again and again. He was a panty thief. His plunder never varied. He showed no interest in shirts, dresses or overalls. Every night, now on the Northside, now on the South, the thief stripped some clothesline of a pair of ladies' panties. In despair the police asked the women of the town to bring in their washing at night. But there was always someone who forgot, and it was into her yard that the scoundrel crept, snatched a pair of panties off the line, and vanished into the night.

In my sleeplessness I mused about this exotic bandit. Polishing my gun, I pondered his curious depredations and contrived to find ways of capturing him. All at once I arrived upon a scheme.

I put on a robe and tiptoed into the room where my wife slept. Opening her dresser, I removed three pairs of her silk panties. Without a sound I went downstairs and through the house to the backyard. Our clothesline ran parallel with the back fence along the alley. There in the moonlight I hung the panties, one black, one white, one pink. A soft breeze lifted them to irresistible proportions. Now I hurried back to my room, turned off the lights, and sat at my window awaiting developments. I was there ten minutes before I realized my scheme was mad and worthless. In the first place my gun was not loaded, nor had I any desire to shoot the famous thief. In the second place, should he arrive on the scene, he would simply snatch the panties and be off, for I certainly had no intention of rushing out and grappling with him.

Alert as a wound, I smoked cigarettes and listened to the night noises. It was late summer and warm. Beyond my window an elm spread itself, luminous in the moonlight. Already the leaves were falling. We lived on a quiet tree-lined street. Approaching footsteps were audible two blocks away, and that was a rare sound, for everyone in the district went to town by car.

But now I heard footsteps. They were very near, in our yard, swishing through the dead leaves. The steps began in the front yard and moved around to the side of the house. I unhooked the screen and looked out the window. All was clear and bright, no movement, no sound. I locked the screen and sat back. Once more I heard the footsteps. This time I snapped on the light, opened the screen and called out, "Who's there?" No answer. I snapped off the light.

Instantly the leaves rustled, the steps moving around the house to the side door. Now I was certain of it: someone was in our yard, a tramp, a prowler, a thief. A man's home was about to be invaded. The situation called for action. I picked up my gun. In the yard the invader's feet plowed through the leaves defiantly.

Alarmed and angry I stood with the gun in my hand, the bullets buried in a sack of silk stockings downstairs on the back porch. I cursed my wife and tiptoed down the staircase. I needed ammunition. The moon lit up the living room, and I crouched low at the foot of the stairs, for the curtains were apart and I could be seen from the outside.

Sprawled flat on my stomach, I crawled through the dining room to the kitchen. My heart banged against the floor, the gun in my hand was sticky with perspiration, and I felt hot and suffocating in the flannel robe. The hiss of leaves told me the intruder was at the side door between the kitchen and the dining room. This was no panty thief, this was a burglar.

An inch at a time, I dragged myself across the linoleum in the kitchen. By now I had reached the door to the back porch. Raising my arm, I turned the lock. There was a sharp click. Instantly the noise outside stopped. Sweat poured from me. I lay prostrate, panting and waiting. Another weary twenty feet lay between me and the broom closet. Again there was activity at the side door, and I thought I heard the knob turn. I kept going, dragging myself along the floor of the back porch to the broom closet. With both hands I reached up and tore the stocking sack from a hook.

Feverish with excitement, I clawed through the stockings, cursing my wife and all women, my fingers snagging the silk as they searched for the elusive box of cartridges. At last I found it and loaded the gun. Now I was unafraid. With six bullets in the .38 I got to my feet and walked boldly through the kitchen to the side door. For hair-trigger action I cocked the gun. The situation was well in hand. I was aware of the consequences. I knew no jury would convict me.

I flung open the door.

"Stay where you are," I said.

He didn't. It was Heinrich, the long brown Dachshund belonging to the Richardsons, our next-door neighbors. Heinrich yelped and skittered through the leaves and under the hedge.

I sat on the doorstep. I was utterly exhausted, my whole body bathed in sweat, my face and robe smeared with dust and lint picked up on the long crawl across the floor. Tangled silk stockings draped my arms and ankles. It had been a terrifying night, and the less my wife knew of it the better. I unloaded the gun, replaced the cartridges in the stocking bag, mopped up the sweaty streak across the linoleum, put everything in order, and took a shower.

Then I remembered the panties out on the clothesline. They had to be returned. Disgusted with myself, I went downstairs once more and into the backyard. It was two o'clock. As I gathered the panties, I heard a voice behind me, and the voice said;

"For lord's sake."

It was Richardson. He was a railroad engineer. He went to work at insane hours, and he was on his way to work now, opening the doors to his garage.

I said, "Hi, neighbor."

But there was a sickening feeling in the pit of my stomach as I walked back to the house, for I knew Richardson stood in his driveway looking at me and thinking of the zany wanted by the police.

For a week I avoided Richardson. He was a fiend for gardening, spending every possible moment in his yard. Whenever the urge for exercise seized me I went to the window, and there was Richardson in his garden, clipping roses or hauling manure. The confinement left me jittery and fogged from excessive cigarette smoking.

One thing was certain: Richardson had not told his wife. Had he done so, it would have come back to me through the grapevine. For Mrs. Richardson and my wife spent most of their waking hours chinning over the hedge. Why had Richardson not told his wife? His silence was ominous. Had he reported me to the police? Had he told any of his fellow engineers at the roundhouse? Richardson had always regarded me with cautious reserve. Now I recalled an election discussion between us. Richardson had said he didn't hold with any Communist ideas. Had he reported the panty episode to the FBI? Anything was possible in a world coming apart at the seams.

I decided to face the man. He was on his knees in the dahlia bed, digging up bulbs. On the pretext of emptying a wastebasket I went out to the incinerator. Richardson looked up and waved a muddy glove.

"Haven't seen you around," he said.

"Been working."

"You work nights too?"

"Sometimes."

"Nice and quiet at night," he said. "Nobody around."

That decided it. Richardson suspected something.

The situation was untenable. One course lay before me —to get out of town until the whole thing blew over.

A telephone call from my agent simplified matters. There was a job at Paramount. He was airmailing the script. I told him I would take the job, that I liked the script without reading it. There was a ten-week guarantee. I promised to be at work Monday morning.

"And leave me alone in this haunted house?" my wife said.

I was shocked.

"I thought you were over that nonsense."

"I won't stay here alone."

I tried to point out the salubrious effects of a brief holiday between husbands and wives—a time of reflection on the past, a time of high resolves for the future. Besides, there was the needless expense of two people in Hollywood.

"I won't stay here alone in this house."

I reminded her that it was our home, our hearthstone rooted in the earth. The lawn, the roses, the trees so dearly loved—these were the ancient responsibilities of the wife while her husband went into the jungle to forage for food.

"You don't go to Hollywood without me."

She phoned a real estate agent, offering our house on a short-term lease. The next morning Mr. and Mrs. Aidlin called on us. They were Berkeley people. Mr. Aidlin was an engineer for the State Highway Division, which was now putting in a new freeway to Marysville. For months the Aidlins had lived in hotels and auto courts. They were desperate for decent housing.

They stood in our fern-patterned living room, Mrs. Aidlin's large sad eyes brimming with eagerness as she clutched her husband's arm. They would take the house under any circumstances, for any length of time, a week or a year.

"But you haven't seen it," my wife said. "Don't you think you ought to go through it first?"

Mrs. Aidlin refused to take another step. She was perfectly satisfied. I took Mr. Aidlin upstairs. He was in his late forties, tall and grey and tired. He peeked into the front bedroom. He put his head inside the bathroom and nodded. Then he went down the hall to my bedroom. He stood in the middle of a wine carpet and suddenly his reserve was gone.

"Oh man," he said. "A room of my own."

He threw himself into the reading chair by the window, unbuttoned his collar and spread his legs wide.

"Oh man," he repeated. "Oh man, oh man."

We had a couple of slugs of bourbon and went downstairs. Mrs. Aidlin and my wife were having tea in the kitchen. The Aidlins were friendly, solid people. Their desire to lease the house was our good fortune. They solemnly promised to vacate in ten weeks. We followed them to their car and shook hands all around. Saturday night they drove us to the depot. I gave Mr. Aidlin the keys to the house and told him to finish the bourbon. We hoarded the train to Los Angeles and they drove back to Harmony Lane.

The *Roseville Tribune* was forwarded to our Los Angeles hotel, and I watched every issue. It was not until the eighth week of our stay that I found on the *Tribune's* front page the story I sought: news of the capture of the panty thief. The Roseville police had collared their man under a railroad bridge near the public library. Thirty assorted pairs of ladies' panties were found in his blanket roll. He was brought to swift justice, sentenced to a week in the city jail, and then given a floater out of town.

A few days later the *Tribune* reported the death of Mr. Aidlin. He had succumbed to a heart attack in his sleep. We had had no correspondence with the Aidlins, and the news of his death was a shock. My wife sent a card of condolence, and Mrs. Aidlin replied with a brief note telling us of her desire to close the house and return to her family in Berkeley.

We carefully avoided the subject, but there was no denying simple arithmetic. Mr. Aidlin was the third person to go directly from our house to the morgue. I remembered the way he looked that first day in my room, how he spread his legs and looked around and was pleased. He had died in his sleep, so he had died up there in my room, in my bed. I felt sorry for Mr. Aidlin, but I didn't like him dying in my bed.

Now that Mrs. Aidlin was leaving, someone would have to look after the house. My wife's mother was ill and my brother was out of town. That left the Old Man. But there were still over a hundred gallons of wine in the basement.

"I'll go," my wife said.

In the afternoon she took a plane. A week later, the studio having closed me out on schedule, I was back in Roseville too. We carried the luggage up to my room, and she sat on the bed and gave me a report. She had talked to Mrs. Aidlin a few minutes before the unhappy woman returned to Berkeley. Apparently Aidlin had never been sick before. When his alarm continued to ring that morning Mrs Aidlin had found him there, a book in his lap.

It was coming. I knew it was coming, and that night as I lay in bed things began to happen. I heard the alarm go off. I heard footsteps downstairs. I heard someone crawling around in the attic. I lay in the bed of a dead man, felt the curvature of the mattress that had once pressed against his body, and stared at the very ceiling which had been his last view of this world. I turned the bed around. I put the pillow at the foot of the bed and slept with my feet toward the top. It was no good. I tried to sleep in the chair, but it had me, the fancies, and I remembered Aidlin sitting there, and I got up and made my bed on the floor. Here in this room he had died, here too Edward Coffin had died, and here I might die too. For a week I fought it, but it got steadily worse. When, in the darkness, I saw both Edward Coffin and Aidlin sitting in the elm tree outside my window, it was too much

I grabbed an armful of blankets and went downstairs to the couch in my workroom. Here all the fancies vanished, and I slept well. I awoke strong and fresh, ready for work. At breakfast I told my wife I had changed bedrooms. From now on, I would sleep in the workroom.

"I can't sleep upstairs. I keep thinking about Aidlin."

"But Mr. Aidlin didn't die upstairs," my wife said. "He died on the couch in your workroom."

We sold the house and headed back to Los Angeles.

Mama's Dream

MAMA ANDRILLI SAT at the kitchen table preparing lunch. The hot white sun of the Sacramento Valley burst out into the room from the south windows—big cascades of sunshine spilling over the red linoleum floor where slept Papa's cats, Philomina and Constanza. Both were males, but Papa recognized only one sex in cats.

In less than an hour he would be home from work. Papa was seventy now, and worse than ever, Except for a weakening of his eyes, he still laid brick and stone as fast as a young mason. But the years—no matter how blasphemous his denials—had taken their toll, and by now Mama had given up all hope of a quiet old age.

When a man reaches seventy you would think he

might mellow. But no: the past ten years, with their three sons married and gone, had been the worst. Now Papa would never soften and grow gentle. Until his last breath he would go raging and shouting, with Mama always there, patient to the end. It had been so for forty years, and now Mama was sixty-eight, with white hair and sometimes excruciating agony in her withered hands. Papa still had his red mustache and only traces of grey at his temples. He still pounded his chest with furious blows as he entreated God to strike him down and remove him from this valley of travail. Years ago, when she was young and strong, Mama took comfort in the thought that she would leave her noisy husband as soon as her children were grown. The notion was a tiny jewel she hoarded in secret. But it was lost now, misplaced in some teapot of the past, and Mama had forgotten it.

On the table stood a bowl of bell peppers, green and fat. Mama cut them into strips for frying and thought again of last night's dream. Papa had slept badly, his kidneys heckling him, tumbling him from bed half a dozen times. Naturally he blamed Mama. Not enough peppers in his diet. Papa was a sort of primitive medicine man with some ancient Italian notions about food. You ate fish for the brain, cheese for the teeth, eggplant for the blood, beans for the bowels, bread for brawn, chicory for the nerves, garlic for purity, olive oil for strength, and peppers for the kidneys. Without these a man faced quick decay.

For a week he had demanded peppers without

avail. This was the result. Coming back to dump his tired body beside her, he had accused her of trying to destroy him, of deliberately withholding peppers so that his kidneys would become diseased, a malady which had cut down his cousin Rocco at the age of thirty-five, thus ending the career of the man who made the best zinfandel in California.

The dream had come after that, a product of shattered sleep, lucid through her husband's grumbling. In it Mama saw herself naked at the side of Highway 99 as a speeding car approached. Nick, her oldest son, was driving the car. Beside him sat his wife Hild. She was laughing hysterically as she blew her nose into a large piece of lace. For all her nudity and shame Mama could not help seeing in horror that the lace was an altar boy's surplice. Hild tossed the surplice out of the speeding car, Nick honked the horn madly, and the surplice came flying back to Mama. At that moment the car went over a cliff with Nick screaming, "Mama, Mama."

Frightened and suddenly aware of her nudity, Mama ran away, the surplice shielding her loins, her backside exposed and gleaming in the moonlight as she ran across a field. In a little while she reached a graveyard where a funeral service was being conducted. In the descending coffin she saw her son Nick. The coffin was open, but Nick was not dead. He was on his knees before a typewriter, his fingers tapping out a message on a yellow Western Union blank. The message read: *They won't give me the last sacraments.* Mama began to scream for a priest, and the mourners around the grave turned to glare at her in annoyance. Once more she was aware of her nakedness and rushed off in shame, her backside shining like a diamond in the moonlight. This ended the dream.

Mama cut the last of the peppers and probed for a meaning to the dream. She was a lonely woman and her dreams fascinated her. She did not believe in dreams, since the Church forbade it, but there was a desire to believe and a wonder at their portent

Nick at his typewriter she understood, for her son was a writer. The surplice meant Nick as a youngster, when he was an altar boy. The disgusting and sacrilegious spectacle of her daughter-in-law blowing her nose into the surplice symbolized the fact that Nick had married a Protestant girl. As for the funeral, Mama dared not make any conjecture. It could mean that Nick was dead back in Los Angeles, just as previous coffin dreams had presaged the deaths of her mother and father, her brother Gino, and her sister Cathy. The telegram was of course bad news. Mama always dreaded telegram dreams. But the most confusing part of the dream was her own nudity. For the last ten years Mama had been dreaming of herself walking around the countryside without a stitch to cover her, and it was completely baffling. For a while she presumed it meant a cold was coming on. She fortified herself with aspirin and put on an extra sweater, but the cold never materialized and she was left more confused than ever.

The peppers were cut now, and ready for frying. Mama put Cathy's pot over the gas jet and lit the flame.

Cathy's pot was not a pot, nor did it belong to Cathy. It was a heavy iron skillet Mama's sister Cathy gave her as a wedding present forty years ago, and yet throughout the years it was ever known as Cathy's pot. Mama's little house was full of things described in that fashion. For the years of sacrifice in the life of Mama Andrilli had removed all sense of possession from her nature. Living around her, one quickly got the false impression that everything was borrowed.

In truth, all the things in the house were hers—and many were gifts from her sons, her brothers and sisters. There were no strings attached to these gifts, they belonged to her completely, but Mama Andrilli had long ago lost any sense of possession. For this reason, the three-room bungalow contained Nick's radio, Stella's sheets, Mike's towels, Ralph's lamp, Rosie's coffee pot, Tony's dress, Bettina's shoes, and Vito's bathrobe. There were also Mike's suitcase, Nettie's tablecloth, Joe's dishes, and Angelo's rugs. A notable omission was anything belonging to Papa, except, of course, Papa's breakfast, Papa's laundry, Papa's hash. But these were not concrete possessions. They were things Mama had to get done.

And now, Papa's peppers. They had to be prepared with solemn precision. Though Mama did all the cooking and was excellent in the Neapolitan style, Papa had altered her technique to suit the tastes of his Abruzzian origins. The difference was a matter of quantity. Where Mama used one clove of garlic, he demanded two. These she cut up now, dropping the small bits into hot olive oil in Cathy's pot. She added sweet basil and rosemary, spicing the oil with breathless caution. After forty years, Papa still sampled his wife's cooking with the darkest suspicions, lest she concoct some unpalatable thing to lay him low.

There was an angry swoosh as she dumped the peppers into the hot oil. Shielding her face, she saw the cats spring up from the floor, their backs arched as they hissed like snakes. Philomina and Constanza knew that Mama's hearing was poor and failing, and they always assumed this hostile position to warn her that someone was at the front door.

It was the man from Western Union. He was no less alarming than an angel of death, and she stared at him with her face suddenly white as he said, "Telegram for Mr. Andrilli."

He opened the screen and pushed the yellow envelope toward her, but she refused to accept it, her arm failing to go out after that missive so symbolic of death somewhere in the clan. The memory of all the telegrams in her past blocked the reflexes of her arm and she stood with bulging eyes while the frightened cats brushed against her and hissed their hatred of the man on the porch. Finally he thrust the message into her hands and she accepted it weakly.

A few more telegrams showed inside his hat and as he hurried away she thought of how many others besides Nick had suddenly gone to their God. Nick! Her Nicola, her first-born. For now she knew the meaning of last night's dream. Her son was dead. She

248

dragged herself to the kitchen table and began to cry, the deep wailing lament that only death can arouse. The crushed telegram fell in a ball to the floor and the cats made sport with it.

Thirty minutes later Papa Andrilli turned into the yard from the back alley and sniffed the odor of burning peppers. He wore a mangled felt hat, tan shirt and trousers. All of him was smeared with grey mortar, for he had just come off the scaffold after a morning of bricklaying. His nostrils flared at the smell. Already tasting his burnt lunch, he slammed the back gate and went charging up the porch steps.

The kitchen was smudged with black smoke. At the table sat his weeping wife, oblivious to the choking fumes. Quickly he turned off the flame under the skillet. The peppers were black and shriveled, but the tragic face of Mama Andrilli drove the anger out of him.

"What happened?" he asked.

Her chin trembled and the torrent from her eyes made him afraid. His own eyes began to sting as he forced himself to be calm and took a chair at the table opposite her. They sat in the heavy pall and he twisted his thick battered fingers and prepared for the worst.

"What is it, *mia moglia?*" he asked again. "Tell your husband the trouble."

"Our Nicola."

It sounded ominous. When in trouble he was always Nicola, otherwise he was just plain Nick.

"What's he done now?"

"The telegram. He's dead."

Papa looked for the telegram, the shock of her words choking his vision with blinding tears. The crushed message skittered across the smooth floor, pursued by the cats. He rose to pick it up, but he could not bear to read it. He could only sit opposite his wife, numbed by the pain in his soul. Then a fresh burst of grief surged from her, and he set his jaw and determined to be strong.

Even now he told himself again that weeping was for women, but the pain in his chest was very great as he threw open the windows to let the smoke escape. Like a thing of horror, the telegram slid crazily over the floor, the cats pouncing upon it and snarling at one another. Mama Andrilli shuddered, her face buried in her arms. He turned from her in misery, wanting to comfort her. But Italo Andrilli was not familiar with sentiment, nor had he ever practiced tenderness.

Ashamed of his inadequacy, he opened the refrigerator door and grabbed a decanter of red wine. He drank quickly, desperately, the shock of cold wine down his throat as he recalled the face of his son, his very hands and feet. There was nobody like Nick, dead before his time, the first and favorite of his children. There was even a touch of genius in Nick, the story-writer, with his books and wild ideas and the reckless ways he spent money. Papa Andrilli had not always approved of the things in his son's books, tales of his own family and their friends. He had been enraged about the theme of one of Nick's books, a tale of infidelity involving an Italian stone-mason and his wife. Even though there was considerable truth in the story, he had torn the book in half and burned it and even thought of launching a lawsuit against his son. But that was in the past; all was forgiven now, forgiven and forgotten. For better or worse, it was not given to all men to be set down in books by their sons.

But Nick's death took away irrevocably one stirring ambition in the final days of Italo Andrilli. Remembering it now, Papa went to his desk in the living room and pulled out a set of building plans. He had made these sketches in pencil on rolled sheets of drawing paper. He placed the wine bottle on the desk and unrolled the plans. Here in neat black lines was his scheme of a master house for Nick and his wife. For weeks at odd moments he had worked over these plans, hoping to show them to his son when he visited Sacramento again.

Papa studied them and wept bitterly as from the kitchen came the pitiful moans of his wife. Gulping down more wine, Papa wept without shame. But his grief was suffused with rising indignation. It was not right that Nick should die so young. No man should be taken at thirty-seven, not even a bad man, and Nick was good. With both fists in the air he cried to his God and demanded an explanation of this terrible tragedy. His mortar-splattered fingers clawed at the drawings, tearing them to shreds as he sobbed helplessly.

From the alley came the clatter and belch of an engine. Only one car in Sacramento made such a noise, his son Tony's.

Two years younger than Nick, Tony had a temperament to match his red hair. He too was a bricklayer, having served an apprenticeship under his father. They were in business together, a stormy partnership in which even the smallest matters were never settled. Unlike Nick or Vito, Tony stood toe to toe with Papa in arguments that frequently ended with fists flying. In spite of his seventy years, Papa still held his ground against a son half his age, but not without a club or a trowel with which to defend himself.

Tony had married at seventeen and soon divorced. It set a pattern in his life. He was now with his fourth wife, a man of intense jealousies, insecure with his women. He worked very hard, never satisfied to get a job done in any fashion. He was always in need of money, for his was a hopeless integrity in a trade where speed and trickery were the measures of success.

Tony and his latest wife lived in a nearby hotel, for Tony always contrived to be as near his mother's cooking as possible. His craving for the Italian food upon which he had been raised brought him back home for at least one meal a day, but Mama Andrilli never knew when he was coming, and it infuriated him when she asked.

As Tony opened the kitchen door Mama rose with a cry so piteous that he stopped in his tracks. She lurched toward him, her hair loosed from its braids, her face thickened by weeping. With fierce strength she clung to him, her hands around his neck, her tortured mouth crushing kisses to his throat and now on his hands as he fought her off and tried to learn the reason for her hysteria. Shouting and struggling across the waxed linoleum floor, it took all his strength to break the locked hands behind his neck.

"What's happened?" he yelled. Then he sniffed the burnt peppers and saw the room still clouded with smoke. "For God's sake, what's going on around here?"

Suddenly Mama was calm, limp in his arms, and he dragged her back to the chair. He blew into her face and fanned her with wild hands. Her eyes were closed, her chin resting on her breast.

"Mama," he begged. "Oh, Mama. Please."

She opened her eyes and began to cry again and Papa staggered from the living room. With bloodshot eyes he leaned in the doorway, the wine bottle almost empty in his limp hand.

"So that's how it is," Tony concluded. Quickly he was across the room, his fists in Papa's collar, shaking him. "What'd you do to my mother?" he demanded. "You drunkard, you dirty old man."

That hurt Papa. He covered his eyes and wept softly. Tony let him go. Mystified, he looked from one parent to the other. The confusion was more than he could cope with. He seized his thumb with his teeth and pounded his own head with heavy blows, now his jaw, now his temple, staggering clouts that left one side of his face crimson. Then he calmed down and dropped to his knees before Mama Andrilli. He touched her gently.

"Tell me, Mama. What happened?"

She sat back, panting, unable to speak.

"It's Nick," Papa intervened. "Your own brother."

"Is he sick?"

Mama flung herself upon the table and began to cry again. Papa's lips quivered, but he could not say more. Tony waited until Mama got control of herself. She crossed her arms over her bosom, one hand on each shoulder, and spoke with careful deliberation, her eyes toward heaven.

"Last night I had a dream," she began. "There was my Nick, in his coffin, with his typewriter..."

Tony leaped to his feet, bit his thumb, and started slugging himself again.

"Dreams!" he yelled. "Always dreams. What do I care about your dreams? I want to know what happened. Is Nick alright? Is he alive, or dead, or in jail, or what?"

But Mama kept talking with the same somber deliberation. "And then the telegram came."

"Telegram? What telegram?"

They looked around. The telegram was not in sight. Tony got down on his knees and peered under the stove. One of the cats was playing with the wadded telegram. Tony swept the animal aside and picked up the crushed yellow ball.

"Why," he said, "it ain't even open yet."

"Don't open it, Tony," Mama begged. "Oh, God in heaven, don't read it!"

254

Tony tore the envelope apart and read the message aloud. He read it with consternation, fury and horror.

It said: *Arriving tomorrow. Fix ravioli. Love and kisses. Nick.*

For a moment there was silence. Then from Mama there came a long, penetrating wail. She threw back her arms and head and let it pour from her throat. Even the cats responded, their backs arching.

"Thank God, " Mama cried. "Oh thank Our Blessed Lord for this miracle from heaven."

Papa sighed and smiled gratefully, but Tony's disgust was inarticulate. Exhausted, he threw himself into a chair and methodically pulled at his red hair. Mama's face was bright with elation, yet still puffed from so much weeping. Seeing her like that, Tony turned his eyes away with an expression of wrenching nausea.

"Fix me something to eat," he said.

Papa Andrilli drained the wine decanter and studied the telegram, his eyes squinting from the bright sunlight. The blood moved up his cheeks and nose as his anger flowed steadily.

"He's crazy," he said, crushing the telegram. "He never did have any brains."

"What's wrong with you now?" Tony asked.

"Him," Papa said, shaking the telegram. "Writing books, writing telegrams, scaring people to death. Who does he think he is, sending telegrams?"

"Why not?"

Papa went to the window and looked out at the fig tree with the young fruit no larger than marbles.

The wine had reached him fast in the heat of the day. He shook his head in confusion.

"What's going on in the world?" he asked the fig tree. "Telegrams, and war, and hamburger eighty cents a pound. When I was a boy I worked for one lira a week. I never got any telegrams in those days. I never sent any either. One lira week, I made."

"Last time it was one lira a day," Tony said.

"Let's have a glass of wine," Papa said.

He opened the trap door near the stove and the cool musty air came from the cellar. He went down the steps and Tony listened to the wine gurgling from the spigot. In a moment Papa was back, the ruby red beads of wine gleaming in the sunlight.

They drank in silence, father and son. Mama put a new batch of peppers in Cathy's pot, and the aroma of garlic and rosemary and olive oil pervaded the kitchen. Papa got a round ball of goat's cheese from the refrigerator and cut up thick chunks of sourdough bread. They sat and drank in silence, thinking about Nick.

The Sins of the Mother

DINNER WAS SERVED. Donna Martino, big and menacing, sat down at the head of the table. The chair squealed a protest. Rosa and Stella sat at her right, Bettina at her left. Papa Martino was down where he belonged, at the foot. A place was set for the other one but she was still upstairs. The sound of high heels clicking overhead made Bettina giggle.

"Shaddup!" roared Donna Martino.

Papa shivered. Lowering his head, he groped blindly for a glass of wine. He felt the black fury of his wife's large dark eyes. For Papa knew the thoughts turning in Donna Martino's mind—how she loathed his softness, scorned his gentleness, how she blamed him for conspiring with the one upstairs—that Carlotta, that traitor, that strangest daughter of them all.

With jutting lips Donna kept her eyes on Papa Martino as she placed the roast before her. With clenched teeth she picked up the carving knife and the sharpener. With savage intensity she flayed the knife against the Carborundum until the sparks flew. Papa Martino put his thin delicate fingers against his throat.

So, at long last it had happened. The ominous predictions of Donna Martino had come true, and the sins of a fanciful father had marked one of his offspring.

The others, thank God in Heaven, had profited by their mother's mistakes. *They* had not married a miserable tailor like Papa. Rosa was the wife of Dr. Faustino, one of Denver's finest dentists. Stella's husband owned four drugstores. And Bettina, the shrewdest of them all, was the wife of Harvey Crane, who the newspapers said would some day be governor of the state.

The daughters were now gathered in a fateful homecoming. Donna Martino had ordered it, asking that they come without their husbands. If there had been any doubt that this family conclave concerned the one upstairs, Carlotta's empty chair removed it. And they were glad—Rosa, Stella and Bettina—their eyes bright with flashing expectancy.

That Carlotta! Since childhood she had waged quiet war against them, against Mama, an undeclared hostility toward their thinking, their friends, their ambitions. But they had been obedient children, bending to the mighty will of Donna Martino, achieving the goals she had set for them.

"Remember my fate," she had said a thousand

times. "Remember, and marry well."

True, it had not been easy for Donna Martino. For in his way, Giovanni had tricked her. Had she known, she might have stayed in Sicily to live out her life in her native land. But thirty-five years ago Giovanni Martino had espoused Donna and come to America alone to make a home for himself and his prospective bride. Ah, that scoundrel! He had been handsome too, his teeth the color of a white moon, his thoughts as seductive as a dream.

She did not see him again for five years. Five years —one letter a week, fifty-two letters a year from her betrothed in New York City. What pirate of a woman's heart was this who wrote of his vast piles of money, the magnificent house he had prepared for her, the fabulous freedom and gaiety of America—he had put it all down in letters which she still read now and then to assuage her disillusioned heart and reassure herself of his shameless cunning.

Well, she had finally come to America the year after the Armistice. She had arrived in humility, anxious to prostrate herself at the feet of her conquering Giovanni.

Mama mia! What a rascal! She had found him living, but barely alive, in a boardinghouse on Mulberry Street. All of his wealth could have fitted into two suitcases. His tales of the merchant prince, his thousands in the bank—all pitiful whimsies of a lonely suitor whose coal-black hair had greyed in five years of toil in the needle trades, whose dim eyes longed for a girl symbolizing his Sicilian homeland where the soft blue sea came up to caress the lemon groves.

Choking back her grief, she had married him anyhow. What else was there to do? He had developed an alarming cough, with fever every afternoon, and his heart was broken. Remembering hard the young Marco Polo of five years before, she had married a memory. He had saved a few hundred dollars and because the doctor had ordered him to a high place, they had come to Denver.

That was nearly thirty years ago. Thirty years, four daughters and Giovanni. For in his way Papa Martino was more boy than man. The mountain air had quickly restored his health, but he never recovered from the devastation of those bad years in New York.

He was a good tailor. His little shop was a few blocks from the old brick house he had managed to buy out of his earnings. Year after year he tailored clothing for his regular customers, his *paesani*. The shop had become a rendezvous for old-time Italians. Here they gathered to play chess and pinochle, to argue the flow of history.

But for Donna Martino, Papa might have failed completely. She made periodic invasions of his tailor shop, driving out the venerable loafers, shrieking at them, swinging a broom as they scattered in all directions. She knew every detail of his business, every bolt of cloth and spool of thread. Sometimes, in order to make sure a job was done on schedule, she planted herself in a chair before Papa's workbench, watching him with big threatening eyes, defying him to waste one moment of time. *Si, si,* without Donna Martino Papa's business would have failed.

But he was a noble lover, that Giovanni, tender and lonely, forever seeking his lost Sicilian groves and finding them full of bloom and blossom in the scented world of her embrace. And when they were together, the wit and cunning of his early times mocked her and made her the shy and beautiful creature he remembered in Mediterranean sunlight.

Papa Martino was a stranger to his children. Baffled by fatherhood, he lived in a world remote from the problems of young people. He accepted fatherhood as the will of God. Beyond that, he had no active participation.

Donna Martino had done it all—brought them into the world, had them baptized, nursed them through illness, sent them through school, given them spending money and advised them as best she could on the mysterious problems of childhood and youth. No, it was not easy for Donna Martino. America was not like a Sicilian village. Here the customs were different, the language new and stubborn. Papa was no help to her in the endless dilemmas of four daughters.

The fact that three of his children were now married sometimes puzzled the old man. Closing his eyes, he tried hard to remember when they had grown to womanhood. The process had been so imperceptible he recalled no phases of it. Yet one by one they had come of age, taken husbands and moved to other houses. He knew nothing of his sons-in-law and cared less. It was specially at mealtimes around the big oak table that he noticed the absence of his daughters. And as each of them disappeared, Mama sat with a melancholy face, determined not to weep, but with uncontrollable tears washing her face. Then Papa realized another girl was gone. Stella first, then Rosa and Bettina, all within four years.

Only Carlotta remained. If the old man had a favorite daughter, it was Carlotta. She was like Donna Martino thirty years ago, tall and brave and beautiful, with Mama's implacable will. She had Donna Martino's quick impatience with his lassitude but she controlled it better. Mama shrieked at him for drinking too much red wine, but Carlotta kissed him first and took the bottle away.

Donna was heavy now and full of the rheumatism. She couldn't walk the few blocks to Papa's tailor shop and the *paesani* were in full control, with as many as three pinochle games going at one time. But Carlotta did the marketing now and visited the shop every day. She did not come like a thundering witch, brandishing a broom. She came with cheeks bright from walking, smiling at Giovanni's cronies. She made jokes with Angelo. She inquired about the health of Pasquale's wife. Better still, she took off her coat and helped Papa with his work. There wasn't much she could do but Giovanni loved having her there, talking of a hundred things, talking mostly of his boyhood in Sicily. Before long the *paesani* were gone and he was hard at work again.

The crisis in the Martino family had its beginnings three months ago in Giovanni's tailor shop. Papa remembered the incident well because of the truck, a big diesel engine job, its motor roaring as it pulled up before the shop. Trucks of that size rarely appeared on the quiet little street and the excitement broke up the pinochle game. Giovanni and his friends hurried outside to examine the red monster.

The serious young man who drove this juggernaut emerged from the cab like one freed from some physical ordeal, his breathing a series of sighs as he pulled off leather gloves and massaged his temples. He looked very tired as he began an inspection of the truck, walking slowly around it, now and then kicking one of the ten big tires. The *paesani* watched in silence. At that moment Carlotta arrived. She stood in the doorway of the shop and watched with uncertain curiosity. If something was wrong with the truck, the young man's expression failed to show it. He suddenly broke off the inspection and started for the tailor shop. Then he saw Carlotta.

"You the tailor?" he asked.

"Hardly." She smiled "But my father is."

Giovanni entered.

"A gentleman to see you, Papa."

"Brancato's my name," the young man said. "Gino Brancato. I need a suit of clothes."

Papa rubbed his hands. "She'sa pleasure, Signor."

But Signor Brancato was a hard man to please. For an hour he fingered bolts of cloth and draped yardage over his leather jacket as he stood before the mirror. Nor was he at first the sort of customer Giovanni liked to serve, neither gossipy nor autobiographical.

It took all that hour for Papa to squeeze from Brancato these simple facts: that he lived on the west side of Denver, that his mother was dead but his father lived with brothers in Philadelphia, that his parents were from the Abruzzi in the south of Italy. Young Brancato was a Denver boy but during the war he had fought in Italy.

Giovanni wanted to know about Sicily. Had Signor Brancato ever visited his home town of Palermo?

"I was stationed in Palermo three months. One of the prettiest towns in Europe."

Here was the key to the soul of Papa Martino. All at once this weary young trucker became friend. With quivering hands Papa led him to a chair and pushed him gently into it. Brancato glanced at Carlotta for help. She smiled sympathetically.

Papa's voice fluttered. There was a little farm, he said in Italian, five kilometers east of Palermo, on the Via Sardinia. The house was of pink stone, with a sloping roof of red tile. Had the young man ever seen it? Brancato frowned, watching Giovanni's face.

"I was there, sir," Brancato said. "The house was on

a hill, above the lemon grove. We used to stop there to buy figs and wine. Very good wine, Signor. Angelica and port."

For a moment it looked as though Giovanni were going to cry. He stared into the eyes of Gino Brancato worshipfully, holding back an impulse to throw his arms around the young man. Instead he took Gino's hand and studied the big knuckles, the thick fingers. He opened the hand gently and smiled into the muscled palm. Then he closed it gently again, as he might a jewel box.

From that moment Giovanni Martino wanted to possess Gino Brancato as a son. For Gino Brancato had drunk the wine of his own youth and savored the figs of that time.

When they returned to the matter of Gino's suit, the three together finally selected a beige gabardine that went well against his tanned face. Brancato was smiling now—a shy young fellow, Papa decided, very much like himself in the old days. He was filled with singing tenderness as he pondered the enigma of God's ways, that such a splendid young man should come to enrich their lives. For Giovanni felt this was destiny. The young man was heaven-sent to marry his daughter.

He was pleased to see that Carlotta was touched by Gino. The magic was in her eyes. Gino Brancato talked a great deal now, as though he had not talked in a long time, and Carlotta listened and smiled.

Giovanni saw them leave together. Gino had asked

Carlotta to have a soda with him. How long they were gone Giovanni could not recall but it was twilight when Carlotta came back to the shop. He left his bench, weary with the delicious fatigue that comes from satisfying work.

Walking home beside Carlotta, old Giovanni's serenity was a shadowy thing he almost feared. With quiet joy he took Carlotta's hand. Her own fingers twined in his.

"You like him, don't you, Papa?"

"Long time ago, thirty-five year maybe, and I'ma like Gino. Strong. With big dream."

And suddenly he began to cry.

Gino came to the shop regularly, always with a gift for Papa—the things the old man loved: round goat cheese, salami, wine. And gifts for Carlotta—small things in small packages: once a pair of earrings, another time a gold locket. And always flowers. Once he came straight to the shop early in the morning after fourteen hours on the road, a black stubble of beard covering his tired face and in his arms a pile of roses for Carlotta.

She never took the flowers home. Papa understood why and assumed that Gino did too. She set them in vases around the shop, their scent making the place cooler.

Usually he arrived a few minutes before Carlotta, wearing the beige gabardine Papa had tailored, looking for all the world like a suntanned banker from uptown.

266

Then he and Carlotta would slip out the back way and get into his small car. They had to be circumspect because Donna Martino had many friends in the community. It saddened Giovanni. There was so little for them to do at that hour: visit a movie or sit in the park—anywhere to be alone, to talk and plan. Giovanni longed to invite the young man to his home and when he apologized for not doing so Gino smiled and told him that Carlotta had explained,

All through the summer things went on like that. Every day Giovanni saw the rising torment of Carlotta's frustration at having to hide her love like a criminal thing. Saying goodbye to Gino, she would come into the shop, breathless and miserable. Three months of deceiving Donna Martino, of hurried clandestine meetings with Gino, were beginning to show.

Giovanni wanted to say words of encouragement but he scarcely knew how for he had never done it before. Besides, there was something formidable about Carlotta at those times, like Donna Martino, tense and explosive. Sometimes it seemed she was about to fall into her father's arms and Giovanni would smile and wait and hope. But she was like the mother, too proud to break.

One afternoon she showed him an engagement ring, a simple gold band with a winking stone in it. She held out her hand and turned it in the sunlight, watching the colors inside the stone. Here at last was a time to talk to his daughter about the future, to speak importantly like a wise parent, to advise her on what to say to Mama. But the sight of the ring stiffened him with excitement. He stared open-mouthed, inarticulate with delight.

"She'sa purty ring," was all he could say.

Carlotta slipped the jewel from her finger and put it in her purse. For it was time to go home now and Mama must not know

"Carlotta," he faltered, "you are happy—no, yes?"

"No, Papa." She kissed his cheek, and the kiss was like a period at the end of a sentence. She didn't want to talk it over with him and though it pained him he knew why. None of his daughters had ever talked to him of important matters. Now it was too late to begin.

The next day Gino came to the shop. And what he had to say made Giovanni feel strong and a man among men.

"Signor Martino," said Gino, speaking Italian, using the proper Italian phrases for such an occasion. "I wish to talk to you of an important matter."

"What is it, my son?"

"Yesterday, Signor, Carlotta consented to become my wife."

"Ah. So?"

"So now, today, I am here to beg the honor of becoming her husband."

Like that he said it. A man's way, a nobly phrased request, straight to the point.

"Ho," said Giovanni, "so that's it."

Gino's eyes showed their alarm.

"You do not approve of me, Signor?"

Giovanni lit a cigar and puffed it slowly. He was determined to act as a father should, stern and dignified.

"It is not a matter to be decided quickly, young man. As a father I have the right to know certain facts. There is the matter of money, Signor Brancato. Money is very important as my wife will tell you. Though I am not rich, Carlotta has known a certain standard."

"She will not want, Signor. I swear she will never know hunger or cold."

"We are in America, my son. It is not a matter of hunger and cold. It is a matter of how much? You gotta say just how much."

Brancato shrugged uncertainly.

"A few hundred, Signor. I am not wealthy. But a few hundred I have. And these."

He stretched out his hands, turning them over near the face of Giovanni Martino. They were eloquent, those thick knuckled fists; they implied so much that the old man was ashamed to say more. For Gino was indeed like himself thirty-five years ago, strong with the old dreams, alive with the old dreams.

"You will have to speak to Carlotta's mother," he said.

"I know."

"I am positive she will refuse."

Gino clenched his fists.

"We must marry soon, Signor. Carlotta is miserable. It is not right that my love should bring her unhappiness."

"Her mother will refuse."

"Then we will marry without the blessing of Signora Martino."

"I will speak to my wife," Giovanni said importantly. "I will get this matter straightened out as soon as possible."

That night Papa broke the news to Donna Martino. They were alone in the living room, Carlotta having gone to the theater with Bettina and her husband. Papa sat near the radio, listening to the ten o'clock news. Opposite him in her deep chair Mama drowsed. She filled the chair like a sleeping mountain. As long as one of her children was out in the night, Donna would remain in that chair, waiting for the front door to open. Nervously, Giovanni watched the drowsing mountain. She was a volcano and she would erupt, Papa knew, the moment she learned the news. He was a mere villager in the foothills with remote chances of survival once she exploded.

"Mama," he ventured.

She murmured sleepily. It made him sit up—alert, ready to flee. He licked his lips.

"A great problem disturbs Carlotta," he began in his native tongue. "It is serious."

The mountain awakened.

"Problem? What now?"

"A young man."

"There is no man in my daughter's life."

270

The explosion did not come. He gathered courage.

"There is, *Carissima*. There has been for three months. You have not been told."

She lifted her face and stared at him with bright terrible eyes.

"Three months?"

"A fine young man, dear wife. His name is Brancato. Gino Brancato."

"I know no such young man."

"They wish to be married."

As if struck by an earthquake, the mountain quivered. But there was no explosion. The hands of Donna Martino tightened.

"So now you tell me."

"It was difficult to tell."

"Is she pregnant?"

It shocked Giovanni. His hands flew to his mouth as if he himself had said this and now he wished to push back the words.

"No, Mama. This is love. Carlotta is so beautiful. She has such nobility, such pride. You should not say, you should not think ..."

"Three months," she interrupted. "Three months of treachery."

"It was not treachery, Mama."

"I am the child's mother. I brought her into the world. I should have been told."

"You would have destroyed it. The young man is not wealthy like the husbands of the others. We were afraid."

"And now you are not afraid. Now, with the child coming?"

He saw that the idea of a child was unshakable in her mind. It was a notion he had not anticipated and because she believed it so firmly he felt ashamed for her as he remembered the strong face, the clear eyes of Gino.

"This young man ..."

"That dog!" she interrupted.

"He asked my permission ..."

"Beast!"

It was useless to say more, to try. He sat humiliated by his own sense of inadequacy. He had hoped to tell his wife everything in the Brancato manner—simply, honestly, as Gino had done that afternoon. But the spark had died too soon and he slipped back into the comforting lassitude of despair.

"Who is this Brancato?" Donna asked. "How did she meet him? Tell me everything. Omit nothing, you hear? Nothing!"

He told her all there was to know. He spoke with deep weariness, almost with relief now that the entire situation had moved out of his sphere and into hers. He even told of his own foolish enthusiasm when he learned that Brancato had been in Palermo. Now it seemed ludicrous and infantile. But he left out nothing for it was her problem now.

As he finished, the sound of a car door slamming came from outside. Then Carlotta's quick steps up the path as the car drove away. The door opened and

272

Carlotta was inside. One look at Donna Martino and Carlotta knew her mother had been told of the man she loved. But Donna did not glance at the face of her daughter. Instead, she kept her eyes fastened to the silhouette of Carlotta's waist. The melancholy face of her father told Carlotta of the old man's ordeal. She bent down and kissed his forehead. It was like ice. And always she felt the searching eyes of her mother. She was angry and disgusted at this contemptible gesture. She turned and faced her mother, ready for whatever might come.

"Bring Signor Brancato to the house," Donna said "I should like to meet the man espoused to my daughter."

"I've wanted to, Mama. From the first."

"I am anxious to make his acquaintance."

A quixotic assertion. No tone of sarcasm, no mockery, no sinister insinuation. Donna's face was soft now, ineffably calm. Even Giovanni was surprised.

"Yes," Donna repeated, "I want to know this young man."

It disarmed Carlotta, freeing her momentarily from the taint of suspicion.

"I'll ask him to come tomorrow night."

So Gino was at last coming to the house. This should have been a high moment but for some reason Carlotta found herself more disturbed than happy. She kissed her parents goodnight.

At the top of the stairs, she turned.

"Shall I ask Gino to dinner?"

"I never dine with strangers," Donna said.

It tingled with sheer malice, telling her that Donna Martino had closed her heart to Gino Brancato, that Donna was scheming to tear him out of Carlotta's life.

The next day Carlotta awoke with a profound sense of its importance. She had slept well but something more than the enchantment of sleep invigorated her. There was the majestic knowledge that somewhere beneath the morning sun walked the man she loved.

There had been other suitors. By Donna Martino's standards Carlotta could have done better than her sisters. Even now she could hear Donna Martino's shrill challenge, demanding that she do something with her life. It mystified Carlotta. For a while she had tried music. Then she had gone to art school. But in the long run all things resolved themselves in this room, this sanctuary with its few beloved books, and her violin. Here was peace. But there were obligations—that vagary called duty to one's parents and the exasperating insistence that a woman must marry well. The room protected her from that.

Rosa had called her a snob. Stella had called her selfish. Bettina had called her neurotic and Mama had denounced her as a fool. But none had sought to take this room from her. And now she was giving up this room. Already it was dimly in the past, the shadow of Gino Brancato upon it. She loved him and she knew not why. He would probably never be a rich man but he gave her flowers and his eyes were haunted by his love for her.

They had agreed to meet at one o'clock. Gino was already there when she arrived, Giovanni looked at them with a face cast in misery. Gino's arm went around the old man's shoulder, hugging him briefly.

"*Paesano.*" He grinned. "Why so sad?"

"Trouble," Papa said. "Tonight, trouble."

Carlotta explained. "Mama would like you to come. Tonight at eight."

"At last."

"It may not be pleasant."

"Leave it to Gino," he said with assurance.

He pulled her out the back door to where his car was parked. It was early September, warm and lazy. He hummed softly as he drove, his cap tilted back, his body slouched comfortably. She leaned against him, pleased at the change in him. Now that she was promised to him the shyness was gone. She liked this touch of confidence even though it made her uncertain about herself. It was very satisfying to feel less strong than he.

Then she noticed that he was turning into her street. She caught her breath and tugged at his arm. He grinned as he swung the car in to the curbing before the Martino house.

"I'm going to miss those nights," he said. "The nights I've driven past here, up and down, waiting for you."

She could not control her uneasiness, the overpowering sense of her mother's presence. She was ashamed of it before Gino but it was there. His serenity seemed foolhardy.

"You'd better go now," she said.

"There's nothing to fear. After tonight we're free."

"It's better if you go."

He took her hands as she glanced over his shoulder toward the porch.

Thinking of her mother's great eyes watching them from behind the front curtain, she tried to withdraw her hands but he tightened his fingers.

"Promise me something, Carlotta."

"Please go."

"No matter what happens tonight, promise you'll do what I say."

"I promise."

He let her go.

"*Angela mia,*" he said.

She reached the porch and watched his car disappear. Then she entered the house. For a moment she was speechless at what she saw. They stood there, her sisters—Rosa, Stella and Bettina. They were alert, watching her. Bettina came away from the window. They tried to be casual but it was no moment for casualness.

Carlotta managed to smile, to say hello.

Bettina nodded toward the street.

"I think he's cute," she said.

Carlotta ignored it, her eyes frozen with anger as they sought Donna Martino through the dining room.

Donna stood in the kitchen door, her face a hard mask of confidence, telling Carlotta that this was only part of the evening's business, that Gino Brancato was to face not only herself but three others who also lived by the proper code of love and marriage.

Carlotta looked at them scornfully. They were like sleek Maltese cats, rivaling one another in their furs, sisters only by accident of blood. But she pitied them too. For in spite of themselves they had not escaped their mother this time. Never had Donna Martino been able to reunite them, not even at Christmas. Instead they had always sent handsome gifts and feeble excuses. But now they had finally succumbed to the mother's summons—and Carlotta knew why; because she had remained indifferent, even contemptuous of their husbands, their possessions, their lives.

They did not speak, nor did Carlotta as she passed through the room and upstairs. They stood quietly, looking at one another. Then the front door opened. It was Giovanni. A houseful of people always delighted Papa. He clapped his hands and shouted hello.

"Hello," they said in unison.

Through the space of two rooms Donna Martino's heavy presence made itself felt. Then Giovanni remembered. His jaw dropped and his shoulders bent a little more.

Carlotta did not come down to dinner. Instead, she got into a grey tweed suit Papa had tailored. She put on low shoes. Then she began to pack.

Long before eight o'clock it was all done, the

luggage stacked near the door, her coat, scarf and gloves spread on the bed. Standing at the window she watched the street below.

As Gino's car drove up she hurried downstairs. In the dining room they turned their heads to watch her rush outside. She met Gino coming up the porch steps. He was in the gabardine Papa had made for him, his arms out to her. He lifted her high off the ground

"All set?" he asked.

She took his hand and led him inside.

They had not left the dinner table. She smiled proudly as she led him in. His fine shoulders, the glow of his sun-drenched face made the room shrink in size. Each step gave her more confidence. He smiled generously. He was making their throats flutter, this Gino, their hearts beat faster. She had been afraid that he might be grim but he was as gentle as a child.

Except for Papa, they did not rise from the table. The old man got up and his adoration of this boy lighted his face. Gino slipped his arm around the old man and hugged him.

The gesture put Papa out of control. He tried to do the honors but he couldn't remember the married names of his daughters and he completely forgot to present his guest to Mama Martino, who sat glaring at him in disgust. To make matters worse, he knocked over a glass of red wine, the crimson streak spreading across Mama's linen tablecloth. That was enough for Donna Martino. She struck the table a mighty whack.

"Jackass!" she shouted. "Sit down!" He apologized

under his breath, groping for his chair. Finding the seat shoved neatly under him, he turned to see that Gino was behind him and he smiled his thanks. Donna Martino pointed to Gino. "You," she said. "Are you able to speak Italian?"

"*Si, Signora.*"

"Good," she said in Italian. "The things I have to say to you I can best say in my native tongue."

"My parents taught me the language."

"Ah. So you have a mother and a father."

"My father lives with my brothers in Philadelphia, Signora. My mother is dead."

"You loved your mother, young man?"

"More than earth and sky."

He appraised them coolly—Bettina with arms folded, Rosa with the proudly tilted head, Stella with her elbows on the table, her chin in her hands. And beside him, Carlotta. Now she locked her arm in his.

"Stop caressing the young man," Donna Martino said. "Have you no self-control? Forget your passion for a few moments."

Anger blinded Carlotta. Then she felt the pressure of Gino's arm, heard him suggest that she sit down. He pulled out the chair at Papa's left and she sank into it, weak with indignation.

"You loved your mother more than earth and sky," Donna continued. "Had someone injured her, you would have killed him. Is that right?"

"Most certainly, Signora."

"Brancato, I am an old woman. You are killing me."

He smiled. "That, Signora, I cannot believe."

She snapped her fingers angrily. "See here, Brancato. I am the mother of four daughters. You can see for yourself that they are beautiful women. Three of them have made fine marriages, Brancato. They have splendid homes, devoted wealthy husbands. It is good and satisfying for a mother to know that her children are protected. It is misery and nights without sleep when one of her children is burdened with poverty."

"That is true, signora."

"You are a poor man, Brancato. You drive a truck —that proves your poverty. A man of means does not drive a truck."

"I am not a rich man, Signora. Some day, by the grace of God, I may have the good fortune of your sons-in-law. I am far from rich. But on the other hand I am not so poor that Carlotta should go hungry."

Donna Martino changed her tactics. Now she was smiling.

"Make your fortune first, Brancato. Let this marriage wait a few years. You are both young. Come back when you are secure like the others, with wealth and position."

Something about Gino's eyes told Carlotta he had had enough. He looked at Donna Martino as though he wished to speak carefully.

"Signora," he said. "I do not think we speak of the same things. I am not here to purchase Carlotta. I am here because we love each other and wish to marry."

Donna Marino rose majestically and leaned toward

him, her heavy arms supporting her.

"I am weary of this jabbering about love. I say it now—I forbid you to marry my daughter. And I forbid my daughter to marry you. I cannot and I will not welcome you as a son-in-law. Because you are a man of strong will I see that I cannot prevent the marriage. But I denounce it. The curse of almighty God shall be upon it for all time, just as it was on my own tragic marriage."

She sat down again, collapsing like some piece of architecture whose foundations had rotted. The dust and debris of her evil fury billowed from her. They could not look at her—not Gino, nor Carlotta, nor the other daughters—and they turned their faces and hid their eyes from her. All but Giovanni. He did not take his eyes from her. His chin was tilted a little, as if he looked down at her, but his face was without emotion.

Gino turned to Carlotta.

"Pack your things," he said.

"I'm ready. I have."

When they returned with the luggage, the others still sat there and Donna Martino had not moved. But they were far from her now, forced back, remote from her. Carlotta choked out a desperate farewell, saying, "Goodbye, Mama."

No answer, but there was a change in her sisters, a reaching out with their eyes as if they were telling her to seize love now, to escape with her Gino.

Papa followed them out to the car. He was so quiet, so calm. Gino told of their plans—marriage in Nevada, home in a few days. Carlotta kissed the old man's cold forehead and Gino shook his hand.

The car drove away and Papa stood alone, uncertain, not wanting to return to the house. The pain of his soul filled the night. This evil thing his wife had said! How was it possible? Certainly he had been a poor husband, deserving her harsh words for his laziness. But God had not cursed his marriage. No!

He dragged himself back to the house. Mama had not moved but his daughters had slipped away from the table, silently pulling on coats and gloves. They kissed him and Bettina tweaked his nose. In the doorway they stood smiling at him, reassuring him.

He watched them get into their fine cars and drive away. Then he turned to see Donna still immobile at the table. He could not stay there. He got his coat and hurried out into the night.

As he walked he remembered a hundred things—Bettina with the measles, Carlotta in her graduation gown, Rosa running away from home on a broomstick, Stella's bad report cards—the murmuring of half-forgotten things. He smiled one moment and wept the next, because God had been so good to him—a loafer and a dreamer—had filled his life with beauty and with children. No, Donna should not have said that. But her tongue had always been a wild and dangerous thing, a flash of lightning, the thrust of a sword. How she had abused him and then repented! That day in New York when she found him poor and sick instead of rich and triumphant—that was a day he would never forget, her anger and bitterness flung upon him, in a torrent of language, until they were all spent and she became helpless and remorseful, begging his forgiveness. It was ever so with that woman. And now, he knew, it would happen again. But it was a hard thing to bear.

By habit his feet carried him to the tailor shop. He unlocked the door and went inside. Sinking into the chair at his workbench, he laid his head in his arms and slept.

It was daylight when he wakened. Someone was tapping the front window. The great figure of Donna Martino loomed at the door.

"I come," he called.

He unlocked the door. She looked at him with a face shattered from hours of weeping, like the earth pounded by rain, and she was trying to smile.

"You should not sleep here," she said. "Your place is at home."

He put his arms around her.

"My wife," he whispered. "My poor beautiful wife."

She wept so hard, so painfully, her flesh shaking, her body shuddering. This was her remorse, more devastating than her wrath, tearing at her bones, choking off her breath. But in a little while she felt better and they walked home together in the fresh morning sun. It was difficult for her, the rheumatism slowing her knees.

"Brancato spoke of the farm near Palermo," she said. "Your father's farm."

"He was there, Mama."

"My mother's farm was not far away."

"Only a few steps down the road." He smiled.

"I wonder if Brancato visited it too?"

"You will have to ask him, Mama."

They did not speak again until they reached the house. He helped her up the porch steps. It was hard going.

"I will ask him," she gasped. "That Carlotta! She is very impulsive, Giovanni. She has a mind of her own."

The Big Hunger

HE HEARD HIS MOTHER coming up the stairs, her feet in soft slippers. For an hour he had lain awake, reading *Crime Comics*, which were forbidden because Mother said they were bad for kids. But Dan Crane couldn't read, not really, because he was barely seven, a crummy age, two years younger than his brother Nick, who read real good, that heel.

"Up, Danny boy," Mrs. Crane said from the doorway. "Breakfast's ready."

Breakfast. Dan's stomach lurched. Every morning the same old malarkey: breakfast. He wasn't hungry. He had gone to bed with a sack of plums and had eaten them all, stowing the pits behind the radiator. Now she was after him to eat again. He lay staring at the ceiling, being very cold to his mother,

"You hear me, son?"

"Okay, Mom."

"And wash your face. And clean your nails."

The commands were so beneath him that he didn't even answer. One thing was becoming apparent: Dan Crane couldn't take much more. Breakfast. Wash your face. Clean your nails. Brush your teeth. Comb your hair. Change your shorts. Hang up your sweater. Go to sleep. Wake up. Be quiet. Speak out. Hold still. Get moving. Open your mouth. Stick out your tongue. Close your mouth. For seven long years Dan Crane had hung on grimly. seven years: his whole life, a slave.

When he tossed back the covers, it pleased him to see the blobs of dirt at the backs of his heels. Take a bath. Use the brush. And suppose he told her to go soak? Then he'd have to deal with the Old Man. Was that bad? Ho ho! He had the Old Man in his power. There was an expression he used—a mystic smile, a look of holy innocence—that melted his father's wrath every time.

His brother's bed was across the room, the covers thrown back, Nick's pajamas folded neatly under the pillow. Nick *liked* wearing pajamas! With a pretense of merely sauntering past, Dan Crane snatched the pajamas in one fist and held them out before him, a sneer on his lips.

Now he had Nick where he wanted him, within a coil of his fist, and it all came back to him—old Bright Boy with straight A's, so clever at drawing too, so helpful to his mother, so impressive when company came, old Bright Boy in person, the pajamas dancing in the air as Dan Crane cuffed them with jabs. Then the pajamas seemed to strike back, and Crane staggered and fell to the floor, for Nick was choking him and his face purpled as he struggled to breathe. He rolled across the floor, the pajamas on top of him until, with superhuman strength, Crane broke the grip at his throat and the tide of battle turned. Now Nick was beneath him, his upturned face receiving sickening blows to the mouth and nose, blood spurting from his nostrils, his eyes flaming in terror. One final bash of Crane's fist and Nick lay very quiet, not breathing. Dan Crane prodded one of Nick's eyes with a forefinger. Nick was dead. Weakly, Crane rose to his feet, aware now of his own wounds, of his torn face, a limp arm, blood trickling from his lips. He stood reeling, panting with exhaustion, offering no word of explanation as the Sheriff came in, his eyes popping at the brutal scene.

"You killed him, Crane," the Sheriff said. "You beat your own brother to a pulp. Gad, what a beating."

"I had to do it, Sheriff," Crane gasped. "It was him or me. You know Nick. He pulled a knife on me."

The Sheriff put out his hand "He was a no-good stinker, Dan. The whole county owes you a vote of thanks."

The Sheriff evaporated, and Dan Crane strode naked toward the bathroom, his chest out, the new day taking on a cheery hue now that Nick was dead. Through the window he saw the bright morning, the sunlight bouncing off the white stucco garage and stinging his eyes. The bathroom clock showed eight-thirty. He studied it intently. Nick always teased him for not being able to tell time. Ha—that stupe! Well, it was a quarter to twelve, and it was ten minutes to seven, and eleven o'clock; so what difference did it make?

From the staircase it came again, *her* voice: "Daniel Crane. Did you hear me? Breakfast!"

"Okay, okay, okay."

He dipped a corner of the washrag in warm water, braced his feet, and took three light swipes at his face, across his forehead and over both cheeks. It was a revolting experience. His teeth were clenched as he wiped the stuff off with a towel. The mirror told him there was no need to comb his hair; it was fine, away from his face and eyes. Maybe it stuck out at the sides, but so what? He examined his fingernails. But Dan was a poor judge of clean fingernails. These many years of observation had finally persuaded him that his nails were two-toned: pink and grey-black. Sometimes, by sheer brute force, his mother dug out some of the grey-black substance. On these occasions Dan screamed in agony, sure that she was prying out living flesh.

There was the smell of bacon and eggs in the hall, of buttered toast and wheat germ, and for a moment it pleased him. But now he chose to have it nauseate him, and his mind conjured up the plate of bacon and eggs too gooey, the wheat germ covered with the sweet slime of honey. This wrenching of his imagination produced the desired effect. Up his gullet came the rancid juices of last night's plums. Crane forced them back. He

288

was sick now, too sick to eat breakfast.

Bitterly, he reflected on his miserable fate. No corn flakes in this lousy house, or puffed wheat, or Rice Krispies, or Corn Pops, or any of the delicious things shown on TV. *His* mother brought home nothing but junk from the store. This junk was supposed to give you perfect teeth. But did it? Crane grinned ironically, his tongue probing a tooth that had been filled only last week by the dentist; across the street lived David Culp, nine years old, who ate nothing but Rice Krispies for breakfast and had big, white, absolutely perfect teeth.

With sullen laziness he pulled on his clothes, being careful not to wear the clean shorts laid out for him, the freshly ironed jeans and T-shirt, the new pair of socks.

The old shorts slipped nicely into place. They were almost like his own skin, and they smelled that good personal smell of none other than Dan Crane. Yesterday's T-shirt was befouled with the pleasant memory of adventures under David's house, a secret hideaway where he and David buried seashells gathered earlier at the beach. Indeed, the preponderant odor coming off Dan Crane was of the sea, the old tired sea at low tide. His jeans clung to his legs like damp canvas, grease and tar lending them an intimate stickiness like buckskin on the thighs of Daniel Boone. His socks were coyly resilient, like a mechanic's soiled rags, with a comfortable, form-fitting hole for each big toe. He knew his mother would beef about the old tennis shoes. He put one to his nostril and sniffed. He could smell nothing except just plain feet. With much tugging and groaning he got the shoes on, the laces snagged in a fiendish cluster of knots no mother on earth could unravel.

He wondered if he could get away with it. His mother might send him back upstairs; then again, she might not. It was worth a try. Slowly he descended the stairs, his chest sliding along the bannister. Then he saw her, his two-year-old sister Victoria, down there at the bottom, and he became alert to the danger, for she was waiting for him to come down to her, and her large brown eyes were full of mischief. She was the anguish of his life, the person in all the world he wanted to tear limb from limb.

"Okay now, Vicky," he warned. "Be careful. I'm just telling you: Watch it."

She knelt at the bottom step and smiled up at him. "Danny," she smiled. "Danny."

Her plump pink fingers were stretched out to him lovingly, but Dan Crane knew her only as a woman of devious cunning who kissed him one moment and bit him the next. Worse, he was not permitted to defend himself. The Old Man gave a lot of orders around there, most of which could be ignored, but one he enforced always: nobody could lay a hand on Victoria —not even if she poked out your eyes, bit your finger, or banged you with a croquet mallet. In her time she had done all these things and more to Dan Crane, and his cup of bitterness overflowed.

"Danny..."

She put her arms around his hips and he felt the

softness of her hair and he could smell her morning sweetness, and suddenly he was sorry he cherished such resentment for her. She kept repeating his name out of a rosebud mouth, adoring him with magic eyes.

"Dear Vicky," he murmured. "Dear little thing."

He sat on the bottom step and she touched his face and stroked his hand, purring with happiness at seeing him again. Her round innocence almost overwhelmed him, and now he was in her power again, hugging her tightly, kissing the soft hair of her neck.

"Kiss," he begged. "Kiss brother."

Like a wafted rose her mouth drifted to his lips, and he closed his eyes in delicious acceptance. But a demon burst within her and her bright teeth snatched his lower lip in a terrible vise. With a shriek he threw out his arms, falling back on the stairs, the little mouth hanging on. When she let go, Dan Crane lay there weeping. He covered his face with his hands and wept hard.

"Victoria!" Mother said. "Bad girl!"

It frightened the child and she began to howl. Mrs. Crane bent down to examine Dan's trembling lower lip. Now he cried with fervor, for he knew the bite had saved him, that he wouldn't have to go upstairs and change, and that he wouldn't even have to eat any breakfast. All he had to do was keep suffering, letting the anguish roar out of him, while his mother held him tenderly, sniffing suspiciously, but comforting him nevertheless.

Like a broken man he staggered into the kitchen

and flopped on the bench in the breakfast nook Through his tears he saw the bacon and eggs, the cereal, the orange juice, the glass of milk. It was more than he could bear. Fresh cascades of misery heaved out of him, his whole body rocking.

"Please, Mother. Oh, Mother, Mother! I beg you, Mother. Don't ask me to eat!"

She ruffled his dirty hair, feeling sand and tar on her fingertips. "Of course not, Danny."

He did not rise at once and rush off. For a few moments he produced more sobs. Even Vicky, contrite now, was touched by his suffering. She slid over to him and brushed his hand with a cheek that was still wet with her own tears.

He wanted to belt her, but he remembered how useful she had been. Sighing hard, he moved out of the kitchen, reeling slightly but not overdoing it. Once on the porch, he dropped the mask of misery, and his eyes danced with the prospect of this great new day. Under his breath he made guttural sounds, turning a phrase as he thought of his mother.

"Sucker, he said, grinning. "What a sucker."

A slinking figure at the corner of the garage caught his attention. It was Johnny Stribling from next door. He was armed to the teeth, a rubber knife in his jaws, a rifle in his hands, and two Gene Autry .45s strapped to his hips. John Stribling was the sworn enemy of law and order in the West. Day and night he roamed the plains, shooting down constables, knifing sheriffs, ambushing marshals. For two weeks, since the beginning of summer vacation, Stribling had left a trail of blood and murder in his wake, his guns going ckh! ckh! with a movement of his tongue against the roof of his mouth.

Crane had done plenty of killing on his own. It took him exactly two seconds to size up the situation. Then he sprang into action. With a spark-throwing burp gun in one hand and a gold-plated Hoppy six-shooter in the other, he jumped off the porch and saluted his neighbor.

"Who you after, Johnny?"

The greeting irritated Stribling, thumping him back to the sordid reality of a Southern California backyard, across which stretched pieces of the Crane laundry—panties, shorts and shirts.

"What's it to you?"

"Want me to play with you?"

Stribling looked him over with lynx eyes. "You wanna be the Law?"

"Nah. I'm Billy the Kid."

"No, you ain't. You gotta be the Law."

"And get killed? No chance."

"Then we got no game."

John Stribling swaggered toward the back gate, his artillery clattering

"Wait, Johnny. I'll play."

The outlaw swung around, his cruel lips smiling. "I just knocked over the bank at San Juan. Killed three men. Shot up the place real good. Big posse out to get me. That's you. Count to a hundred, then come and get me."

"Okay."

Dan Crane couldn't count to a hundred. After nineteen he just mumbled stuff, but he knew about how long it took to get to a hundred. The sheer stupidity of the Law ground out his joy in the game. The Law was no good. The Law was old people, like his mother and father and his teacher, telling him what to do, what to eat, when to eat it. The Law put you to bed, made you get up. The Law washed your face, poked a washcloth into your ears, sent you to school and to church. The Law offended him, gave him a bellyache, insulted him. And in the end, the Law even destroyed the outlaw. With a heavy heart he stood there, wanting no part in the victory his role represented.

Then he set out to find the enemy. He knew where Stribling would be holed up, for they had played the game a hundred times. Down the alley five houses, among the big leaves of the Becker fig tree, John Stribling would be hidden. He had only to go around and enter the yard from the street, tiptoe down the Becker driveway, and Stribling would be a setup for his burp gun. But Crane was in the grip of tragedy, and the old instinct for pursuit wasn't there. On sullen feet he trudged down the alley, no stealth in his tread, his heart almost welcoming the outlaw's bullet.

"Ckh! ckh!" came the deadly fire from the fig tree.

Crane staggered, feeling the hot cutting pain of the

bullet under his heart. The burp gun dropped from his fingers as he careened drunkenly and fell. With a howl of triumph Stribling leaped from the tree and rushed over. Crane was badly hurt. The bullet had burst through his back, and plenty of blood was spurting from the wound. Feebly, he groped for his six-gun. With a grin of evil pleasure Stribling waited until Crane's hand touched the gun. Then he let him have it with the rubber knife, leaping on the broken body and jabbing away. There was a quiver as life drained from Crane's battered form: then he lay quite still. He was dead. The game was over. It was time to start all over again.

Crane died twice more that morning. As Hopalong Cassidy, his heart was cut out and thrown to the Arizona buzzards. As the Lone Ranger, his demise was even more horrible. Stribling lashed him to a tree and shot off both ears; and when he still refused to divulge the hiding place of the gold shipment, the outlaw sliced off his nose with the rubber knife. Crane collapsed in a pool of his own blood, moaning pitifully, but carrying his secret into eternity.

The killings might have gone on all morning if they hadn't found the ginger-ale bottles There were ten empties in a gunny sack, tossed among the alley's high weeds, and they were as good as gold, worth five cents apiece. The boys loaded the booty into a wagon and hauled it to the Safeway. When they emerged, each with a quarter, they were rich men, lavishly spending their money on bubble gum and candy bars down at the drugstore.

It was an intimate, secret orgy. Hidden on the roof of the Crane garage, they lay on their bellies and ate in silent hoggishness. The hot noon sun melted the chocolate so that they scraped it off the wrappers with their teeth and licked it from their fingers. Then they rolled on their backs and popped the warm delicious bubble gum into their jaws, chewing slowly, their eyes closed to the sun, reveling in the sweet juices trickling down their throats.

"Danny!"

It was his mother, calling him from the back porch.

"Whaddya' want?"

"Lunch is ready."

Crane moaned. The very thought of lunch turned the bubble gum to gall. He spat it out in disgust.

They climbed down from the garage, dropping to the fence and then to the lawn. Stribling went next door. Crane turned on the hose and let the water trickle across his mouth, wiping himself dry with a sleeve. He looked at the kitchen door and thought a moment. It was probably cream of tomato soup, a sandwich and a glass of milk. There was no way out, except plain revolt. He was in an ugly mood, a heaviness at his stomach. With a hard face he walked into the kitchen.

Tomato soup it was, and milk, and a sandwich.

Nick was just finishing. He downed his glass of

milk and pushed back his chair.

"That was real good, Mother. Thanks."

"Twerp," Dan sneered.

"Who you calling a twerp?"

"You, bub. *Do* something."

Mrs. Crane broke it up. "Sit down, Danny. Eat your lunch."

"I'm not hungry."

"But you didn't have any breakfast."

"I'm still not hungry."

"Don't you feel well, Danny?"

"Never felt better in my life."

Anger made her voice sharp. "Dan Crane, I won't have you defying me. Go to your room."

Crane swaggered upstairs to his room and threw himself on the bed. He stared at the ceiling and dreamed of owning a burro, just a friendly little jackass, so that he could pull out of L.A. and go up around Sacramento, his grandpa's country, where the hills were full of gold, where a man could strike it rich and shed his family. He smiled as he pictured himself a rich man, tossing nuggets to his weeping mother, who was sorry she had mistreated him in the old days.

At three o'clock, he heard the gurgling voice of Victoria through the wall, and he knew his sister had wakened from her afternoon nap. He pictured Vicky in her crib, pink and bright-eyed, singing to herself, and the fatal urge to see her overcame him.

She lay among dolls and teddy bears, her feet in the air, as she crooned to her toes.

Dan stood over her in mute adoration, enchanted by her sleepy eyes, her sweet red lips. As always, her beauty melted his killer instinct, and he babbled to her. "Pretty girl, pretty, pretty, pretty."

Her pink fingers explored his eyes and ears, and he sucked quick kisses when they touched his lips. Her small nails probed his nostrils. She seemed to wait until he was completely spellbound. Then she let him have it again. The nails dug. There was a fierce pain. He saw it on his fingers and down the front of his T-shirt—not the blood of Hopalong Cassidy, not the blood of the Lone Ranger—but the rich, red, priceless blood of Daniel Crane.

"Mother, help! Oh Mother!"

She found him in the bathroom, reeling with fear, holding a towel tinged with scarlet against his face. Two ice cubes wrapped in a washcloth quickly stopped the bleeding, and Mrs. Crane forgave everything and told him to go out into the world again. He did not protest when she suggested changing his clothes. Then he stood before her, in clean clothes, subdued and rather sad. Suddenly his arms went around her, and his wild kiss left her blinking in wonder, for Crane was a hard man who opposed mother-kissing.

He left her standing there bewildered, and sauntered down the stairs. The smell of liver and bacon and baked beans was coming from the kitchen. The madness of hunger seized him, and he hurried into the kitchen.

The liver and bacon sang in the frying pan, and the beans sizzled in a brown pot in the oven. But everything was too hot to handle. He opened the refrigerator, took out a half-pound block of yellow cheese and an apple and stuffed them under an armpit. He raised a bottle of milk to his lips and drank most of the quart without a pause. Then he closed the ice-box door and walked outside.

Dinner was ready an hour later, but Dan Crane could eat none of it. A leaden cheddar satiation crushed his stomach, and when Mr. Crane served up the liver and bacon, the baked beans, and salad of lettuce and cucumbers, Dan stared helplessly at his plate, while he listened to his brother saying, "Gee, Mother, I love liver and bacon, and the beans are wonderful."

"What's the matter, Danny?" Mr. Crane said.

"Not hungry, Dad."

"But you haven't even *tried* the liver and bacon," Nick said with bright impatience.

Dan lowered his chin and scowled.

"I'm so worried about that boy," Mrs. Crane said. "He has simply stopped eating altogether."

Mr. Crane studied Dan's frowning face. "He'll eat. He just isn't hungry. That right, Danny?"

Dan Crane stared across the table at his father, and waves of love and tenderness flowed from his eyes. The frown gave way to a softness around his lips, and two tears spilled on his empty plate.

"Oh, Dad," he sobbed. "You're the only one in the world who understands me."

"I try," Mr. Crane said, smiling at him. "I do the best I can. Leave the table, if you want."

"Thanks, Dad."

Dan pushed his chair and moved toward the front door. From the dining room came his mother's voice, full of concern. "Talk to the boy. I'm so worried. He hasn't eaten for days."

Sitting on the porch steps, his chin in his hands, Crane waited for his father. He thought of a better life for himself, away from all this, the life of a tramp, him and his father riding boxcars, hitchhiking rides on the highways, living like free men, traveling the whole earth together, pals to the end.

Mr. Crane opened the front door and sat down beside his son. A big geyser of self-pity was rising in Dan's throat, pushing upward, finally bringing tears. He sobbed quietly. Mr. Crane put his arm around the boy's shoulder.

"Tell me, Dan. What's wrong?"

Dan couldn't think of anything, so he kept on crying, until an idea came forth. "I'm lonesome, Dad. Nobody likes me. That's why I don't eat, Dad. Because I'm lonesome all the time."

It took Mr. Crane five minutes to knock down this excuse and convince Dan that he was not lonesome, that, in fact, he had many friends, and that he was truly loved by his own family.

He pulled out a handkerchief and stroked away Dan's tears. Dan watched the wrinkles in his father's forehead, the concern in his eyes. He was doing a lot better than he'd ever dreamed he could, and he decided to go all the way with it.

"I miss school, too, Dad," he lied. "I want to get back so I can learn to read and write."

"That's fine, kid. And you will, but don't rush it. You've got plenty of time."

Dan's arms went around his father's neck. "Gee, Dad. You're great. No foolin'."

Mr. Crane dug a half dollar from his pocket. "Go to the drugstore and get yourself a chocolate malted, Danny boy. Good for you. Full of protein."

As in a dream, Dan Crane walked to the drugstore. He climbed up on the stool at the fountain, the fifty-cent piece in his fist. He almost ordered a chocolate malted, too, but happily his eyes fell on a luscious picture on the mirror behind the counter, a triumph of ice cream, crushed nuts, maraschino cherries, sliced bananas, whipped cream and colored syrups.

"Banana split," he ordered.

At midnight, a frantic hunger got hold of Dan Crane, a hunger for simple things like bread and meat and beans. Lying in his bed, while across the room his brother Nick snorted softly, he felt the vast emptiness of his stomach.

Quietly, he slipped out of bed and tiptoed into the hall and down the stairs. Like a naked ghost, he drifted into the kitchen. His practiced hand made no sound as the refrigerator door opened. He looked over the lighted interior. The baked beans were in one bowl, the liver and bacon in another. Dan hugged them to his chest, enduring without a murmur the shock of their coldness against his skin.

A minute later he was in bed again, the food before him as he lay on his stomach, the covers over his head. It was very cold food, but that was as it should be, for he was Dan Crane of the Northwest Mounted, living in an igloo in the Far North, and he was eating bear meat, and Nick's snores were the howls of wolves outside the igloo. Crane of the Mounties ate two pieces of cold liver and three fistfuls of iced beans before sleep laid him low. He barely got the food out of bed and behind the radiator; indeed, his hand went limp and he had no strength to pull it back under the covers before a great wave of sleep carried him away.

It was morning when he awakened, and there it was again, her voice, coming up the staircase:

"Up, Danny boy. Breakfast!"

Jeepers, what a dame. Dan Crane moaned. He wouldn't eat. He never wanted to eat again.

The First Time I Saw Paris

I WAS COMING along the Avenue George V about eight of an evening, wading through a river of heat, coat over my shoulder, wondering how in the hell those Frenchmen did it, all day long neat as penguins in starched collars and neckties, and their women forever chic in bell-shaped dresses, some wearing furs even in the heat. But most of the chicks in furs were Americans, the mink stoles a badge of global identification, as positive as the Stars and Stripes, meaning we're off to Maxim's and then a strip joint, absolutely naked, Darling, and when we got back to the hotel Harry was like a boy again.

Then on this corner leaning against the wall of the French Red Cross was this old woman, old as Paris, the oldest and lousiest and ugliest human being I ever saw in Paris in nine whole weeks, with skin like Notre Dame and stringy grey hair sweat-matted, it could have been a pigeon's nest, and a cotton dress such as you find in deserted shacks down in East Texas, something they use to stop up a leak under the sink ... and her ankles, ponderous as posts, swollen, fish-white, thrust into some shredded leather called shoes, and she was crying, her face in the crook of her elbow, sobbing—the river deep sobs of my son my son is dead, or my husband, they put him away forever and now I am alone—such a heart-twisting thing that I stopped and stared, and felt I should do something, do what? At least say something, are you hurt, do you need a doctor, do you want some money Madame?

But I went along with the rest of them, everybody immune to the torment of another human being, and floating past in the heat of the evening, but when I got across the street I thought wait, you can't do this, leave her like that, you have to go back and help her, but why should I? Nobody gives a damn, so why should I? Well, maybe someone will come along, and I waited, and the only thing that stopped to investigate was a little grey Scottie, and he was at the end of a chrome chain, and he went over and sniffed the fish-white ankles and got yanked back to respectability by his mistress.

Then a gent came along lugging a coat over his shoulder like me, maybe he was a baker, or maybe a plasterer, the dust of his good day's labor coating him gently, and he stopped and rubbed his chin and went on again, and looked once more over his shoulder and went away forever. Him and me, I said, him and me.

My God, nobody gives a damn, what a civilization, Jacques Fath and their pastries and Judas do they rook you in those bistros with all the broads, what a country, no wonder they got beat. Not even two gendarmes who came and stood two feet from her and hooked their thumbs in their belts and stared at the sky and obviously said God we sure could use a little rain.

I said well you dope, are you enjoying it or something, so why do you stand here watching, are you getting your jollies? So I turned and walked another block to my hotel, through a crowd of kids waiting for The Presley to come out, and I went inside and asked for my mail. No mail. All at once I almost burst into tears for my beautiful California, and I crossed to the bar which is so magnificent with twenty-foot walls of paneled mahogany simply wonderful, and I sat in a red chair and looked around for a kid I know from Fresno who comes rushing in there to grab a beer once in a while, but I didn't see anybody except a Hindu princess, an Italian movie star, a countess who is really not a countess, four luscious whores proud of their profession, and horribly expensive, and the usual dapper Frenchmen in their dark suits and starched collars they wear like sweatshirts. I drank two highballs while chicks almost too exquisite for touching went floating into my eyes.

And all at once there she was again, that old woman down on the corner—was it possible she was still there? It could not be possible, and what if it was, and it came over me again, this thing, this terrible twist of divine idiocy that goads me and louses me up, always wanting to know about people, can't leave people alone.

She was still there, I saw her from half a block away, she hadn't moved in the heat of the evening, and it began to irritate me and I said it's a racket, she's a beggar you dope, people slip her coins in sympathy, how stupid can you get? But nobody slipped her anything except a slewing of the eyes, and when I reached the corner and she was across the street, her grief came over, hulking and crawling and crippled in the heat of the evening, and it hurt me without letting up, and I knew I had to help that woman or it would pound and pound in me, and maybe chip off another little piece of my own death upon the earth.

I crossed the street and stood before her, and my masterful French took over, and I said is there something wrong Madame, can I help you, Señora, no Français, Ma'am, parla un poco Italiano, you need—I give, what's wrong, old girl? And I touched the skin of old Notre Dame, my hand softly upon the gargoyle, and wondered suddenly frightfully could she be a saint, because it was possible because saints can be the strangest of people in the damndest of places.

She turned and looked at me, her eyes very small and crinkled up, and tears as big as raindrops running down in the heat of the evening. I said, Please, Madame, you no cry no more, I help you, you want a doctor, you want some food, some wine, anything your heart desires, and I pulled out some sheets of huge money made out of paper, and I said you take, pour vous, merci, if you please, gracias, my pleasure. She shook her head and seemed to say oh you idiot, and cried all the more.

I got the panic then, lost control, and I grabbed this gent, he carried an umbrella and wore a checkered vest and could have been the French Ambassador, and I said, for God's sake find out what's wrong with her, and he looked surprised and turned and spoke to her in a low melodious and intimate way, gentle as her son, and she spoke back in a low and intimate way, gentle as his mother.

He turned to me and said, "She wishes nothing, except to be alone with her pain." He bowed like the French Ambassador and walked away.

I sighed in the heat of evening and walked back to the hotel, past the kids waiting for The Presley, and I ordered a drink, and there was a moment when I choked up at the dignity of man, and suddenly Paris was a great town.

Editor's Notes

THE NOTES THAT FOLLOW provide basic information about the stories in this book. Readers interested in learning more may wish to read my *Full of Life: A Biography of John Fante.*

Fante wrote "Horselaugh on Dibber Lannon" in late 1936 or early 1937 when he was still unmarried and living with his parents in Roseville at 211 Pleasant Street. The narrator's reference to Pope Pius is to Pius XI (Achille Ratti), who was pontiff from 1922 to 1939. Pageants were religious plays, often allegorical, staged in Catholic primary and secondary schools at Christmas and Easter time.

Fante was living in a Long Beach apartment with Helen Purcell at 926 East Fourth Street when he wrote "Jakie's Mother" in early 1933. The manner of Petey's death in the story recalls the death of Fante's favorite cousin Mario Campiglia, run down by a car in East Denver when he was a young boy. The parlor mourning scene, with Petey laid out in his coffin, prefigures "One of Us," the story Fante would later write based more closely on his cousin's death.

"The Still Small Voices" is an even earlier story, written in early 1932 when Fante was living in Long Beach and receiving his mail via General Delivery. The title page of the manuscript indicates that this was the first of six brief sketches; the other five do not survive.

"Charge It," published in the April, 1937 issue of *Scribner's Magazine*, is an early treatment of what would become the following year Chapter 4 of *Wait Until Spring, Bandini*.

Although the manuscripts of both "The Criminal" and "A Bad Woman" are without dates or addresses, each shows signs of being written in the late 1940s, in the aftermath of the chaotic war years.

The anonymous narrator of "To Be a Monstrous Clever Fellow" prefigures the Arturo Bandini of *The Road to Los Angeles*, which was finished in 1936 but not published until 1985. Like Arturo, this story's narrator is a self-obsessed young writer who plays fast and furious with his literary references, some of which today may be obscure. Aside from readily recognizable figures like Voltaire, Nietzsche, H.L. Mencken, Sinclair Lewis, Sherwood Anderson and Ralph Waldo Emerson, he invokes the names of James Gibbons Huneker (1860–1921), the American musician and literary critic; George Jean

Nathan (1882–1958), the American drama critic who worked with Mencken on *The American Mercury*; E. Boyd Barrett (1883–?), the Dublin-born psychologist and author of *The Jesuit Enigma* (1927) and *Ex-Jesuit* (1931); James Branch Cabell (1878–1959), the prolific American writer whose novel *Jurgen: A Comedy of Justice* (1919) became a literary cause célèbre when it was banned and then acquitted of obscenity charges; Everett Dean Martin (1880–1941), American social psychologist and author of *The Behavior of Crowds* (1920) and *The Meaning of a Liberal Education* (1926); and William Jennings Bryan (1860–1925), the American orator and perennial Democratic presidential candidate. In this story Fante also used the names of several people whom he knew in his personal life. Sister Mary Ethelbert was one of his teachers at Sacred Heart of Jesus grammar school in Boulder. A Father Benson was a prefect at Regis High School in Denver at the time of Fante's attendance, and Paul Reinert and Dan Campbell were fellow students and teammates on the Regis baseball team, the Clovers. Reinert went on to become a Jesuit priest and the President of St. Louis University.

"Washed in the Rain" appeared in the October, 1934 issue of *Westways*. Here again Fante indulges his penchant for blending fact and fiction—and playfully confusing the two. "When I told you I took a girl named Helen Purcell to the Santa Barbara Biltmore, it was the truth," the narrator confesses, using the name of Fante's actual girlfriend of the time—only to contradict himself by going on to say, "but there isn't any Helen Purcell that I know about."

Fante wrote "I Am a Writer of Truth" on MGM stationery in early 1936, when he was a client of the New York literary agent Elizabeth Nowell. In a remarkable correspondence which lasted the better part of that year, Nowell got Fante to read Knut Hamsun's great novel *Hunger*, which in turn exerted a decisive influence on Fante's style in *The Road to Los Angeles, Wait Until Spring, Bandini,* and *Ask the Dust.*

When "Prologue to *Ask the Dust*" was published by Black Sparrow Press in 1990, the last page of Fante's untitled manuscript was missing. That page has here been restored. It was early 1939 when Fante wrote this remarkable précis of the story which would become *Ask the Dust.* Page one of the manuscript indicates that Fante originally addressed the piece to William Soskin, his editor at Stackpole Sons. Before he ever sent the pages to Soskin, however, Fante showed them to his neighbor Daniel Mainwaring, a former newspaperman turned movie publicist who would go on to a successful career as a novelist (under the pen name Geoffrey Homes) and a screenwriter (*Out of the Past, The Body Snatchers*). Mainwaring urged Fante to rethink the strategy of telling the end of his romance at the beginning, with Camilla's desert disappearance featured in the story's first paragraph. After initially resisting Mainwaring's advice Fante relented, and the result was *Ask the Dust.*

The story published here as "Bus Ride" was

written as Chapter 2 of Fante's unfinished novel about Filipino migrant farm workers in California, *The Little Brown Brothers*. The story picks up with its protagonist Julio Sal where the action leaves off in the short story "Helen, Thy Beauty Is to Me—," which was to have served as the novel's first chapter. Fante worked on this novel with high hopes through the early to mid-1940s, finally abandoning the project in 1946.

Although the protagonist of "Mary Osaka, I Love you" is named Mingo Mateo, Fante planned to use a revision of this story, in which Mingo's name would be changed to Julio Sal, for the conclusion of *The Little Brown Brothers*. That plan was never realized. "Mary Osaka, I Love You" appeared in the October, 1942 issue of *Good Housekeeping*, preceded by the following "Editor's Note":

> This, we think, is one of the fine stories of the year. For obvious reasons it was submitted to the Executive Office of the President, Office of Emergency Management, Washington, D.C. The Government's viewpoint is that it can have no objectionable propaganda effect. Said the Office of War Information, in part: "The Government recognizes that there is a large number of loyal Japanese-Americans, and has considered the difficulties they face during this war period... The War Relocation Authority in establishing its Relocation Centers has acted for the protection of loyal Japanese-Americans. These Centers are not internment camps; American citizens in them retain all their rights of voting, access to courts, etc."

Mary's paean to America over which Mingo swoons is a catalogue of all-American personalities and phenomena: among others Artie Shaw and his big band, Joe DiMaggio and his baseball artistry, Cab Calloway and his jazz, President Roosevelt, ladies' slacks, and so on. Against all that is good about America the story pits a single villain, "a man named Yamamoto." Commander of the Imperial Japanese Fleet, Admiral Yamamoto (1884–1943) masterminded the bombing of Pearl Harbor on December 7, 1941. In the words of the *Los Angeles Times*, Yamamoto's cold-blooded sneak attack was "the act of a mad dog, a gangster's parody of every principle of international honor." Despite his initial success, by the end of the war Japan was defeated and Yamamoto was dead.

"The Taming of Valenti" appeared in the April, 1941 issue of *Esquire*.

Fante wrote both "The Case of the Haunted Writer" and "Mama's Dream" in the late 1940s when, after wasting the latter half of the decade on golf and alcohol, he was struggling to regain his novelist's focus.

"The Sins of the Mother" was originally published in the December, 1948 issue of *Woman's Home Companion* as "The Wine of Youth."

In "The Big Hunger" (*Collier's*, August 2, 1952), Fante returned to mixing fact with fiction. Although the protagonist's family name is Crane and not Fante, young Dan has the same name as did Fante's own son Dan, and likewise Dan's brother Nick and sister Vicky.

Fante wrote "The First Time I Saw Paris" in the

summer of 1959, while he was living in Paris and writing a screenplay for producer Darryl F. Zanuck. Elvis Presley stayed for a time at Fante's hotel, the Hotel Prince de Galles on Avenue George V. When writer and rocker were introduced, they shook hands affably, Fante afterwards referring to Presley as "quite a nice kid." "The First Time I Saw Paris" is concerned with an even more numinous encounter, which crystallizes when the narrator reaches out to touch the withered skin of the old weeping lady, "my hand softly upon the gargoyle, and [I] wondered suddenly frightfully could she be a saint, because it was possible because saints can be the strangest of people in the damndest of places."

John Fante, pray for us.

JOHN FANTE was born in Colorado in 1909. His first novel, *Wait Until Spring, Bandini*, was published in 1938. The following year *Ask the Dust* appeared, followed by *Dago Red*, a collection of stories, in 1940.

Meanwhile, Fante had been occupied extensively in screenwriting. Some of his credits include *Full of Life, Jeanne Eagels, My Man and I, The Reluctant Saint, Something for a Lonely Man, My Six Loves* and *Walk on the Wild Side*.

Fante was stricken with diabetes in 1955 and its complications brought about his blindness in 1978, but he continued to write by dictation to his wife, Joyce. He died at the age of 74 on May 8, 1983.

Fante's selected stories, *The Wine of Youth*, and two early novels, *The Road to Los Angeles* and *1933 Was a Bad Year*, were among the works published after his death. *The John Fante Reader* (Ecco, 2003), a collection combining excerpts from his novels and stories, as well as previously unpublished letters, is the most recent addition to the posthumous body of work and a long-awaited tribute to an extraordinary career.

STEPHEN COOPER is the recipient of a National Endowment for the Arts Fellowship. He is the author of *Full of Life: A Biography of John Fante* and the editor of *The John Fante Reader*. He lives in Los Angeles with his wife and their two children.